Dear reader,

Here we go for the 4th installment of the World War One Alternate Series. I think you naval lovers will really like the start of the book, with action right off the bat, to change the pace from the other books, which were dominated by diplomacy at the start. Trust me, when you turn the page here, you won't stop reading until you are done with the prologue!

On another subject, things are going well for me all around. I am now full time in my writing thing, as I have left my regular day job. This means for you, my dear readers that I will be able to churn out a lot more books. As if I wasn't fast enough, hahaha. And speaking of my dear readers, I wanted to thank one of my avid fans who has been helping with my work. Eric Roser has transitioned from reader, to proofreader, and now to editor. Along with my other proofreader, Dr. Kevin Plaisance, their hard work has made my writing into a more polished product, many thanks!

Speaking of books, you might have noticed I have started republishing the Blitzkrieg Europa Series under a 2nd edition label. For those who liked my original series, I would suggest you pick it up, as I have overhauled the entire thing, with a lot more stories on Erich Walder and Skorzeny, a lot more character development, and, most importantly, complete proofreading of all the works by two proofreaders. I've even added more text on, for example, the invasion of the United Kingdom since I felt I had been pretty thin on that part of the story. The final work is almost double the size of the original one (120,000 words VS 70,000 words for the original).

I published Blitzkrieg Europa in December, now Batte Europa is about to hit the shelves in January; and I am not only doing a 2nd edition of the Blitzkrieg Europa Series, but I will also be adding books. Thus, the 3rd installment in the series will be called Battle Russia and will take place between Battle Europa and Struggle Europa. I have also overhauled the link between Pacific Alternate and Blitzkrieg Alternate with a lot more reference to what is happening in the Pacific. All in all, I believe that it will now be a complete work with the level of quality you've come to expect from my more recent book series. I hope you enjoy it!

Speaking of proofreaders, I would like to thank Kevin Plaisance and Eric Roser for their great collaboration. It is thanks to them that my books have been upgraded in quality.

Before I sign out and leave the book to you, I would like, once more, to thank you for reading my books.

PROLOGUE
Naval War

Fleets in Motions Part 1
German sortie, British reaction, March 11th, 1915

"Admiral Pohl," said the man's Chief of Staff, Henning von Hotzendorf. *"Yes, Vice Admiral?" "The entire fleet is out, both from Brest and St Nazaire; we have just received the telegraph message." "Very well,"* answered Hugo von Pohl, the overall commander of the German High Seas Fleet. *"The ships should join together within a few hours and then we can proceed to our mission."* Finished Hotzendorf.

The High Sea Fleet Hugo von Pohl		
Chif of staff Henning von Holtzendorff		
1st Battle Squadron, 1st Division (Vice-Admiral Wilhelm von Lans)		
BB Ostfriesland (Flagship)	BB Oldenburg	4 CA
BB Helgoland	BB Thüringen	5 DD
1st Battle Squadron, 2nd Division (Rear-Admiral Friedrich Gädecke)		
BB Posen (Flagship)	BB Rheinland	4 CA
BB Nassau		3 DD
2nd Battle Squadron, 3rd Division (Vice-Admiral Reinhard Scheer)		
Pre-Dread BB Preussen (Flagship)	Pre-dread BB Hessen	3 CA
Pre-dread BB Deutschland	Pre-dread BB Lothringen,	4 DD
2nd Battle Squadron, 4th Division (Kommodore Franz Mauve)		
Pre-dread BB Hannover (Flagship)	Pre-dread BB Schlesien	4 CA
Pre-dread BB Dantzig	Pre-dread BB Prussia	1 DD
3rd Battle Squadron, 6th Division (Rear-Admiral Carl Schaumann)		
BB Prinzregent Luitpold (Flagship)	BB Sharnhorst	4 CL
BB Kaiser	BB König Albert	1 DD
4th Battle Squadron, 7th Division (Vice-Admiral Ehrhard Schmidt)		
Pre-Dread BB Wittelsbach (Flagship)	-	2 CL
Pre-Dread BB Mecklenburg	Pre-Dread BB Wettin	2 DD
5th Battle Squadron, 8th Division (Rear-Admiral Hermann Alberts)		
Pre-Dread BB Braunschweig (Flagship)	Pre-Dread BB Zähringen	1 CL
Pre-Dread BB Elsass		
5th Battle Squadron, 10th Division ((Kommodore Alfred Begas)		
Pre-Dread BB Brandenburg	Pre-Dread BB Kaiser Karl der Grosse	
Pre-Dread BB Kaiser Friedrich III (Flagship)	3 DD	

He stayed silent after that, the enormity of the moment hitting him.

He was again going to fight the dreaded British Grand Fleet. He walked to the door, giving way to the outside steel balcony circling the bridge, and picked up his binoculars.

From his vantage point on the fleet's flagship (dreadnought battleship Ostfriesland), he was able to see the magnificence of the powerful Kaiserliche Marine. Gulls flew overhead, yapping away like they always were. The air was crisp and fresh, with the unmistakable tinge of salt smell characteristic of the Atlantic Ocean. A fog remained over the water as it was early morning, and he saw his ship's bows slashed through it. His fleet seemed lost in a world of white vapor. He took a deep breath, feeling the tingles of nervousness creep up his spine. Before this mission was over, there would be a fight.

Hotzendorf followed him right behind. *"What about Rear-Admiral Funk's 3rd Battle Squadron,"* asked von Pohl. *"Already underway and steaming full speed south to breakout as planned into the Central Atlantic."* *"Excellent,"* answered the Admiral, looking this time at the Pre-Dreadnought battleship Brandenburg, his former command until 1905. The ship was as sturdy as they got but was now almost obsolete with the appearance of the new types of battleships, the powerful dreadnought class, like the Ostfriesland. He decided that those years were simpler times. Then, he could sail without fear of being gunned down by the English. *"I hope Funk gets through the British net and makes it to safety."*

Hotzendorf stayed silent as he didn't have any more news of Funke's squadron, but did on their own fleet. *"Sir, Destroyer Markoff reports that they chased away the British picket destroyer but weren't able to sink it,"* said the communications officer as he walked outside on the balcony coming from the wireless telegraph room. *"We can bet they have relayed the news."*

"We have been detected," said Hugo Von Pohl, resigned, and giving a look of seriousness to his Chief of Staff. He took a deep breath, crossed his arms behind his back, and closed his eyes for a moment

to calm himself. He then returned inside to face his bridge officers and sailors, flanked by Hotzendorf and the communications officer. *"Gentlemen, the enemy knows we are out. But have no worries,"* he said, lifting a finger in the air, *"this was expected, and part of our plan. We knew they would see us the moment we sortied,"* he said, sensing the palpable worry from his people. *"We keep on as planned. Remember, we are a diversion, so we shouldn't be out for long."*

His people were nervous because the strength disparity between the High Seas Fleet and the British Grand Fleet was humongous. A straight-up fight was not going to end well for the Germans if they got sucked into one.

They looked at their Admiral for a moment, not saying anything. Then, they went back to their tasks with renewed vigor.

(..) 100 miles southward (...)

Rear-Admiral Felix Funke was alone in his cabin onboard his flagship, the dreadnought battleship Grosser Kurfurst, a 26,000-ton Konig-Class battleship launched just a year prior to the Great War. Along with her three sister ships, König, Markgraf, and Kronprinz (all part of the 3rd Battle Squadron he commanded), the warships were amongst the most powerful in the entire Kaiserliche Marine. They were armed with ten 12-inch guns, each in a super-firing position, four to the front, four in the rear, and one twin gun turret in the center. Super-firing was the design in which gun turrets were built closely together, with one above the other, to attain optimal firing capabilities and the best traverse angles.

3rd Battle Squadron, relief fleet (Rear-Admiral Felix Funke) - To German West Africa		
BB Grosser Kurfürst	BB König	4 CL
BB Markgraf	BB Kronprinz	1 DD

He commanded a powerful squadron, and had been supplied with three of the fastest coal colliers in the Reich. He thus had the battleships mentioned earlier, along with four light cruisers, one destroyer, and three colliers.

His mission was straightforward, if not at all simple. He was to make for the harbor of Swakopmund in German Southwest Africa, the German colony just above South Africa. There, he was to give assistance to Admiral Maximilan von Spee, who was to try and exit the Pacific soon through the tip of Chile (Cape Horn). And in between, he was to sink as much enemy shipping as he could.

Admiral von Pohl had devised the plan in which he would sortie with the entire High Seas Fleet and entice the British to battle. All the while, Funke had set sail in the early hours of the morning during full darkness, with all lights out.

His ship's range was 8,000 nautical miles, while the harbor of Swakopmund was 5,125 nautical miles away from St-Nazaire. But this was the optimal range, and that was why he had colliers with him. He raced at near full speed and that consumed a lot more coal than cruising speed. And, if his ships were ever involved in a battle, it would be even worse. Thus, he didn't have enough coal for a one-way trip if he kept going at full speed like he was, hence the reason for the collier's presence.

His cabin was pretty large compared to what he'd seen in smaller ships, because the Grosser Kurfurst was built to be a fleet flagship, and that meant it had an *admiral of the fleet cabin.* These were larger in order to accommodate small conference rooms to house his captains when the commanding Admiral needed to have a meeting with them. Once in a while, captains from other ships were invited to a conference for face-to-face meetings. It was also big enough for a naval staff officer setup, although, at present, most of those were on the ship's bridge.

He was currently sitting at his conference table, fingers on his chin and looking out over naval charts and maps. *"Where are you, Beatty,"* he

---

muttered questioningly.

The fact of the matter was that Funke was referring to the commander of the British Mediterranean Squadron, who was pretty certain to sortie and try to intercept him the moment it was known the German fleet was out and sailing south. Hell, maybe he was already looking for him. Since he knew that the enemy had spies in the harbor of St-Nazaire (Germany occupied a French port, after all), he was convinced he would have to fight his way south if he wanted to make it to German West Africa.

Looking at the course plotted out by his people, he wondered if this was the right call. The obvious move was to sail to the open sea and hope to lose themselves in the immensity of the Atlantic. But that was also the exact same thing his admiral counterpart would think. He felt a little lost without the rest of the fleet to back him up.

It wasn't that he lacked the training, but he did lack the high sea experience, like the rest of the Kaiserliche Marine, which had stayed pretty much confined to the North Sea, apart from some exceptions. He hoped that everything would be all right and wondered when and if Beaty would catch up to him.

(...) Dreadnought battleship Neptune 150 miles southwest (...)

As a matter of fact, Rear-Admiral Funke wouldn't have to wonder and ponder for a long time since the British Mediterranean Squadron was already at sea and not very far from his position. *"Is this confirmed?"* *"Indeed, Sir. Submarine HMS E20 spotted a German fleet coming down south at what looked like battle speed,"* started the communication officer. *"Then, the message was relayed by HMS E19 and then HMS L14 right to us."* In 1915, the British submarine's wireless telegraph range was 50 miles.

Since the Royal Navy could not anchor in front of Brest and St Nazaire, they had established a network of destroyers and submarines that crisscrossed the sea in patterns. Their job was to act as a tripwire net in case of a German fleet breakout attempt. The idea was that when one of them spotted the enemy fleet of ships, it would relay the message to all the others in range, and they would do the same, for the news to reach London and Gibraltar in no time. Some of the message relays would also be done with more powerful land stations based in the French part still under the control of the Entente armies. These stations had a much greater range. During a clear day, messages could travel 300 miles, while the number was doubled or even tripled during the nighttime because the ionosphere refracted long-wave radiation.

The news thus reached Admiral David Beatty within an hour of the German 3rd Battle Squadron sailing out of St-Nazaire.

BRITISH MEDITERRANEAN FLEET (Gibraltar)		
Admiral David Beatty, 1st Earl Beatty		
BC Invincible	Pre-dread BB Russell (6th battle squ.)	9 DD
BB Conqueror	Pre-dread BB Cornwallis (6th battle squ.)	4 CA
BB Neptune flagship	Pre-dread BB Exmouth (6th battle squ.)	
BB Benbow		
BC Tiger		
BB Agincourt		

The British Mediterranean Fleet had already been sailing northward and was near the Spanish northern coast in order to beef up the blockade of the High Seas Fleet in St-Nazaire and Brest. The reason for the sudden departure from the Mediterranean was that the French navy had recently won a very important battle in the Strait of Otranto against the only potential threat in the Western Mediterranean, the Austro-Hungarian Navy. There was thus no threat as it was a sure bet the Austrians were licking their wounds in their base at Polan on the Adriatic Sea, and their fleet remained bottled up.

The fleet Beatty commanded was very powerful, and it was assumed that it would eradicate the 3rd German Squadron's four dreadnought battleships because it had three dreadnought battleships (Neptune, Benbow, and Agincourt), three dreadnought battlecruisers (Invincible, Conqueror, and Tiger), three pre-dreadnought battleships (Russel, Cornwallis, and Exmouth) plus nine destroyers and four heavy cruisers. The trick was, of course, to find and intercept the Germans.

Admiral David Richard Beatty, 1st Earl Beatty, was a rising star in the Royal Navy; having first been spotted during the Sudan Operation and then during the Boxer Rebellion, he was now one of the top British admirals and could even hope to become the Commander-in-Chief of the Grand Fleet once Jellicoe retired.

The man was resolute, relentless, and professional. He walked outside on the steel balcony, scanning the northern horizon as if to divine the German fleet's position. Beside him stood his second in command, Rear-Admiral Gordon Moore, doing the same, but this time with binoculars. *"There isn't any point in trying to see the enemy from that distance, Rear-Admiral Moore,"* said Beatty as he gave him a slight nod to the ribs with his left elbow. Moore laughed softly. *"I know, Sir, just a habit."*

"What do you think the enemy commander will do," asked Beatty in return. *"Will he do the obvious and sail for the deep Atlantic, or else try to feint us and sail close to the Franco-Spanish coast?"* Moore thought for a moment before answering. *"Well, sir, we don't even know where the German fleet is headed. For all we know, it's out to sink convoys, and that is exactly what they will encounter if they sail due south toward the shipping lanes coming from the Mediterranean."*

Beatty grunted as his second-in-command had just laid the gist of his dilemma. A large convoy was sailing just twenty miles south of his fleet, and if it encountered the German fleet while he was gallivanting in the Central Atlantic looking for the enemy ships, it would be destroyed, and his career would be over. He thus needed to decide if he wanted to risk it because the obvious enemy move was to sail for the Atlantic and try to lose itself in its immensity. But there remained a chance it was out to kill the convoy south of the Mediterranean Squadron.

"Rear-Admiral," he spoke again, still looking at the horizon (it was a sunny day with no clouds, and visibility was excellent, with the sun reflecting on the water as if on a mirror). *"I know we discussed this, but what are your thoughts about splitting the fleet down the middle to try and cover both options?" "An interesting option, Admiral,"* answered Moore.

The British fleet had six dreadnoughts and three pre-dreadnought battleships, plus a good superiority in cruisers, and support ships. Splitting the fleet would mean that if it came to a battle, the ships fighting the Germans would do so on even terms, which wasn't ideal if you wanted to guarantee a victory.

"It's certainly the safe option to make certain we reach both our objectives of protecting the convoy, and intercepting these bastards," countered Beatty. "Mmmm," he mumbled.

And then he decided. *"Rear-Admiral, please give the necessary order to split the fleet with the dispositions we have previously discussed,"* said Beatty in one long sentence without a pause for a breath, *"We'll just have to rely on our skills and our ships and fight the Germans on even terms in order to have the best of both worlds."*

(…) The other fleet (…)

Admiral of the Fleet John Rushworth Jellicoe, 1st Earl Jellicoe, felt excitement rising from the very depths of his soul as his fleet exited Southampton Harbor at battle speed. The German High Seas Fleet had been spotted exiting Brest and St-Nazaire, splitting in two. One of the fleets was angling southward, and that would be Beatty's problem. His job was going to be to face the entirety of the enemy battle fleet.

The British Grand Fleet was the strongest and most powerful fleet in history. It included no less than eighteen dreadnought battleships, four dreadnought battlecruisers, and an incredible twenty-nine pre-dreadnought battleships. It was screened by well over a hundred and fifty support ships ranging from heavy cruisers to destroyers and mine-sweepers.

THE GRAND FLEET (BRITISH HOME WATERS)		
1st Battle Squadron		
BB Iron Duke	BB Colossus	BB Vanguard
BB St. Vincent	BB Hercules	CL Bellona
BB Collingwood	BB Emperor of India	5 DD
BB Malborough (back from operation Ares)	BB Conqueror	
BB Ajax (back from Operation Ares)	BB Superb	
2nd Battle Squadron		
BB King Georve V	BB Monarch	Cl Boadicea
BB Centurion	BB Thunderer	5 DD
BB Audacious	BB Orion	
3rd and 4th Battle Squadron (combined)		
Pre-dread BB King Edward VII	Pre-dread BB Hindustan	CL Blanche
Pre-dread BB Britannia	Pre-dread BB New Zealand	5 DD
BB Bellopheron	BB Temeraire	CL Blonde
Pre-dread BB Dominion	Pre-dread BB Commonwealth	
5th Battle Squadron		
Pre-dread BB Agamemnon,	Pre-dread BB Venerable	Pre-dread BB Implacable
Pre-dread BB Prince of Wales	Pre-dread BB Queen	10 DD
Pre-dread BB Bulkwark	Pre-dread BB Formidable	
Pre-dread BB London,	Pre-dread BB Irresistable	
7th Battle Squadron		
Pre-dread BB Prince George	Pre-dread BB Jupiter	CL Sapphire
Pre-dread BB Caesar	Pre-dread BB Majestic	
8th Battle Squadron		
Pre-dread BB Albion	Pre-dread BB Vengeance	CL Preserpine
Pre-dread BB Canopus	Pre-dread BB Goliath	5 DD
Pre-dread BB Glory	Pre-dread BB Ocean	
9th Battle Squadron		
Pre-dread BB Hannibal	Pre-dread BB Mars	Pre-dread BB Magnificent
Pre-dread BB Illustrious	Pre-dread BB Victorious	
1st and 2nd Battlecruiser Squadron (combined)		
BC Lion	BC Princess Royal	12 CA
BC New Zealand	BC Invincible	10 DD
Pre Dread BB Lord Nelson	4 CA	3 CL
		7 DD

The fleet was so large it was very difficult to command it all through wireless telegraph and signal flags. But if it came to a fight, Admiral Jellicoe was pretty certain that his incredible numerical superiority would tell and win him the day.

"Sir," said the Captain of the British battleship Iron Duke, the ship where Jellicoe had installed his flag. *"The fleet is underway."* The Admiral of the Fleet nodded in silence, turned toward the bridge viewport to look at the southern horizon, and crossed his arms behind his back.

(...)

With all of the fleets in motion in the Atlantic Ocean, everything was lining up for a major naval action that they would talk about for years in history books.

Manzanillo, Revolutionary Mexico Part 1
German Pacific Squadron, March 7th, 1915

The harbor, and city of Manzanillo were located on the Pacific Coast of Mexico. It was one of the most modern harbors in the country, and used to be the main base for the Spanish Fleets when the country was still a colony. The harbor was one of the best natural anchorages in the area, and was thus a great place to house and protect ships.

The sight of a full German battle squadron inside of it was a peculiar sight, and not something that pleased the Americans nor the British. But the Mexicans didn't care, as they were in a state of war with the Americans following the occupation of the city of Veracruz on the Gulf of Mexico by American troops. Revolutionary Mexico was in the midst of a civil war with factions still fighting and was in no shape to fight the United States. Regardless, some of its rogue elements had raided across the northern border and triggered the attack on Vera Cruz by the U.S. Army. Regardless of the fact that it was the instigator of the contention between the two states, Mexico didn't harbor any love for their northern neighbors. Hence, it was pleased to have a German fleet in its midst.

The Reich had long sought to use Mexico against the United States because the Germans understood that if war came one day, the Yankees would never side with the Germans but instead would support their British cousins. While they understood that the Mexicans would never be able to face the Americans in a stand-up fight, it was surmised that war between the two countries could have a serious impact on the transport of supplies, and divert important U.S. resources or troops to a non-European theater.

To that effect, the Reich entertained a large diplomatic delegation headed by an ambassador known as Paul von Hintze, and had even started to make gold payments (twelve million in gold bars were delivered in the fall of 1914) to the Revolutionary government of President Venustiano Carranza.

Thus, when von Spee requested to enter Manzanillo, the Mexican government granted his request, because first it was an ally of Germany, and second because it was almost in a state of war with the United States.

German Pacific Squadron

Admival von Graf Spee

BB Westfalen stern damage, boiler damage, deck damage	CL Emden stern and forecastle damage
BB Kaiserin stern and boiler damage, 1 rear turret destroyed	~~CL Nurnberg~~
~~CA Kaiserin Elisabeth (Austria-Hungary)~~	~~CL Leipzing~~
Collier ship Oldenwald	~~Collier ship Brukenheim~~

It wasn't that the German Admiral had originally intended to stop in Mexico on his long journey home. It was because he was forced to do so following the important damage his ships had received during the Naval Battle of Western Samoa against a British squadron.

The battle, while ending in a German victory, was one hell of a destructive fight, and was a sort of Pyrrhic success for von Spee. The Kaiserin Elizabeth, their Austro-Hungarian heavy cruiser, was sunk, along with the light cruisers Nurnberg and Leipzig. Collier Brukenheim was also sunk, hit by a shell from the heavy cruiser Australia.

But the real problem was that both Kaiserin, and Westfalen had sustained heavy damage. Everything could have been shrugged off as battle damage, and the German commander would have continued on southward, but both battleships sustained heavy boiler damage. As a consequence, it became no longer possible to think the German Pacific Squadron would sail the great distances needed to round Cape Horn and reenter the Atlantic.

Von Spee had thus looked to find a place where he could have the boilers repaired, and that place (the only friendly country in the entire Western Hemisphere) was Mexico.

To say that the endeavor had displeased the United States was an understatement. Von Spee was no politician and had thus created a big problem for the Reich, as well as for Mexico. For him, it was all about repairing its ships.

For American President Woodrow Wilson, who had been quite content to stay neutral since the start of the Great War, it was as if the Reich had sided with his enemy, Mexico. The moment it became known that von Spee was in Manzanillo, a U.S. Navy Squadron was dispatched to blockade the port.

US Navy Asiatic Squadron
Admiral A G Winterhalter)
CA BROOKLYN,, Flagship   4 DD
CL CINCINNATI
CL GALVESTON

The Americans didn't have a lot of ships stationed in the Pacific for a lack of enemies. At the time of the Great War, the only perceived threats to the United States' territorial integrity were coming from Europe or Mexico. Japan was not considered an enemy because it was too far to act in any way against the American West Coast, or Hawaii. After all, it was also a staunch British ally.

The U.S. thus only entertained the so-called "Asiatic Squadron, based out of Manilla and sailing to and from San Diego once in a while to patrol U.S. territories across the Pacific. The reason for so few ships was also because the transit time was very long. While the Panama Canal had just opened in August 1914, greatly shortening sailing time from the Atlantic to the Pacific, the U.S. military had yet to change its fleet positioning.

It was thus with a paltry three-cruiser strong squadron, screened by four destroyers, that American Admiral AG Whitaker patrolled just offshore the Manzanillo harbor, preventing von Spee from exiting Manzanillo. The U.S. government had earlier given a note to the Reich ambassador in Washington D.C. for the immediate surrender of von

Spee's ships and internment for the duration of the conflict.

It was in this setting that Admiral von Spee read the telegram he'd just received from Ambassador von Hinze back in Mexico City. The man who had just given him the message clicked his heels and gave him the military salute before exiting his Admiral's stateroom on dreadnought battleship Westfalen.

He took a long breath and then looked at the empty air for a moment. He had not imagined that the sailing of his fleet into Manzanillo would create such a diplomatic crisis. Being isolated from world news, he had not known the American Army was occupying the city of Vera Cruz and that there was a state of war between Mexico and the USA. *"Would it have made a difference if I'd known?"* he asked himself. He decided that it wouldn't have since his ships had needed urgent repairs, and Mexico was the only friendly country with capable shipyards for thousands of miles.

He crumbled the piece of paper, walking to the edge of his cabin, stopping by the hatch as if hesitating. The content of these orders was problematic at best, and would create even more problems for Germany. At the very least, the boilers on both his battleships were now repaired, and his fleet could resume sailing toward the south, and onward to the Atlantic Ocean.

Hesitating another second, he exited the cabin and made his way to the ship's bridge to carry out his orders.

(...) Oval Office (...)

"Is this for real, Robert," asked a dejected Woodrow Wilson, the President of the United States. *"I am afraid it is the answer the Kaiser has just given us, Mr. President,"* answered the U.S. Secretary of State, Robert Lansing.

Wilson stayed silent for a moment, frustration bubbling inside of him. *"Who is this man to speak to the United States in this way,"* he said to himself. All the while, Secretary Lansing sat immobile and seemingly without emotion on the other side of the Resolute Desk. *"Sir, it's the same man that was instrumental in the start of that terrible war in Europe. A damned hothead if you ask me."*

By sending ships to blockade Manzanillo, and ask for the immediate internment of the German Pacific Squadron, Wilson had thought, just as Lansing did, that they were doing so from a position of strength and that the Germans would do everything to avoid war with the United States of America. It was also what both men wanted. They had no wish to join in the European conflict, and their electors had no taste for it either. The end result they had wished for might not have ended in complete victory and internment, but they expected a little more negotiation than this since many representatives of Congress were asking for blood. They thus had to make a good show of it. But this... answer was not what they had thought they would get in return for their just demands. After all, the country was at war with Mexico, and there were serious rumors the Germans were providing aid to the recently-in-power President.

"This answer is unacceptable, Robert."

(...) Berlin, half a day earlier (...)

"Your Majesty," said German Imperial Chancellor Theobald von Bethmann Hollweg, the man also responsible for the Reich's diplomacy and foreign relations. *"Are we certain this is the type of answer we want to give them?"* For a moment, Kaiser Wilhelm the 2nd hesitated before giving his answer. As much as the man was a bully, at heart, he was also a coward.

Both men were in one of the many ballrooms of the Berlin Palace. The Emperor was preparing an evening with a slew of German nobles, and since he was busy directing operations for his lavish diner, Bethmann Hollweg had to come to meet him there. The Kaiser had sent everyone away for the duration of their discussion, and thus, they were left with a large, half-done dinner table, a hearth where a fire burned fiercely, and several magnificent crystal chandeliers above their heads. The wooden floor was polished to a shine, and thus, the setting for the talks was grandiose.

The notes von Bethmann Hollweg had taken down as the core of the answer to be drafted to the U.S. President's demand of internment for the German Pacific Squadron (following his Emperor's dictations) was only going to make the situation even worse than it was.

"We are, Chancellor," said the German Emperor. *"These upstart Americans have no say in European affairs, and it isn't like they can do anything about it with their paltry 100,000-man army against my millions of soldiers."* Bethmann Hollweg made a face before countering. *"Your majesty, it isn't about what the Americans are fielding now; it's about what they will field if we go to war with them, notwithstanding the fact that we already have millions of enemies arrayed against the Reich on both sides of our borders."*

"Chancellor, they already sell goods to our enemies, and we cannot attack their ships with our U-boats and battleships. Hell, even British ships sail with their flags to protect themselves." Wilhelm paused to slam the dinner table he was sitting in front of with his closed fist. *"I will not lose two of my precious battleships because the Americans*

have a case of badly mistaken pride." He looked at Hollweg with fiery eyes. *"They are not a major player, and they will act accordingly."*

"Your Majesty," started the Chancellor before being interrupted by the Kaiser, lifting his left hand. *"Von Bethmann Hollweg, I order you to take a hard line against the Americans, diplomacy be damned. I want to provide my brave Admiral von Spee with the means to get back to the fatherland. Is that clear?"*

(...) Washington D.C. A few hours later (...)

"So, now, what are our options, Robert," asked Wilson in a sad tone, still looking at the German diplomatic message. *"There aren't many but two, Mr. President. The first one,"* said Lansing, lifting one finger facing Woodrow, *"is to fold, and let the German ships leave without incident. The second one,"* he continued, lifting a second finger, *"is to order Winterhalter to enforce the blockade and engage the Germans. The Kaiser may be bluffing, after all."* He shook his head in bewilderment. *"It's hard to believe he wants to fight us as well."*

"But if we do order the Admiral to engage, won't the odds be abysmal?" Lansing made a gloomy face mixed with some worry. *"They will, Mr. President. If the German Admiral fights as this message says, then we are dooming our sailors and officers to death."*

The Kaiser's answer to American demands had been quite simple, riddled with aggressive words and posture, and could be summed up with, *"Let my ship's pass, or they will destroy you."*

"I see," answered Wilson, putting his fingers to his chin as he obviously hesitated to take a decision. *"What If we send battleships to the Pacific through the Panama Canal? It would be only a week or so if we do."* *"Indeed, Mr. President, which is the first thing I would do, but as we both know, the Germans will probably be long gone by then."*

"Very well," countered Wilson, taking a deep breath as if he was

winded. In fact, he felt defeated because he didn't have the means to enforce the United States' will over the damned Kaiser. *"Our electors do not want war with Europe, and, after all, they are just ships. Have the Navy order the Admiral in Manzanillo to keep a menacing posture, but under no circumstances he is to fire at the Germans unless he is attacked like the Kaiser's message seems to be implying."*

Lansing looked at his boss with a neutral face. *"Mr. President, I know this isn't what we want, but at least we won't be condemning our sailors to their deaths."*

"Indeed," answered Wilson, standing up. *"Robert, let's go for a walk. I need to cool my head a little,"* finished the leader of the USA in a frustrated tone. *"Yes, Mr. President."*

As they walked the halls of the White House to the outside (it was a beautiful day in Washington D.C.), President Woodrow Wilson was lost in his thoughts, and those thoughts were not very positive toward the Reich. *"You've won the first round, you bastard,"* he said to himself. *"But I will win the last one."*

The American march to war had begun.

Manzanillo, Revolutionary Mexico Part 2
German Pacific Squadron, March 8th, 1915

(...) Dreadnought battleship Westfalen (...)

"Admiral, the Kaiserin is now exiting the harbor," said the lookout officer, reporting for his men atop the masts observing the other German battleship moving out of Manzanillo. *"Any reaction from the cruisers offshore?"* *"None so far, Admiral,"* said the man sometime later, as he received the answer from his lookouts.

"Very well. Get the Westfalen underway, and order cruiser Emden and collier Oldenwald to stay on our port side shadow in case the Yankee admiral decides to get lively." *"Yes, sir."*

The four German ships, great blackened and damaged hulks that they were (only their boilers were repaired in the Mexican harbor), slid silently amidst the morning fog, and the slowly rising sun. It was not yet 7 AM, and the German ships were attempting to run the gauntlet in front of the U.S. Navy vessels blockading the harbor.

Their bows slashed across the morning fog, and they let go several blaring horn noises to let everyone know they were underway, especially the Americans facing them at the harbor's exit.

(...) U.S. Navy Cruiser USS Brooklyn (...)

Launched in 1895 before the dreadnought era, the 10,00 tons and eight 8-inch gun ships were no match for what was sliding out of the harbor. The Brooklyn was considered an *"armored cruiser,"* what would later be dubbed a heavy cruiser. The other ships in the squadron, Cincinnati (3,500 tons and with five 5-inch guns) and Galveston (3,800 tons, four 5-inch guns) were near it, guns trained on the German ships. *"Let's hope they don't get too lively,"* said Admiral A. G. Winterhalter to no one in particular on the bridge of the armored cruiser. His new set of orders was to let the Germans pass but still show that the United States Navy would not be intimidated. He was in complete agreement with these instructions, as this would enable him, his men, and his ships to live to see another day. *"Mr. Simpson,"* he said to the ship's captain. *"Yes, Admiral?" "Please relay once more the order to stand down and do nothing as the Germans exit the harbor."*

The American sailors had strict orders to refrain from engaging the ships of von Spee, but it ended up being a Mexican who set up the powder keg that day.

(...)

The tension in the land fort facing the sea was palpable as Hector Don Miguel, the Captain in charge of the 7-inch 1898 Howitzer acting as a naval fortification for Manzanillo, watched the German ships exit the harbor. The man was mad at the Americans because the U.S. Army that invaded Vera Cruz had killed two of his cousins, and he wanted revenge.

"Range," he said to one of his men. *"But Captain, we have been ordered to stand down and not provoke the Yankees,"* answered the gunner. *"Shut up and execute your order, soldier,"* answered Don Miguel. From his own crooked point of view, Mexico needed to fight the Americans. The bastards had already stolen lands (Arizona, New Mexico, Texas, and California) in the last war forty years ago. Land that used to be owned by his family. His grandfather had almost been bankrupted because of it. The country needed a strong ally, and the Germans were just the right fit.

While the battleships had been in the harbor, Miguel had been content to just watch the U.S. Navy cruisers offshore as he was certain Germany had joined Mexico in its revolutionary war and the struggle against America. But when he heard that the Kaiserliche Marine ships were departing, and that there was no alliance or support from Germany apart from friendship (the content of the German-Mexican alliance and diplomatic relations had not been made public to men like Don Miguel), he decided to take the matter into his own hands. The trick was to fire on the enemy cruisers and hope the two fleets would interpret that as the opening of hostilities.

"Range 2,100 yards, Sir." "Excellent. Have you got a firing solution?" "Yes, Captain. Ready to fire when you give the order," answered the gunner. *"Well, then, fire when ready."*

The old howitzer gun, reminiscent of an old war, was obsolete and not at all made for this type of fight. But it did fire, and made an impressive cloud of smoke, and the blast reverberated across the harbor.

(...)Dreadnought battleship Westfalen (...)

Admiral Maximilian von Spee was silently congratulating himself as the ship was out of Manzanillo. His gamble was paying off. The boilers were repaired, and he could resume sailing toward Cape Horn. The Japanese fleet had not pursued further than the Caroline Islands, and the British Fleet he'd defeated in Western Samoa was not in any fit state to try and intercept him.

During the fight with the Royal Navy Squadron, his fleet sunk battlecruisers Furious and Majestic, and two cruisers (Good Hope and Monmouth) and made the British flee from the scene. He'd learned from reading (after translation) in the local newspaper that the press had called the engagement the Battle of Western Samoa and that the British Admiral, a certain Cradock, was dead along with his flagship, the Furious.

This meant that for all intents and purposes, he had a clean run to the Atlantic, provided he got out of his current predicament with the Americans. While he had no doubt he would destroy the three smaller ships, they could damage his already banged-up vessels, and he wanted to avoid that. He thought again about the Kaiser's message to force the blockade and not worry about the details and smiled. The

Emperor was a fighter.

"Admiral," yelled his Chief of staff, Vice-Admiral Max von Krenk, while pointing at a large and high water column that appeared near the bow of one of the American ships. *"I can see, Lieutenant,"* he answered, his mouth slowly opening and closing.

When the second column of water splashed near the U.S. ships, he came back to his senses. *"Who the fuck is firing at the Americans? Get me the captain of Kaiserin and Emden!"*

But it was too late. Von Spee saw the tell-tale flashes of the American ships firing away at his fleet. Seconds later, the shots hurled over the German ships and exploded in the water 1,000 yards too long. "Sir," said the wireless telegraph officer, running from the telegraph room. *"We're not the ones firing at the Americans,"* he started with bewilderment on his face. *"It's the fucking Mexicans!"*

(...) Armored Cruiser Brooklyn (...)

Admiral A G Winterhalter felt dejected at the German betrayal and wanted nothing more than revenge on the dastardly bastards. He was mad as hell, and he had given the order to his ships to fire back. What was weird was that the explosions were small and that he hadn't seen the big battleships fire yet. He decided the fire came from the light cruiser and the other ship (what looked like a collier) hiding in the shadow of the Westfalen's port side. As the sound of the ship's guns reverberated through the hull, he finally thought about looking in the harbor's direction. And as right as rain he then saw what was firing at him. *"It's the Mexicans!"* He thought for a moment about ordering his ships to stop firing, but as the first Kaiserin-Westfalen volleys catapulted water about 600 yards ahead of his ships, he saw that it was of no use. The battle had started, and while the Mexicans had started it, he was the one responsible for attacking the Germans.

"Signal the Germans, we are surrendering!" The Admiral looked with

worry at the distant German warships and hoped that their next volley wouldn't hit before they saw the white flag indicating he was giving up the fight.

As luck would have it, there was not enough time. On Kaiserin's third volley, light cruiser Galveston was slammed with two 12-inch shells and exploded in a myriad of flaming debris.

Events had taken a life of their own, and a full-blown international incident between the German Empire and the United States of America was going to bring both countries to the brink of war.

(...) Dreadnought battleship Westfalen (...)

"Sir," yelled the flag officer. *"The two remaining enemy ships are lowering their flag!"* *"Well, that was to be expected,"* answered the Admiral. *"Striking the colors"* was a universally recognized sign of surrender for ships at sea. *"They seem to have stopped firing as well and are now concentrating their fire on the fort who fired first."*

Von Spee felt relieved he wouldn't have to fight any more to get out of Manzanillo, but at the same time felt a powerful dread creeping up his spine. He'd destroyed an American ship, and he may be the man responsible for the war between the United States and the German Empire. *"Give the order to stop firing and signal the Americans that we will be leaving now."*

Following the sinking of cruiser Galveston at Manzanillo month of March 1915

(…) March 8th early afternoon (…)

The news of the sinking of the Galveston and the Battle of Manzanillo hit like a lightning bolt on an exploding tree. One of the first to know, U.S. President Woodrow Wilson was mad as hell, and when the news hit the media the next day, the entire United States went into an uproar about what the Germans had done.

The New York Times

CRUISER GALVESTON SUNK OFF MEXICAN COAST!
German squadron attacks and sink U.S. Navy ships.

Galveston sunk by German battleship Westfalen off Manzanillo, Mexico. Probably 1,255 dead. Captain Turner killed. Ship exploded following hits from Westfalen's 12-inch shells. Washington believes that a grave crisis is at hand.

Boston Evening Globe

Galveston Sunk!

Dastardly attack by German battleships off coast of Mexico in response to American blockade. German Kaiser defiant. German fleet at large in the Pacific. General outrage across the country!

THE SEATTLE STAR

1,200 American sailors killed off Mexican coast!

German battleships attack American fleet and sink the cruiser Galveston. Over 1,200 confirmed dead. War with Mexico, as the forts in the harbor also attacked the U.S. Navy. President Wilson's answer still expected over the grave international incident!

THE WORLD

German battleship shells destroy cruiser Galveston!

Terrible loss for America today. Over 1,200 sailors dead. Imperial Germany attacked American ships without provocation and refused internment. U.S. Government response still in limbo.

(...) During the month of March and April (...)

The outrage in the United States grew to a roar, and electors flocked to their Congress representative's offices to demand war or a stronger stance against Germany. President Wilson, knowing the country was not ready to fight the Germans, tried to channel the American public anger and was largely successful in putting the lid on the fire. But it wouldn't take much more to ignite conflict between the two states, and that little something would soon happen when a certain ship called Lusitania would sail out of Liverpool on May 1st, 1915...

All the while, the Germans acted as if they didn't care. Not even an official apology from the Kaiser was sent to Washington D.C. Wilson, not stupid and knowing that war was imminent with the Central Powers, took the outrage by the horns and passed several war budget bills to start increasing the size of the U.S. Army and U.S. Navy. The United States of America was gearing up for war.

As it happened, and even with the immensity of the Atlantic, it didn't take long for the four fleets out for blood to find each other. The High Seas Fleet under Pohl ended up doing a quick turnabout after sailing for six hours, while the British Grand Fleet managed to catch up with the German warships as they neared Brest once more. After all, the Kaiserliche Marine ships were only a diversion, even if it was a very large one. South of them, Admiral Beatty's splitting of his squadron produced the intended result, with his ships intercepting the German 3rd Battle Squadron of Read-Admiral Felix Funke in the open Atlantic. The first battle was called the Battle of Brest, and the second one was the Battle of the Azores, as it happened near the neutral Portuguese Islands.

Battle of Brest

The line of German battleships, guns trained on their enemies 13,000 yards away, was magnificent. The dreadnoughts were lined up in a long battle line like in the Age of Sail. The line of warships extended beyond view. The guns of the powerful vessels blossomed with fireballs and large clouds of smoke. The might of the Kaiserliche Marine was indeed impressive.

The day was clear, without one cloud over the horizon. The German fleet had three Zeppelins flying cover above it to help with gunnery range and spotting. The sun was bright, reflecting on the ocean. If it hadn't been for the hundreds of powerful warships firing at each other, it would have looked like a perfect day to be out on the water.

Running a parallel course to the German fleet was Jellicoe's even bigger Grand Fleet. The Royal Navy battleships and battlecruisers were also lined up in a battle line and were mimicking what their enemies were doing: firing away with all the might of their guns. The British numbers made the sight even more impressive. To the poor German sailors on the decks, gun turrets, and other battle stations, it was as if a continuous line of fiery blasts and smoke was blossoming and expanding at the same time.

All the while, the light wind pushed the gun and funnel smoke around, making for a hell of a log of a foggy grey cloud in the battle area. From a distance, it looked as if a plethora of coal-burning factories were all mingled together, churning out the black smoke. Both fleets had opened fire sometime before, and had yet to score any hits. Nonetheless, both battle lines were surrounded by catapulting geysers of water. Most ships fired high or short, but not one had hit home yet.

Naval gunnery was an imperfect art. Even if Britain, Germany, the United States, and the other world powers employed newly developed central fire control systems, the hit ratio was not higher than three to four percent, and most fights happened between 10,000 to 20,000 yards, which was considered the optimal firing zone. When the range decreased, the hit ratio climbed, but not by a corresponding decrease in distance. Even at 6,000 yards, it was very hard to hit a moving object while your own ship was bobbing in the waves and also moving, not forgetting that it was also being fired at.

While such a percentage seemed low in comparison to the 5% hit ratio of land battles, the effect of the shells when they hit was simply devastating. One 12 to 15-inch shell was often sufficient to inflict critical damage on even the most armored vessels like the dreadnought battleships.

Shortening the distance between the two fleets was the only way to improve accuracy. But, given the incredible three-to-one quantitative British superiority in battleships of all sorts and sizes, Hugo von Pohl was not interested in closing the range, and thus, his ships were under orders to keep the range at 10,000 + yards.

This was something that was written in the German Tactical Orders, which underlined the nervousness over a short-range battle for the

Kaiserliche Marine because of the number's discrepancy in case of a fleet-to-fleet battle: *"A short-range action is not to our advantage. We must attempt to stay within ranges from 10,000 to 12,000 yards. Superior German gunnery will thus keep its advantage over the more numerous British."*

With the hundreds of shells fired on both sides, hits started to be scored. The first significant hits were made by dreadnought battleships Iron Duke and St. Vincent directly on pre-dreadnoughts Deutschland and Lothringen's superstructures. The hits reverberated loudly on the two warship's hulls, producing tremors reminiscent of a small earthquake. A second or two later, a volley from Centurion bracketed the German dreadnought Nassau's forward turrets. When the smoke cleared from above and around the ships, Admiral von Pohl saw that the three ships were reminiscent of a sailing fireball. Their hulls looked like they were half mangled, but they sailed on, and most of their guns fired back in anger seconds later.

The Germans were not to be outdone. All ships threw their shells at the powerful British battle line, and some hits were finally scored on the dreadnoughts Marlborough and Conqueror. The first was slammed with a rain of shells from four German pre-dreadnoughts and instantly morphed from steel behemoth to fiercely burning gun platform. The German 10 and 12-inch shells created an impressive sight but failed to penetrate both ships' armor.

It didn't take long for German Admiral von Pohl to order the destroyers to screen his battleline with a heavy smoke screen and try to avoid damage as much as possible. As this was being done by the smaller ships, more hits were scored by the British, this time on pre-dreadnought battleships Mecklenburg and Wettin. The first saw a shell from the battleship Orion plow through its armor and into the boiler room (the hit was located just below the no.1 funnel), resulting in a catastrophic explosion that shell-shocked most of the crew on the ship, throwing many off-balance and onto the steel deck. Over forty sailors died on impact. When the smoke cleared (the ship eventually sailed out of its own smoke cloud), a gun turret was destroyed, and several blackened spots of mangled armor dotted the ship in many places. A gaping hole smoked off the deck on the front of the vessel. Hurt badly, the German warship started to veer off-course as if its helm was gone. The Wettin didn't fare much better, with a flurry of shells landing on its forecastle, stern, and central bridge tower, killing its command crew, along with over 450 sailors. The wall of fire that rolled across the ship's hull killed another 300, and when the moment was over, the ship also veered off-course, obviously not being steered by anyone anymore.

Both ships would be finished off by four British Pre-Dreadnoughts (Hannibal, Illustrious, Mars, and Victorious) that were ordered to stay behind to shell the two stricken German battleships into oblivion as the battle lines continued to sail and fire at each other at over twenty knots. The entire 9th Battle Squadron thus slowed down, encircled the Germans, and shelled them to burning hulks. The Wettin's ammunition store exploded first, while the Mecklenburg capsized as it was clouded in fire and exploding debris.
Dreadnought battleships Monarch, Colossus, Agincourt Monarch, and Hercules on the British side, with Ostfriesland (Fleet flagship), Heligoland, and Oldenburg on the German side, struck each other in succession with multiple volleys and bracketing volleys (near misses). The Germans were (sadly for their crews) the sore losers in the exchange, being overwhelmed by the British superior number of shells. Ostfriesland was damaged seriously on the bow and lost its forward turret. Oldenburg received serious damage to its waterline, with water gushing in and reducing its speed significantly. Heligoland was unlucky enough to have its ammo magazine hit and was thus raked with a catastrophic explosion, leaving it dead in the water (it would be sunk by the British cruisers a few minutes later).

On the British side, Colossus was seriously hit with a flurry of shells from the excellent Ostfriesland's gunnery. It was covered in fireballs and then was raked with a plethora of explosions, sending debris everywhere around in a star-like fashion. The ship was crippled and sunk, torpedoed by a U-boat an hour after the battle. Hercules lost a turret, hit by the dying Heligoland. Monarch received two 12-inch shells at the waterline level and on the stern. The ship's helm was destroyed, and the stricken battleship drifted off-course. It would be saved by protective destroyers and would need to be towed away to Britain for major repairs.

The next significant hit was done by the dreadnought battleship Rheinland, who was able to slam armored cruiser Berwick squarely in the middle of the ship, destroying the control tower and the gun control; it killed most of its command crew, including its captain. The cruiser, smoking, burning, and severely wounded, was not going to fire a shot again that day. It started drifting, and Rheinland redirected its fire on another target (light cruiser Proserpine), soon stricken by a bracketing volley. The small ship exploded as it capsized, making for a hell of a blast.

The Royal Navy's Pre-dreadnought battleship Glory was hit by an enfilade fire of the pre-dreadnought Hanover and three armored cruisers. Multiple fireballs exploded across its superstructure, and over 200 sailors were killed. Its captain was knocked unconscious as the central tower was slammed hard, with the entire viewport window on the bridge shattering to pieces.

The cannonade finally slackened as the German ships slipped away behind their wall of smoke, content to slink back into Brest. Most of its ships were wounded to a certain level, ranging from superficial to heavy. The British fleet received a lot of damage as well, but a little less because it had been able to bring more firepower to bear down on von Pohl's fleet.

The High Seas Fleet diversion had worked, enabling the 3rd German Battle Squadron under Felix Funke to slip past south, but the entire gambit was very costly, once more showing the Germans that they just didn't have enough ships to face the Royal Navy in a straight up battle.

Battle of the Azores

The incredible day of naval combat wasn't yet over, as the western half of the British Mediterranean Squadron approached the 3rd German Battle Squadron, having spotted its dirty and very obvious smoke columns in the distance.

In the boiler room of the German dreadnought battleships, the heat was almost unbearable as the men toiled in front of their furnaces, shoveling coal into the hungry fires of the ship's boilers.

Above the bowels of the German ships, the gunners ran to their battle stations and prepared for battle while the lookouts concentrated on getting as accurate a bearing on the enemy as possible. The helmsman on the bridge got busy starting the typical zigzag pattern, and the officers near them, including Rear-Admiral Funke, looked on with apprehension at the battle that was about to begin.

On the British side, events in motion were much the same. The gunners were already at their stations and thus started calculating their first firing solution since the ships were still at 20,000 yards of each other and quite out of range.

The only differences were in some of the British dreadnoughts, with their engines running on oil, quite a new concept in 1915. Their boilers were thus fed by machines and not men, although it wouldn't change much else in the battle.

The men were ready and willing, happy to have an enemy to fight. The two fleets closed together, although the Germans tried as best they could to keep the range long in order to avoid a fight. Rear-Admiral Funke was under orders to try and escape unscathed to German Southwest Africa, after all.

(...) British Mediterranean Squadron (...)

The first ship to fire was the squadron's flagship, Neptune. The ship was flanked by Invincible and Agincourt. The other dreadnoughts were with the second half of the fleet that had sailed on to protect the convoy in the Bay of Biscay. Pre-Dreadnought Russel, five destroyers, and 2 armored cruisers flanked the British fleet. The four battleships fired each in succession over a minute, depending on the turret and the gunner's own firing solution. The gale and the roll of the ship also affected when a ship fired.

"The firing solution was too short, Admiral," said the battleship's gunnery officer. *"Indeed,"* answered Admiral Beatty as he watched the high geysers of water at least 2,000 yards short of the moving target that was the German fleet racing southward.

He was wondering if he would get any hits on that day, as only his forward guns could shell the enemy since they were pursuing. The Germans had the same problem, with only their rear turrets able to fire. *"Sir,"* said the lookout officer. *"The enemy is firing; the lookouts can see the gun flashes."*

A few seconds later (it took a full 20 of them for the shells to travel the distance), the enemy fire hurled overhead in a loud whistling noise, only to crash and explode harmlessly into the sea beyond the British vessels.

(...) German 3rd Battle Squadron (...)

"Are they gaining on us," asked Funke, trying to hide his nervousness. The lookout officer went over to the plotting table, and they made some calculations for half a minute. "Rear-Admiral," started the plotting officer. *"It doesn't look like they are, sir. They intercepted us sailing southward, but the turn of their ships has made them lose a lot of speed and momentum, and it is unlikely they will catch up since we are steaming at full speed."*

BB Grosser Kurfürst	BB König	4 CL
BB Markgraf	BB Kronprinz	1 DD

"Orders, Sir," said the helmsman. Some of his men had seen the size of the enemy fleet and were tempted to turn and give battle. The entire German naval doctrine was based on the fact that they needed to maneuver to get in a position to fight on even terms, which appeared to be the case. To say that he was tempted to order the turnaround and give battle was an understatement. With quick action, he could sink a couple of British dreadnoughts and win prestige for the Reich and his personal career. The enemy appeared to have three dreadnoughts and one pre-dreadnought, while he had the four very modern battleships of the Konig Class.

The tension on the bridge was palpable as everyone around him saw the dilemma he was faced with. They went about their business but kept watch and a close ear to what the Rear-Admiral would say next. The only real sound in the room was the booming sounds of the guns and the reverberation across the ship's hull, felt to the men on the deck and elsewhere as a slight tremor beneath their feet.

"Keep current heading and make sure the boiler room keeps the pace by rotating the stoker crews to let them rest. The heat must be unbearable down there." "Yes, sir," answered the ship's captain, betraying the same kind of disappointment as the rest of the men and officers on the bridge.

Sensing their mood, Funke felt compelled to speak up. *"Gentlemen, must I remind you that we are under orders to avoid a battle. Our mission is to join Swakopmund, drop the supplies and soldier reinforcement there so German Southwest Africa can continue to resist the damned South Africans, and save the Pacific Squadron that will soon exit from the Pacific."* He walked amongst his men, putting his hands on their shoulders and smiling. *"Rest assured, you will get your battle, gentlemen. The British are most unlikely to let us sail back northward without incident. But when we do give battle, it will be with our Pacific brothers, the battleships Kaiserin and Westfalen."* The men and officers alike cheered his inspiring words.

The ships of Maximilian von Spee had already reached legendary status in Germany, and even more in the Kaiserliche Marine. These ships were the embodiment of resilience and the German fleet's fighting spirit.

(...) An hour later, the bridge of dreadnought battleship Neptune (...)

British Admiral Beatty turned around, arms crossed behind his back and with what passed as a neutral show of face, as he tried hard not to let his disappointment show to his men. The immediate chase was over, the German funnel smoke now a very distant dot on the horizon. *"Keep current pursuit and battle speed. We stay on the funnel smoke heading. Let's not lose them."* At that, he walked the distance between where he was by the viewport to the hatch, giving way to the bulkheads outside of the bridge. *"I will be in my cabin; let me know if anything changes." "Yes, Admiral,* said the Captain of the Neptune.

As he walked back to his cabin, his thoughts swirled in his mind as he tried to divine the German fleet commander's intentions. The bastard was sailing into the deep Atlantic with what looked like four modern and fast dreadnought battleships, flanked by large transport ships that he was certain (the submarine report had spoken of this already) were colliers carrying coal for his ships.

The Germans were sailing for a long-range mission; that much was obvious. He wondered if they were heading for Togoland, Cameroon, German Southwest Africa, or simply to hunt for convoys. That region of the Atlantic was not populated with a lot of convoys as most sailed through the Suez Canal from the Pacific and Indian Ocean.

And then he stopped in mid-stride, thinking about something bold.

Something truly out of character. *"No, they wouldn't,"* he said with a shocked smile. But indeed, they could, he decided. The more he thought about it (he had already turned back to walk back to the bridge), the more likely it made sense. *"The fucking bastards,"* he said out loud, a sailor hearing him. *"Admiral, are you okay,"* asked the worried sailor. *"Yes, don't worry about it, sailor."*

He finished his walk back to the bridge and smiled again, seeing the surprised faces of his men. *"Helm, head for the Falkland Islands,"* he started to say. *"Send a message to the rest of the squadron to do the same."* "Sir," said his second-in-command, Rear-Admiral Gordon Moore, making a puzzled face. "Just do what I said, Gordon, and make for Port Stanley," Beatty countered. *"What do we do about the Germans on the horizon, Sir?"* Beatty smiled for a third time in the last ten minutes, but this time in a feral way. *"That's just it, Rear-Admiral. That is where the damn weasels are going."*

The Falkland Islands were a small island colony off the coast of Argentina, and the British entertained a sizeable naval base there along with an important coaling station. It was perfectly positioned to block any traffic coming from the Atlantic OR the Pacific, right where von Spee would be if the plan was for the German Pacific Squadron commander to rejoin the fatherland. And the British had just seen the relief fleet.

March-April on land
The war on the ground, Spring 1915
France, East Prussia, Italian Alps, Carpathians, Middle East

France

Following the end of the Anglo-French offensive on Verdun in February, the entire Western Front settled down into trench warfare and stalemate. The French forces lost steam as their accumulated shell and ammo supplies dwindled to nothing. When the German reinforcements rolled in from the East and from Paris, casualties became untenable for the Allies, and the push was called off to wait for better conditions. Now that Spring dawned, the Entente continued to have offensive minded plans. The French and British were again accumulating men and material for a renewed attack, but this time on a different spot of the frontline: Paris.

Now that the Imperial Army had reinforced Verdun and taken troops from elsewhere on the Western Front, it was surmised by Foch, the Entente Commander-in-Chief, that other areas were weakened, especially since their spies now spoke of a major German offensive in the East.

Germany– West			
Verdun - Alsace border			
10th Army	General Max von Pritzwitz	200,000 soldiers	Verdun Area
German 9th Army	General Theodor von Baben	190,000 soldiers	Verdun Area
Paris-Nante frontline			
1st Army	General Alexander von Kluck	300,000 soldiers	Paris-Nante frontline
2nd Army	General Karl von Bülow	220,000 soldiers	Paris-Nante frontline
3rd Army	General Max von Haussen	178,000 soldiers	Paris-Nante frontline
Paris Rheims			
4th Army General	Albrecht Herzog von Württemberg	185,000 soldiers	Paris Rheims
North-Channel and Atlantic Ports			
5th Army	Wilhelm Kronprinz von Preußen	92,000 soldiers	North-Channel and Atlantic Ports
Belfort-Swiss Border			
6th Army	General Konrad Krafft von Dellmensingen	110,000 soldiers	Belfort-Swiss Border
Reserve, Western Germany			
7th Army	General Josias von Heeringen	125,000 soldiers	
New levies- training, Germany			
Reserve Army		525,000 soldiers	

The Kaiser had soldiers everywhere on the map to support his failing allies, and this was an opportunity for the Entente. It had about a corps-sized expeditionary corps in Italy and the Balkans, divisions in the Ottoman Empire, and a full army in Austria-Hungary. Added to the troops they now had arrayed against the Russians in Poland and Lithuania, it was a disaster in the making for the overstretched Reich.

In total, the German Army fielded 2,150,000 men against the Entente in the West. While with trenches, artillery, and maxim machine guns, it was deemed sufficient to hold them off on the defensive

As the thaw transformed entire fields of battle into a sea of mud, the Allies bid their time and accumulated supplies just south of Versailles, where their offensive would be launched. March was thus spent preparing for the attack, and the first half of April was the same, with the soldiers being put in position. A full seven months after the start of the Great War, British recruitment efforts were finally coming to fruition, with 650,000 men ready and trained from the United Kingdom to France from January to the Middle of April.

British Empire-West			
1st Army	General John French	112,000 soldiers	Verdun Area
2nd Army	General Douglas Haig	95,000 soldilers	Paris-Nante frontline
3rd Army	General Smith–Dorrien	95,000 soldiers	Paris Rheims
4th Army	General Henry Rawlinson	350,000 soldiers	Paris-Nante frontline
Reserve Army (England)		300,000 soldiers	Southern England
Imperial forces	Australian, New Zeland, Canadians	100,000 soldiers	Paris-Nante frontline

The total of British imperial troops was close to 900,000 by the dawn of May 1915, and the War Ministry was working diligently on bypassing the million marks by the end of the year. This number was beefed up by about 100,000 soldiers from the Empire (Australians, New Zealanders, and Canadians), freshly arrived in France.

Regardless of the defeats of the Fall of 1915, the French Army was still powerful and bore the brunt of the Allied effort in their own country (as it should be).

France			
1st Army	General Auguste Dubail	500,000 soldiers	Verdun Area
2nd Army	General de Curières de Castelnau	320,000 soldiers	Verdun Area
3rd Army	General Maurice Sarrail	300,000 soldiers	Verdun Area
4th Army	Fernand de Langle de Cary	315,000 soldiers	Paris-Nante frontline
5th Army: .	General Louis Franchet d'Espèrey	276,000 soldiers	Paris-Nante frontline
9th Army	General Charles Lanzerac	245,000 soldiers	Paris-Nante frontline
10th Army	General Louis Ernest Maud'huy's	312,000 soldiers	Paris-Nante frontline
6th Army	Général Joseph Maunoury)	300,000 soldiers	Belfort-Swiss Border
8th Army	Newly raised	300,000 soldiers	Vichy area (reserve)

When all was said and done, the French Army fielded a little over 2,600,000 soldiers on the Western Front and was slowly but surely moving troops from the Verdun area to the Paris-Nantes frontline for the offensive to reclaim Paris. The trick was to move enough artillery guns to smash the German defenses, as no amount of human meat would win over the steel bullets the machine gun nests and rifles could pour into any attack from their defensive trench lines.

Planes were also starting to make an appearance on the battlefield. They were first used as recon for the ground troops, but the fighting between aircraft was picking up in pace, and some of them also started to specialize in dropping bombs on the ground forces.

As the stalemate solidified across the Western Front, the armies and commanders on both sides started to look for alternative solutions to the problem of breaking through the enemy defenses.

East Prussia-Lithuania-Poland

Following the victory at Konigsberg in the Winter of 1915, the German Army was now poised to make a play for Lithuania and Russian Poland toward Bielorussia. The Ludendorff-Hindenburg dynamic duo was thus making plans to smash the (numerous) Russian armies in the area. The idea was to break through the frontline to invade the Baltic provinces, fork northward toward the Russian capital (St-Petersburg), and force the Tsar to sue for peace.

A successful Central Powers offensive in the area would force the Russians to diminish the pressure on the beleaguered Austro-

Hungarians holding on by a thread to their Carpathian frontlines.

East Prussia			
550,000 soldiers	Commander	Soldiers	Area of operation
8th Army	General von Hindenburg and Luddendorf	350,000 soldiers	East Prussia

Poland			
500,000 soldiers	Commander	Soldiers	Area of operation
German 9th Army	General August von Mackensen	190,000 soldiers	Lithuania
German 12th Army	General Max von Fabeck	220,000 soldiers	East of Warsaw

Counting on a total of 760,000 soldiers and a solid artillery park, the two German generals hoped to compensate for the superior Russian numbers (a staggering 2,100,000 soldiers).

Northwestern Front (Lithuania and Baltic States)			
1,490,000 soldiers	Commander	Soldiers	Area of operation
1st Army	General Paul von Rennenkampf	350,000 soldiers	Baltic States
10th Army	General Vasily Flug	400,000 soldiers	Baltic States
Northwest Army	General Yakov Zhilinskiy	333,000 soldiers	Baltic States
Southwest Army	General of Infantry Nikolai Ivanov	410,000 soldiers	Baltic States

Poland			
650,000 soldiers	Commander	Soldiers	Area of operation
11th Army	General of Infantry Andrey Selivanov	250,000 soldiers	East of Warsaw and Belarus
12th Army	General Aleksey Churin	200,000 soldiers	East of Warsaw and Belarus
13th Army	General Mikhail Vassiliavich Aleksayev	200,000 soldiers	East of Warsaw and Belarus

General Rennenkampf, for his part, had licked his wounds after his defeat in Konigsberg and awaited the German attack in the extensive (built over a 65 square miles surface) and powerful Kaunas Fortress. The Russian general wasn't doing the *"switching to the defense"* because he didn't want to attack. It was due to his troops experiencing chronic supply problems, rendered worse by the fact that General Brussilov's forces in Galicia and the Carpathians were getting the brunt of what was available. The tsarist supply system was not efficient and was marred by corruption. It was worsened by the paucity of modern roads and rail lines. The worst part about it was that none of the high leadership (from the Grand Duke to the Tsar himself) seemed to care about fixing the problem.

As April gave way to May, the German 8th, 9th, and 10th Armies were about to launch their offensive to slam the Russians into oblivion.

Italian Alps and the Apulia enclave

The Italian Army entered the Great War with a small force of 300,000 soldiers. It was unprepared, attacked by surprise in Taranto and on its Western border, but it didn't fall apart.

Italy			
France-Italian border			
1st Army	General Giovanni Villani	310,000 soldiers	Franco-Italian Apls
Apulia			
2nd Army	General Luigi Capello	280,000 soldiers	Southern Italy
Reserve - mobilizing			
Milan and Bologna	General Armando Diaz	290,000 soldiers	Northern Italy
Entete Italian thearer			
France-Italian border			
10th Army	General Louis Ernest Maud'huy's	312,000 soldiers	Paris-Nante frontline
Apulia			
5th British imperial Corps	British, Australians, South Africans, Gurkas	34,000 soldiers	Apulia Enclave
11th French Corps		24,000 soldiers	Apulia Enclave

While the Franco-British operation in Taranto (Ares) was a complete success and resulted in the conquest of all of the Italian bootheel (Apulia), the Italian troops were able to stabilize the frontline at its narrowest part and setup an impenetrable trench line a week later. The opposite was also true, as the Allies didn't need a lot of troops to man their own sides of the no man's land and were well supplied with artillery and machine guns. Complete stalemate was the end result and by the beginning of May, there were serious talks in Franco-British leadership circles to evacuate the troops. The only reason it wasn't done as of yet was because the relatively small number of Allied troops tied down five times their opposing numbers, meaning that those Italian fighters were not battling against France. The Otranto barrage and the Entente's will to keep the Austro-Hungarian Fleet bottled up in the Adriatic.

In the Alps, the situation was much the same, where gains were measured in feet. The frontline was jagged, and the fighting was happening in the high peaks, with every road and access to each other's countries blocked and defended by powerful forts.

Carpathians

If one thing was certain at the dawn of the 1915 Summer, it was that Austria-Hungary held on by a tiny thread, and that it wouldn't take much for its armies to fall apart in the East. Germany should have sent more to help but couldn't. The Dual Monarchy Army was demoralized, its troops and guns suffering from a chronic lack of supply, and it was badly led. To make matters even worse, it had suffered a lot of casualties since the start of the conflict. Furthermore, it had lost all of Galicia (about one-fifth of the Empire's landmass), and it didn't look like it would hold the line in the Carpathians.

Austria-Hungary East			
997,000 soldiers	Commander	Soldiers	Area of operation
1st Army	General Viktor Danki von Krasnik	210,000 soldiers	Recently moved to Southern Carpatians and Transylvania
4th army	General Moritz von Auffenberg	235,000 soldiers	Carpathian and galicia
3rd Army	General Rudolf Brudermann	95,000 soldiers	Romania
2nd Army	General Heinrich von Kummer	230,000 soldiers	Carpathian and galicia
5th Army- Mobilizing		225,00 soldiers	Hungary
6th Army - mobilizing		200,000 soldiers	Austria-Bohemia

Fielding close to 1,300,000 at the end of April 1915, the K.U.K. force lost 546,000 men since the beginning of the war, the highest amongst all of the fighting nations. All of its remaining brittle strength was arrayed against the Russians in the East, and the Austrian Emperor held his breath, wondering if he would still be in the war by Summer's end.

Ending the Habsburg Empire was exactly what General Aleksei Brussilov was aiming for as he put the last finishing touches on his major offensive that was about to start in early May 1915. Having just been reinforced by the powerful and newly raised Moscow Front (600,000 soldiers), the Russian commander had almost 2,000,000 men under his command. While General Rennenkampf suffered from critical supply issues in the North, Brussilov's forces had been given priority, and the result was that he had a full two weeks' worth of shells for the artillery, plenty of machine guns, and enough ammo for his men to fight all the way to Vienna if they wanted to.

When he sent the go-ahead signal, it wouldn't be pretty for the poor Austro-Hungarians.

Middle East

Ottoman Empire			
206,000 soldiers	Commander	Soldiers	Area of operation
3rd Army	Hafiz Hakki Pasha	15,000 soldiers	Bessarabia
1st Army	Enver Pacha	65,000 soldiers	Syria, Lebanon
2nd Army	Ahmet Izzet Pasha	45,000 soldiers	Caucasus and Eastern Turkey
4th Army	Djemel Pacha	35,000 soldiers	Sinai and Palestine
5th Army - mobilizing	Mustapha Kemal	45,000 soldiers	Constantinople area

The Ottoman Army remained relatively small at the dawn of the Summer of 1915, especially since it had lost over 250,000 men in the ill-fated Caucasus offensive in the fall and winter of 1914. The Turks were lucky the Caucasus was not a priority frontline for the Russians, who only entertained 150,000 men.

But the Turks were doing their part (at least they tried), first with their fleet actions, the intervention in the Balkans along with the Bulgarians with the attack and victory in Romania, and now with the plan of attacking the Suez Canal. Planning had been well underway for an offensive into the Sinai and into Egypt in January 1915. However, for logistical reasons and because troops had been needed to help the Bulgarians with the Romanian offensive, it was postponed to the early Summer.

For this attack, the influential Djemel Pacha (the Governor of Syria) had under his command the Ottoman 4th Army, 35,00 strong. The idea was to attack and occupy the critical Suez Canal infrastructure, from which all Entente shipping coming from the Pacific and Indian Oceans was transiting. If the Turks could seize it for the Central Powers, it would be a major blow to the British Empire and the Entente.

To say that the Canal was critical for the British Empire and the Entente as a whole was a major understatement. Its fall alone would create havoc in the convoy systems the Allies needed to supply their armies and bring the troops from their Pacific, Asiatic, and Oceanic colonies.

While 5,000 men had defended Egypt at the beginning of the war in the Fall of 1914 (the so-called Egypt Defense Force), the British had quickly moved to reinforce the colony and the Canal zone with troops coming from across the Empire.

British Empire Colonial forces			
EEF (Egypt expetionnary force): General Viscount Edmund Henry Hynman Allenby			
3rd Indian Division	General Climbety	11,000 soldiers	Suez Canal
7th British Brigade	Colonel Estmart	5,000 soldiers	Suez Canal
3rd South Africa Division	General Onedvort	9,500 soldiers	Suez Canal
1st West Indies Regiment	Colonel Smart	3,000 soldiers	Suez Canal
14th British Division (new)	General Combs	14,000 soldiers	Suez Canal
15th British Division (new)	General Dobys	13,000 soldiers	Aden (for landing in Kuwait)

In total, 42,000 soldiers defended the country against a Turkish attack, while a division was in Aden, poised to execute a planned landing in Southern Iraq (Kuwait) with 13,000 men and a sizeable fleet to protect and execute the landings.

While things had stayed pretty quiet since the beginning of the Great War in the Middle Eastern theater, things would now get lively as Summer dawned on the fighting nations of the Central Powers and the Entente.

Apulia Enclave
A fight and a plane, early March 1915

Slow motion...

French Private Soldier Armand Bonnier jumped over the dead body as a flurry of bullets passed under him and tore his jacket sleeve. In slow motion, the bullets seemed to shatter the air around, and the tiny blue fabric on Armand's sleeve splintered outward.

Normal motion...

He landed hard on the ground and stumbled into a roll, slamming his back on an old, half-demolished horse cart in the middle of the area. The sound of thunder (artillery shells) was overbearing, and high columns of dirty earth and debris rose in the air every now and then as the Italian artillery continued to pound the French forces in Armand's sector.

Slow motion...

Moments later, a biplane aircraft barrelled above, barely missing him as he was standing up. His battle helmet (he'd just received it a week before as the French were starting to equip all of their soldiers with them) rocked backward and fell on the ground in a splatter of mud. The ground was wet with the rain from the night before.

Normal motion...

Again, he turned to see the plane continue as it zipped past him, in a loud noise of a failing engine landing about a hundred yards from him, between the second and the third Trench line. The first line was already gone, with the Italians having taken it, and the 14th French Infantry Division was in full retreat. The attack had been preceded by a relentless artillery shelling for three days without a pause.

The fighter struck the ground hard and seemed to bounce back upward, but a few yards further, it landed again, this time turning in a weird semi-circle before slamming its side on a destroyer British gun. And then it lay still between two large enemy shell explosions, unscathed.

Other soldiers around him ran, splashing watery, brownish mud everywhere. Some fell as they got hit by enemy bullets, others yelled, and then, even more, stood their ground, firing from some cover in the ground between the two trench lines. Bonnier ignored them all in his bid for survival.

Slow motion...

Armand ducked back down as the chattering of an enemy Vickers machine gun fired. He'd learned from experience that when that noise was heard, it was time to go to ground. If you dickered around, you died. He dropped flat on his belly, landing in a large puddle of mud that scattered slowly in every direction, the small water droplets glinting in the afternoon sun. For a moment in time, he was sliding down and dodging for his life. The bullets, again seemingly looking like they were shattering the very fabric of the air, zipped above.

Normal motion...

Lifting his head from the watery mud and gasping, he heard the noises of explosions and rifle fire again as the battle remained in full swing. Looking at the plane, he didn't see anyone moving nor any attempt to get it back up in the sky. Looking backward, he saw the green-gray-olive uniforms of the Italian troops approaching in great yells and with bayonet-tipped rifles. It was time to go. He got up again, mud sliding down his body, and he ran, this time right for the plane. He had a crazy idea, and since he knew the enemy would either kill him or catch up to him.

Slow motion…

The explosions all around him lifted dirt in the air, which held there for milliseconds before arcing up and down. From his perspective, things were moving really slowly. Left to right, bullets whizzed past, seemingly suspended in mid-air.

Normal motion…

A minute and a half later and completely winded, he reached the plane, and the sound of battle invaded his ears again. For a moment, he turned his head left and right, looking for his friend Philippe Cren, but he was nowhere to be seen. They had both been separated by the enemy assault sometime before. The Italian breakthrough was large and powerful, and he surmised that they would only be stopped by the third line of defense.

The concept of trench defenses was based on layers upon layers of barbed wires and mutually supporting trenches, including as many as five lines. Thus, if the frontline ones fell, there were backups. While the trenches further back tended to be less extensive and could harbor artillery batteries, it was better than an open field to stop an enemy offensive. But by the time an attack reached the third line, and having faced machine guns and terrible casualties in the first two assaults, most attacks lost steam, which again appeared to be the case in this fight.

"Any…" he tried to catch his breath. *"Anyone alive in there,"* he said as he faced the pilot's open canopy. Silence. He could see the man's head was sideways and that blood was oozing from it. He jumped on the wing, looking at the pilot. *"Dead,"* he said out loud to no one in particular.

The biplane he looked at was a Voisin III, a French multi-purpose aircraft with two seats, one for the pilot and one for the gunner. He saw that the second spot, with the man supposed to man the

Hotchkiss M1914 Machine gun, was empty. With no time to wonder why, he picked up the dead pilot and threw him down. *"Sorry, pal, but I don't have a choice,"* he said once more. He jumped in the seat, finding it disgusting and sticky because it was full of the dead man's blood. Then he remembered he needed someone to turn the propellers to help the engine start.

"What the hell, Bonnier? Do you really think you can fly this thing without me," yelled a voice. He looked at the man. *"Cren, What the hell!"* *"Been following you. Quick, now, we gotta get it started."* Philippe followed that by putting his hands on the propeller. "Ready?" *"Ah, yeah, I think,"* he said. *"Ah, Cren, on your way into the plane, he yelled through the noise the starting engine was making. "Bring the pilot's goggles!"*

The plane started again, and then Philippe climbed on board, putting the goggles on and sitting in the front seat where the Hotchkiss was located. *"Hurry the fuck up, Bonnier,"* he said, pointing at the incoming Italians just fifty yards behind them. Their bullets whizzed past, and some even lodged into the plane's fuselage. He tried to remember Rolland Garros' instructions, and also his own limited flying and take-off experience. The plane started to roll on the ground, and thankfully, the stretch he was on wasn't too bumpy and hole-riddled.

As he concentrated on getting the plane into the sky, he was suddenly startled by the chatter and clinking noise of the Hotchkiss machine gun as Cren fired in the direction of the Italians.

Slow motion...

As the plane lifted off the ground, the Hotchkiss empty bullet casings fell everywhere into Cren's seat and on the side of the plane. They hit the fuselage and slowly turned, somersaulted, and twirled on the wings and then down into the empty air.

The blazing rounds barreled down toward the Italians, mowing dozens down and giving the rest the urge to take cover. They did so as the bullets raked the ground and their comrades, in gusts of blood ever-so-slowly falling on the ground.

"Here we go," said Armand as he closed his eyes for a moment and then the plane was up in the sky, thundering above the remaining Entente lines southward.

CHAPTER 1
Politics, Strategy, and Diplomacy

The name Schönbrunn meant *"beautiful spring,"* and the reason the palace had been given that name was because it used to be the Habsburg's summer residence. Thus, since they moved in when Spring arrived, the name had stuck.

The 1,400-room baroque-style building covered several acres of land with gardens and statues. It was made of yellow bricks, had two wings, and a large central building. It, sort of, looked like the Versailles Palace South of Paris, on which it was re-modeled after in the 17th Century.

Austro-Hungarian Emperor Franz Joseph, the old monarch who had been in power since 1848, was born there and had lived most of his life in the building, as he commanded over the destinies of his Empire.

The Emperor's apartments and plethora of audience chambers and bedrooms were located on the second floor of the central building. Franz-Joseph and his Chief of the General Staff, Conrad von Hotzendorf, were meeting in the so-called Gobelin Salon, a room that used to be one of the main audience chambers for the famous Marie-Theresa Empress in the 17th Century.

The room was richly decorated with a central square wooden-motif floor surrounded by an expensive-looking red carpet. Paintings covering the four walls represented life, war, and the glory of the Empire at the time of the great Austrian leader. In the center of the room lay a small table with six green-covered chairs.

"You know, General, this room used to be where my parents lived before they died. My mother really liked these paintings and spent almost every evening of her adult life here. My great ancestor Marie-Theresa used to receive heads of state in this very place." "Impressive, Your Majesty," answered Hotzendorf politely. Everyone at the court knew of this, but he entertained the notion that he didn't too please

his master. *"It's also in this room that the Dual Monarchy was decided,"* continued the old monarch. Again, Hotzendorf went through the motions, acquiescing graciously. *"This is an important place in our history, Your Majesty."* After all, the Emperor was over 85 years old and didn't have all his head anymore.

The 1867 establishment of Austria-Hungary was a decision by Franz Joseph to create two autonomous states (Hungary and Austria) within the Empire, unified by the same foreign policy and army. This solidified the Empire and had been a great political move. At the time, the Austrian sovereign thought he had assured the future of the Habsburg dynasty, but now he wasn't so certain.

"General Hotzendorf," continued the Emperor, leaning backward in his chair, a deep worry on his face. *"Your Majesty?"* The Habsburg leader looked at the military commander with his piercing eyes. *"Will I be going down as the last Austrian Emperor in history?"*

Conrad knew the discussion and the entire meeting would be about this, but he hadn't seen the entire concept in that way. He hesitated before his answer, as he decided that this man might be old, but he wasn't stupid. *"Your Majesty, your army will fight to the last bullet to avoid this fate."* Hotzendorf had always been patronizing of the aging Emperor. *"Well, I know that, but will you resist the incoming Russian offensive?"* *"We will, Your Majesty, I promise."*

Franz Joseph grunted. *"Well, that isn't what this report says, General,"* answered the monarch, pointing to the opened folder on the table before him.

"General," continued Franz Joseph, *"your failure to date in the conflict was not due to the military and not because of incompetence. Your plans were well made, and, according to many, you have a firm grasp of strategy. But your failing lies in the army you have, against the one you think you have."* *"But..."* stammered von Hotzendorf. *"Your Majesty doesn't understand..."* the Austrian Emperor lifted his hand to forestall the military commander.

The aging man took some time to answer, again looking at the General with fierce eyes. *'If we really have to go under, then we should at least go decently,"* he yelled, slamming his fist on the table.

"But, Your Majesty, what do you mean?" "General Hotzendorf, you are dismissed from command and named to lead the 1st Austro-Hungarian Army. I am replacing you with General Svetozar Boroević to be chief of staff of the Austro-Hungarian Army."

The northern door of the Gobelin Room (there were four doors, one on each wall) opened to give way to Prime Minister Karl von Stürgkh, the Emperor's right-hand man for political affairs, and overall management of the Empire's day-to-day operations. The man had been a close ally of von Hotzendorf when the war started, and also one of the war hawks who had pushed hard for a punitive move against Serbia. But things had changed since the future of the Empire was at stake.

"Prime Minister von Stürgkh will show you out, General," said Franz Joseph. Von Hotzendorf bowed in silence before storming out of the room. *"Will you need anything from me, Your Majesty,"* said von Stürgkh. It was late in the evening, and there wasn't much to do now that Vienna was asleep. *"No, Prime Minister. Please go through with General Boroevic's official nomination in the morning. "Of course, Your Majesty."*

The two men were quickly gone, and Franz Joseph was left alone in the room. He was tired but wasn't ready to go to bed. He stood up, crossed his arms behind his back, and walked toward his mother's favorite painting. He liked to look at the intricate details as his mother did since it helped him think.

General Svetozar Boroević was considered a good defensive general, and he had been one of the only commanders who did well in the Galician debacle. He had also done a good job in the Carpathians, which gave a sense of hope to the old Emperor. He didn't want to leave the war and for his empire to shatter in pieces, and that was why he'd decided to make the change now while it wasn't yet too late. A victory could change everything, but another defeat, like the grave naval reverse in January 1915, would topple his government. Losing dreadnought battleships and naval battles did not help any nation's prestige.

Tomorrow, he was to have yet another meeting with his Foreign Affairs Minister, Leopold Graf von Berchtold, and the German Ambassador to Vienna, Baron Heinrich von Tschirschky. He needed more men, and the only place he could get them was through the Kaiser.

"The President and the Secretary of State will now receive you, Ambassador von Bernstorff," said the secretary as she hung up the phone. The lady was sitting at a desk right next to Robert Lansing's office. *"Very well, thank you,"* said the German Ambassador in a heavy accent.

The man had been summoned by the American President and his Secretary of State to discuss the latest developments in the very strained American-German relations. Things were coming to a head following the major and tragic incident the month before in Manzanillo, Mexico. The moment had been discussed at length and had almost seen the Americans declare war on the Reich, especially following the Kaiser's arrogant attitude. But Congress, wanting to stay out of the war, had voted against it, and anyway, even Woodrow Wilson had no stomach for it.

But now things were again coming to a head due to Germany's action in the Atlantic and also its continued ties with Mexico, the United States' southern neighbor. Von Bernstorff had no illusion about the discussion about to happen with the two U.S. leaders. They would demand Germany cease all support to Mexico and also stop attacking neutral shipping or else any American ships. They might go as far as asking not to attack British shipping as well, as the ships were filled with American goods and often had American citizens. If that happened, the Ambassador already had an answer, which was, in nice diplomatic flowery words, to go to hell.

Following the sinking of the USS Galveston in Manzanillo, The American President had, through an executive order, instructed that U.S. vessels could defend themselves against U-boat attacks or sightings. Von Bernstorff didn't know what the Kaiserliche Marine's orders were about this, but knowing the Kaiser, they probably had received no special instruction to be careful with U.S. ships. While U-boats would not attack a vessel sporting the American flag since the two countries were not at war, the torpedoing of ships was not an exact science. From his point of view, and because of German support to Mexico and the sinking of the Galveston, it wouldn't take much for Washington to declare war on the Reich.

Lost in his thoughts, he entered the room, where two serious-faced men awaited him. *"Mr. President, it's a pleasure to see you,"* he said again in his German-accented English. He extended his hands. *"Likewise, Ambassador von Bernstorff, although I would have liked to meet you in happier circumstances."* The two men shook hands. He only smiled back and turned toward Robert Landing. *"Mr. Secretary of State,"* he said, shaking hands with the other American. *"Mr. Ambassador,"* answered the U.S. top diplomat.

Within a minute, they were sitting down on the reception couches in the room. No drinks or niceties were offered, as this was a summoning from the United States of America to a foreign nation it didn't have good diplomatic relations with. Lansing didn't waste any time. *"Mr. Ambassador, we are not happy with your conduct of the war in the Atlantic and of your continued support to our enemy, the Mexican Revolutionary state. We first want to inform you that we will be sending an expeditionary corps south of our border to stabilize the situation and put an end to this quandary. Second, we want to stress our deep worry and displeasure over the German conduct of naval warfare in the Atlantic against our British allies and shipping in general."* Lansing took a breath, waiting to see if President Wilson wanted to add anything, but the U.S. leader didn't. *"The U.S. Navy has been ordered to sail out and escort both American and British convoys, and any attack on our ships will be considered an act of war by Germany upon our country."*

Ambassador von Bernstorff tried to keep a straight face, but a small show of displeasure at the harsh words appeared at the corner of his mouth. His instructions from Berlin were simple. *"Do not be intimidated by the Americans. Convey to the U.S. President that Imperial Germany would not accept any restrictions on the conduct of the war against its enemies, the British and the French."* He also had another set of instructions, this time in the form of a message. *"Mr. Secretary, Mr. President,"* he started, joining both hands together as he spoke. *"My Government has instructed me to convey to you the Reich's displeasure at American support of France and Great Britain in the form of arms sales and other types of support and sees its Mexican ally in the same way you regard the British and the French. Furthermore,"* he said, taking a breath, *"we do not feel obligated in any way to the United States in regard to the conduct of the naval war against the Entente, especially in British, French, and international waters."*

Both Americans looked at each other for a moment, turning back toward von Bernstorff, and this time, it was Wilson's turn to speak. *"Let me put it plainly to you, Mr. Ambassador. Go tell your Kaiser that if we have one more incident, Congress will vote for war against Germany."*

President Woodrow Wilson was not a fan of old European secret diplomacy and considered the old monarchs of Europe relics of a bygone age. Von Bernstorff was offended by the U.S. leader's direct words, but it was what it was, and these Americans had no respect for tradition and diplomatic language. *"I understand, Mr. President,"* he finally answered, again in a hushed tone, showing he was not happy with being spoken to in that way. *"Will that be all?"*

Robert Lansing looked at him with a plain face. "Yes, that will be all, Mr. Ambassador. Consider yourself warned and make sure you convey to the Kaiser, and in no uncertain terms, that we are serious about this and that the American public will demand justice for anything else Imperial Germany may do."

The atmosphere in the room was as cold as it could get, and it was obvious to von Bernstorff that it was time to leave. He stood up, politely bowed to both Americans, and then spoke. *"Mr. President, Mr. Secretary of States, I will take my leave now and hope the next time we speak will be in better times."* The other two didn't answer, and he left the room, the secretary closing the door behind him.

"The bastard didn't take us seriously," started Lansing. *"Oh, but he did, Robert,"* countered Wilson. *"But I am afraid his asshole of an Emperor has decided that war with the USA was also acceptable." "Indeed, Mr. President,"* answered the Secretary of State.

"Who does he think he is, to bully me like this with his 100,000-men army," boomed the Kaiser, mad as hell following Bethmann Hollweg's (German Minister of Foreign Affairs) reading of Ambassador von Bernstorff diplomatic note following his meeting with both the U.S. President and the Secretary of State.

The top people of the Reich were meeting once more in one of the formal meeting rooms of the Berlin Palace, where they'd gathered many times before since the start of the war. The room itself had Italian marble for flooring, a nice blue glass chandelier, and a big hearth where a blazing fire burned bright to keep everyone warm.

The following people had come for the meeting that morning: Helmut von Moltke, the Chief of the General Staff (and thus head of OHL); the Minister of War, Erich von Falkenhayn, the Chief of the Operations Division; Colonel Gerhard von Tappen, and the Chief of the Information Division (intelligence), Lieutenant Colonel Richard Hentch. Paul von Hindenburg, the Commander-in-Chief of the Eastern Front, was also present to give everyone around the table an update on the soon-to-start Lithuanian offensive, along with the defensive dispositions in the Carpathians. He also was to report on the implications of the change in the overall military commander in Austria-Hungary, whom he had met a couple days before.

At the head of the table and facing them all was the Kaiser, Wilhelm II. To the right was Rear Admiral Roman Berger, the Chief of the Admiral Staff's deputy for this meeting, as Admiral Hugo von Pohl was still in Brest and St-Nazaire in France. And, of course, the German Foreign Affairs Minister (and Imperial Chancellor), Theobald von Bethmann Hollweg.

They had just sat down for the meeting, and the diplomatic note had, of course, taken the discussion by storm. War with the United States was imminent, and it would only take one more serious incident to get the Americans mad enough to declare war. None of the men in the room felt like it would be a great development, as the USA was an industrial powerhouse and had the potential to raise a large army because of its population size.

"Your Majesty," started Bethmann Holweg cautiously since, contrary to his Emperor, he knew how bad the American entry into the conflict would be for the Central Powers. *"The Americans have cause to be mad at us. While I agree with you that they are doing a little too much posturing, it remains a fact that we have sunk one of their armored cruisers, killed 1,500 sailors, and are encouraging their enemy, Revolutionary Mexico."*

"Well, they are trying to meddle in our affairs, and they haven't got the strength to defeat us," countered the Kaiser. *"Your Majesty,"* said the Chief of the Admiral Staff's deputy, Rear Admiral Roman Berger. *"The Americans have the third largest fleet right behind us, with ten dreadnought battleships and twenty-three pre-dreadnoughts. Their sudden appearance in the Atlantic would not be good for the Kaiserliche Marine."* The Emperor, who loved his fleet, was checked for a moment by the Rear-Admiral's comment.

Von Hindenburg spoke up to save face for his Emperor. The man was gaining in influence since his incredible victories in the East, and some were even murmuring that he was one day going to be the head of the OHL in replacement of von Moltke the Younger. Wilhelm the 2nd certainly liked the man as he liked every hero in the war and trusted him and his advice. *"I think we have exposed the matter of the consequences of an American entry into the war in previous discussions. The real subject here is what we do from now on. Do we accept the fact that there will be conflict with the USA, or else try to avoid it?"* He paused, looking at the Kaiser and the rest of the people around the table. The OHL was split halfway between wanting conflict with the United States and trying to avoid it.

"We all know what avoiding war with the U.S. means, gentlemen. It means stopping to attack British shipping, and letting the Entente get supplied by the Americans. The bastards are already selling arms, food, and ammo to our enemies. I am of the same opinion as the Kaiser. They can go to hell, and we'll slam their small army to oblivion if they dare to cross the Atlantic."

Wilhelm took heart at the words from his general, and smiled at Hindenburg for the support. Everyone else around the table decided that the old officer was ambitious and that he was doing this to get overall command, and he might well succeed by the way the Kaiser looked at him.

"It is decided, then," said the German leader with a firm tone. *"While we will not provoke the Americans by directly attacking their ships,"* he paused to close his fingers into a first and slammed the table. *"We'll keep the course we are on and hope for the best."*

The subject quickly moved to the Western Front after a quick ten-minute recess. The German officers and the Emperor sat back at the table, and the head of the Information Division, Lieutenant Colonel Richard Hentsch, started his presentation, standing beside a wooden board with a large operational map of the Western Front pinned on it.

"As discussed informally at the start of the meeting," he started, nodding silently at the Kaiser since he'd spoken to Wilhelm about a couple of the things he was about to present to the rest of the group, *"we will have to stay on the defensive in the West pertaining the results of the offensive in Lithuania and Poland,"* he gave a look to Hindenburg who nodded, *"and the defensive action in the Carpathians. The Reich just doesn't have the troops to attack everywhere. With two million soldiers entrenched from the Atlantic Coast to Alsace, we believe we have enough of them to hold while the Imperial Army masters the Russians and saves the Austro-*

Hungarians."

Erich von Falkenhayn, the Minister of War, lifted a hand since he had a question. *"Yes, Minister?" "To add to what you have just said, Lieutenant Colonel,"* started the man, fishing folders from his briefcase and distributing them around the table, *"here is what we plan to deliver to the Western Front in terms of ammunition ordinance and supplies. Field Marshal Karl von Bulow, the commander in the West, has assured me he will hold the Anglo-French at bat with these supplies and the men allocated to his theater."*

"Very well, thank you, Lieutenant Colonel Hentch," said von Moltke the Younger, the chief of the German General Staff and boss of the OHL. *"We'll talk about the details later in the meeting when the Kaiser has left; thus, I would like to move to the next part of the meeting."* He nodded toward Hindenburg. *"General?"* The old Prussian commander rose from his chair and moved to a different wooden board, this time with a map of Prussia, Poland, and the Carpathians. *"Thank you, Sir,"* he answered out of respect for his commander.

Hindenburg took a wooden stick and pointed at Lithuania. *"The offensive preparations are done; it took about a month and a half to accumulate enough artillery shells and the necessary supplies for the attack. The Battle for Kaunas will start soon. Our first objective here is to storm the Russian fortress and then advance northward toward St-Petersburg to force the enemy to slack off its attack on our beleaguered Austro-Hungarian ally."* He paused, putting his stick on Eastern Poland. *"Furthermore, to support the German 8th Army's offensive on Kaunas, the 9th and 12th armies will attack east of Warsaw and fork northward to add pressure on Rennenkampf's defensive dispositions. The goal is to overwhelm the Russian troops and to try and outflank them."*

"What about the defense on the Carpathian Front," asked the Kaiser worriedly. He had just spoken to the Austrian Ambassador the day before, and the Austro-Hungarian Emperor had asked for more

support. *"Your Excellency,"* answered Hindenburg by pointing his stick at the Carpathians. *"General Max von Gallwitz's 11th Army will be bolstered, as you requested this morning, by 50,000 men from my own 8th Army to bolster weak sectors of the frontline. I should also meet with the new Chief of the Austrian General Staff later this week, and I am told the man is an expert on defense. Because of this,"* continued von Hindenburg with a serious face, *"I think the Austro-Hungarians can hold while I smash the Tsar in the north and force him to send reinforcements there. Without von Hotzendorf to squander troops away in futile offensives, they should do okay. I also believe we should send them shell supplies; they will need them to stop the Russian hordes."*

"Austria needs to hold, or we are doomed," said von Falkenhayn, with the full nodding approval of von Moltke. *"Losing their soldiers would be a disaster, as well as the link with our Balkan allies and the Ottomans."* Everyone was in agreement with the statement. However, it wasn't just about wanting it, it was about defeating the Russian bear.

The discussion over the Eastern Front subject lasted for a while before things switched to the Middle East, where an attack on the Suez Canal was imminent by the Ottoman 4th Army. The matter was discussed at length, and a report from Liman von Sanders, the German military attaché in Constantinople, was read. It was decided that things were going well in that theater, and thus, the matter was put to rest within twenty-five minutes.

The last subject on the agenda was the naval war. Things there were going okay, but the naval defeat near Brest overshadowed the discussions. The German High Command knew that any sortie by the High Seas Fleet would end up in the same way, since the Royal Navy was so superior in ship strength. It was decided to put more emphasis on the U-boat war and to send some of the best imperial surface units on raiding missions.

They also discussed the news of Rear-Admiral Felix Funke about to arrive in Swakopmund, having out distanced the British Squadron pursuing it, and there were many speculative talks if von Spee would make the rendezvous in the middle of May in the Falklands.

The meeting ended with everyone in high spirits, and the war could continue.

Bordeaux, Southern France
Temporary French Capital Army HQ, April 30th, 1915

The leaders of the fledging French Republic were assembled in the mayor's building, looking out to sea and to the magnificent Bordeaux Harbor, where many warships came and went. In the background, a couple of battleships were also anchored. It was a beautiful sunny day without much wind, with the gulls yapping away overhead.

Things were not looking good for France. It had lost over one-third of its territory. What was worse is that that part (the north and Paris) was the industrial heart of France. Modern wars, as the fighting nations were starting to understand, were fought and won by the side that had the most shells, guns, and ammunition. The French Army was currently consuming more than it produced, and this was untenable in the long term. They bought what they needed from the Americans and the British sent them what they could, and yet it wasn't enough. It was doubtful the Army could resist a prolonged German offensive if the Kaiser and his generals decided to concentrate in the West. The only saving grace for France was that the enemy was busy surviving against the Russians.

"This has the looks of the last-ditch offensive," said the French President, Raymond Pointcaré. *"Is it that bad on the ground, General,"* countered Admiral Augustin Boue de Lapeyrere to Ferdinand Foch, the Commander-in-Chief of the Army. Lapeyrere was the recent victor of the Battle of Otranto against Austria Hungary, where the French fleet had defeated the Austro-Hungarian one for a much-needed national morale boost. He thus enjoyed the temporary deference given to military victors, and everyone valued his opinion on any matters pertaining to the military and the war. Foch grunted before answering.

"It's not too bad because the Germans are concentrating their offensive forces in the East since they need to stop the Russians from destroying their Austrian allies in the Carpathians. Hindenburg has just

saved Konigsberg, but the Tsar still has large armies poised to invade again if the Germans aren't careful. Russia is giving us a reprieve, one that we must use, for if the German Army defeats the Tsar, then we'll receive the full brunt of the Kaiser's bayonets and cannons in 1916." The admiral's face dawned with understanding. *"Put in that light, it does look like the last-ditch offensive, but it isn't, Mr. President, then countered Lepeyrere. What Foch is saying is that we must win; if not, things might be truly difficult in 1916 or late 1915."* Pointcaré seemed mollified by the Admiral's words since imminent doom was not at hand. But Prime Minister Viviani was not.

"General Foch, what tells us that you will succeed this time? Trench warfare is a true stalemate, and the Verdun example is a good representation that even if we break through, the Germans will just send reinforcements there, and we'll have only won a few miles."

Foch smiled. *"True, Mr. Prime Minister. But if you remember, we advanced thirty-seven miles during our Verdun offensive." "Yes, and,"* answered Viviani irritatingly. *"Well, Mr. Prime Minister, the new offensive is in the Paris area, and, at last news, the frontline was 21 miles from the center of the city."* The politician smiled and finally got to what the French general was aiming at. Reclaim Paris for French pride and morale. After all, a full one-third of the national economy was centered on the capital. Retaking it would help war production immensely.

President Pointcaré also instantly rallied to Foch's idea of an offensive. *"Well, General. Presented in this way, it doesn't look that bad after all,"* he said, pausing to take a sip of his wine. They were in a room with three large windows, letting the sun in, and they were all enjoying a little bit of cheese and wine to kill the rest of the afternoon and to accompany their meeting.

"What will you need from us apart from what we've already given you?" Foch paused at the President's words. *"Attacking in this age isn't easy. What I will need is your support and all the supplies you can*

send me." He paused, crossing his hands and fingers together in one mingled fist. *"There will come a time when it will be looking dark, but this is when we cannot falter and need to keep up the assaults to break the enemy line."*

"Very well," answered Viviani as he nodded to the President. *"Speaking of support and supplies, I have a meeting with the U.S. Ambassador to France again tomorrow, and this time, it's the Americans who have called the meeting. Apparently, things are getting worse with the Germans, so I guess they want to help us more and talk some strategy,"* he smiled. *"General Foch, a certain General Pershing will be along with the Ambassador and a few other people; I was wondering if you could attend the discussions with me."*

"Indeed," said Foch with a large smile, knowing that meant American full support for France. *"According to the rumors, the recent meeting in Washington D.C. between the German Ambassador and the U.S. President didn't go well. Badly enough, even, for the United States Army to want to make the trip to talk to us about collaborating, it seems."*

Pointcaré refiled his wine bottle as he smiled with enthusiasm. *"That calls for a toast, gentlemen,"* he said, with everyone following suit moments later.

Things weren't rosy for France, but they were looking up. The discussion continued for some time, and then everyone went back to their tasks at hand.

The British leadership was again meeting for another important meeting, and First Lord of the Admiralty Winston Churchill had the impression that everything was always critical these days. They were in the same room as usual, intricately decorated with wood paneling, an old but expensive-looking rug, and a chandelier above. In the back of the room sat a fireplace, but there was no fire as it was a hot day outside. A large central table with twelve chairs was positioned in the middle, where the British leaders were having their discussion on the situation, and their next steps.

Winston was chewing on his cigar, his mind far away into the Middle East and towards the next adventure. The British forces were on the verge of opening a new front. The 15th Division was already in Aden with a fleet escorted by two old armored cruisers. His plan was to get the troops into Southern Iraq to a place called Kuwait. He was impatient to talk to Kitchener about getting more troops there once the landing was successful.

The main objective was to capture Basra northward, as well as the fort in the Fao Peninsula (Al Faw in Arabic language) just north of Kuwait City, a small Arab town in Southern Iraq bordering the Arabian Sea. Churchill, as well as the Indian Viceroy in New Delhi, were concerned that Turkish troops were in a position to strike the Anglo-Persian Oil Company from Kuwait and Basra, both in Ottoman territory. It was decided to use the Indian troops of Force D (15th Division), along with British Royal Marines, to execute a landing and capture the Turkish bases before they could be thus used.

The operation relied on speed and shock action, and he was worried the Ottomans had a strong garrison in the Fao Fortress. The two armored cruisers with their 5-inch guns would support the landing troops and duel with whatever guns the Turks had in place. And... *"Winston, are you with us,"* said Asquith, seeing Churchill was far away. *"Ah yes, Mr. Prime Minister, I apologize. I was thinking about the landings in Southern Iraq."* Asquith made a face and smiled. *"Winston, always the adventurer and dreamer,"* everyone laughed out loud. *"So, the question to you was, Winston, any news of the German fleet at large in the Atlantic?"* Churchill also smiled, put his chewed cigar in the ashtray, and spoke.

"None, Sir. But Admiral Beatty assured me that he knows where the Germans were going, and he was waiting for them there." "And where is that," countered Kitchener, facing him on the other side of the table. *"Ah, the Admiral is certain the German squadron at large is going to meet up with Maximilian Von Spee in the Southern Atlantic, and thus, he has moved the entire Mediterranean Squadron into Port Stanley and is just going to smoothly wait for the bastards in the Falkland Islands."*

Kitchener smiled. *"Well, let's hope he is right."* Everyone around the table laughed once more. *"Lord Kitchener,"* said Churchill, smiling as well. *"I have full confidence in Admiral Beatty."*

"Gentlemen, can we get back to the subject at hand," said Asquith, trying to take control of his meeting again.

The Kings in the Balkans
End of April, in Athens, Sofia, and somewhere in Moldavia

Jassy (Iasi), Cetatuia monastery April 29th, 1915

The Cetatuia Monastery was a beautiful medieval structure protected by sturdy walls. It was located by the Bahlui River, a tributary of the Prut River. It was built on a hill overlooking the old city of Jassy, now called Iasi. Jassy had been the site of many battles in the past, and used to be part of the Principality of Bessarabia and Valachia during Ottoman times. Fought over by the Turks, and the Russians for centuries, the territory and the city were now part of the Russian Empire.

But ever since the unfortunate Romanian entry into the Great War and their cursory attack on Transylvania (Austria-Hungary), it was now the temporary capital of the new King Ferdinand the 1st, the nephew of the late King Carol the 1st, who died at the beginning of the 1915 year. The fight for Romania itself was brief and intense, and in the end, Ferdinand's armies were overrun by a combined attack from the Bulgarians, the Austro-Hungarians, the Germans, and even the Ottomans. The forces of the four countries blitzed all over the country, occupied the capital, Bucharest, and pushed the surviving Romanian Armies (1st, 2nd, and 4th) out of Romania and into Moldavia, a region that was owned by the Russian Empire.

Now, the Romanian troops continued their struggle against the Central Powers with Russian support and from Russian territory. It was a peculiar situation, but it was either that or full surrender, something that King Ferdinand I wasn't ready to contemplate.

"At the very least, your Majesty," said the commander of the Romanian 4th Army and overall commander of the Royal forces, General Constantin Prezan, *"the view is nice."* Located on the top of the so-called Cetatuia Hill, the religious building was built by Prince Gheorghe Duca several centuries ago.

The building was well preserved and surrounded by fortifications with towers on the corners. It provided great protection for the fledgling Romanian King. The name itself, Cetatuia meant fortress in Romanian. *"I suppose it does, General,"* answered the King as he looked down on the city, seemingly quiet.

The two men were standing on one of the corner towers of the fortification and were having a discussion about the military situation. *"Your Majesty, as I was saying,"* continued Prezan, lighting his tobacco pipe and scratching his long beard. *"The military forces are in tatters. We lack in everything, including food, ammunition, and artillery shells. There is no hope of any supplies getting through from the Entente Powers in the West, and the Russians aren't giving much."* The general paused for a moment, exhaling a large cloud of stinky, billowing smoke. King Ferdinand didn't budge, as he was also a smoker and didn't care much for the smell, except that it gave him the idea of fishing out his cigarette pack and following his military commander into the act.

Once he was done, he stayed silent, taking a long drag as well, then exhaled, which seemed to calm him down. His smoke drifted in the light spring wind. *"Can you resist the next assault, General? The enemy is said to be moving to finish the work they have started earlier this year."* Prezan hesitated before answering, concentrating on the horizon in the hope it would give him an answer. *"Your Majesty, my men will give everything they have. The Russians have also sent some troops to help as they do not want the Central Powers to enter Moldavia. I would thus say with a measure of confidence,"* he paused, again taking an intake of smoke from his pipe, *"that the enemy doesn't have enough troops to pierce our lines. We lack in everything, but we still have the men, and it comes down to it; your brave soldiers will fight with their swords and bayonets."*

The Central Powers, with Bulgaria and Turkey in the lead, were indeed about to launch a new offensive aimed at knocking Romania out of the war for good.

ROMANIA

405,000 soldiers	Commander	Soldiers	Area of operation
1st Army	General Ioan Culcer	280,000 soldiers	Moldavia
2nd Army	General Alexandru Averescu	55,000 soldiers	Moldavia
4th Army	General Constantin Prezan	74,000 soldiers	Moldavia

To meet the onslaught, the Royal Army still had 405,000 soldiers in the form of the 1st Army (Ioan Culcer), the 2nd Army (Alexandru Averescu), and the 4th Army (Prezan). The 3rd had been destroyed during the invasion of Romania itself.

BULGARIA

176,000 soldiers	Commander	Soldiers	Area of operation
1st Army	General Kliment Boyadzhiev	75,000 soldiers	Bessarabia
2nd Army	General Georgi Todorov	31,000 soldiers	Bessarabia
3rd Army	General Toshev	33,000 soldiers	Bessarabia
49th German Division	General Anton Dankt	16,000 Soldiers	Bessarabia

Ottoman Empire

3rd Army	Hafiz Hakki Pasha	15,000 soldiers	Bessarabia

Austria-Hungary East

3rd Army	General Rudolf Brudermann	95,000 soldiers	Romania

They were faced with the might of a little over 300,000 Central Powers troops, including men from four nations. While not all of these troops were doing well, they were recently victorious (and thus had high morale) and were somewhat better supplied than their Romanian counterparts. By no means did the Turks and the Bulgarians have better troops, but the Germans and Austro-Hungarians were modern armies and were well-equipped.

The multinational forces were under the command of Bulgarian General Kliment Boyadzhiev, closely supported by the German military mission commander to Bulgaria, General Anton Dankt, also commander of the German 49th Infantry Division. Of note, the German contingent was also very well supplied in artillery, with the

4th Artillery Regiment with its heavy Howitzer guns. Given the Romanians' paucity of guns, the Germans were thus the kings of the battlefield. The main advantage of the Central Powers in the coming fight was that their soldiers and gunners had enough ammo to fight compared to their beleaguered Romanian enemies. Even the Russian reinforcements to the area (66,000 men) were not of the best quality, and since priority was given to Brussilov and his about-to-start offensive, they also didn't come with a lot of supplies.

"I certainly hope so," answered Ferdinand, meekly. The man was utterly discouraged and wondered how his country would get out of its current predicament. *"When do you think the enemy attack will begin,"* he continued. General Prezan hesitated for a moment, calculating. He had no serious reports or information giving him a date. However, from the looks of the enemy preparations and the few deserters who spoke to his frontline commanders (many Romanians fought in the Austro-Hungarian Army and tended to desert when they had the chance), it was likely that it would commence very soon. *"The battle will start in early May, Your Majesty."* The Romanian military commander gestured wide with his arms toward the faraway frontline. *"We have built a solid trench network, and our defenses are ready. We will weather the storm,"* he finished confidently. *"I certainly hope so for our sakes, General,"* answered the King as he took a long smoke intake from his cigarette. The billowing and wind-dissipating smoke drifted away, just like Ferdinand's dreams of victory.

Vrana, Bulgaria
Royal Palace, April 28th, 1915

The Vrana Royal Palace was located near Sofia, the Bulgarian capital. Surrounded by a magnificent park, it was one of the most amazing and beautiful places in all of the country. It covered a large area and was the private estate of the Bulgarian ruler. There were many trees, planted by Ferdinand himself that he hoped one day would grow to a large size and live to hundreds of years. They would, and the future population of the country would come to this place as tourists to get a glimpse of the old days.

The Palace was a two-story building. On the ground floor, there was a large study, a dining room, a very large library, and a large veranda covered in windows. On the second floor were located the chambers for the Royal Family and guests. The royal palace was beautifully decorated with art and paintings. The southern facade was covered with lacquered wood. The tiles on the roof were a bright red, making the sunshine on them at sundown.

King Ferdinand I, ruler of Bulgaria, was busy watching a few bird specimens he'd spotted in the morning, but in a casual way, and from the inside of his veranda. The man was passionate about birds. This was why he'd chosen Vrana since it was a nesting place for many bird species in the area. He had his arms crossed behind his back and was standing up. In fact, he wasn't really looking at the birds. He was indeed seeing them, but he was concentrating on other matters, matters of state.

A small table was right beside him, with a steaming teacup that had been put there by one of the palace servants a minute earlier. The King was pondering on the war, which was certainly going well for Bulgaria. The Army, along with the help of the Turks and the Germans, had defeated the Romanians across the northern border and shattered its military forces, occupying the country in a matter of weeks.

His mind was far away in a place called Moldavia, where his forces were about to launch the offensive supposed to break the Romanian's will to fight. Ferdinand had his eyes set on Romanian territory that Bulgaria had wanted for a long time, some of it lost very recently in the Second Balkan War. Namely, the region of Southern Dobruja was annexed by Romania in the Treaty of Bucharest following Bulgaria's grave defeat against a coalition of Serbs, Turks, Romanians, and Greeks.

"So, as I was saying, Your Majesty," said Dimitar Geshov, King Ferdinand's Military advisor. *"Our troops are about to launch the assault along with the Germans on the southern sector of the front with the aim of driving all the way to Iasi, and the troops we have ordered to Southern Dobruja have taken possession of the territory for the crown."* "Very well," answered the King with satisfaction. "Any news on the promised German military shipment of arms and supplies?"

The General hesitated for a moment. *"Ah, well, sir, the German Ambassador has told me that there have been some delays because of the Austro-Hungarian difficulties in the Carpathians. Germany is giving priority to the area, for if it falls, the war is over for our Austrian ally." "Of course, it was to be expected. Could we have been so stupid as to rely on German promises like we did?" "Ah, but Your Majesty,"* countered Geshov, who had been one of the top supporters of joining Germany (his argument had been the supplies themselves), *"it will come, I guarantee it."*

King Ferdinand's eyes stayed glued to the outside. He was busy trying to figure out what was the large blue bird in the distance. He wasn't certain it was a European Roller. *"Make sure the Germans follow through on their promise. The Turks are also saying they are behind on their shipments." "Very well, Sire."*

Apart from the Kaiser's broken promises, things were doing well for Bulgaria, and it was well on its way to getting rid of its traditional Romanian enemy. There would remain the question of the territories the Greeks and the Turks took from Bulgaria following the Second Balkan War, but at least they were being compensated with traditional lands they wanted over Bulgaria's western border since they had defeated Serbia.

The bird flew closer, and the King was happy to see that it was, indeed, a European Roller. He was looking forward to taking a walk and trying to find its nesting place. It was Spring, after all.

Tatoi Summer Palace
April 30th, 1915

"Finally," said King Constantine as he crossed the open door of the Tatoi Summer Palace. The day was finally upon him and his family, and they were moving to Tatoi once more. The magnificent palace was only for the summer months, and he'd longed to be here during the cold winter months. He didn't like Athens so much, as it was too busy and there were too many people in the Royal Palace in the center of the city.

The Tatoi Summer Palace was a sprawling 10,000-acre property of buildings, gardens, and a magnificent, groomed forest overlooking the city of Athens. Close enough, but also far enough from the bustling capital, it was a haven of peace for the Greek King. *"Your Majesty,"* said one of the servants, saluting him as he walked past, carrying a heavy wooden crate containing several of the previous years wine bottles. The man moved to the side and went down a stone stairway, where the wine cellar was. *"Is the swimming pool ready,"* he said to another servant. *"Unfortunately, no. Your Majesty, but it should be within the week,"* *"Very well,"* answered Constantine in a happy mood. *"Be patient, husband,"* said his wife, Queen Sofia. As Crown Prince of Greece (before his ascendency to the throne), Constantine married her in 1889. She was a granddaughter of Queen Victoria and sister of Kaiser Wilhelm II, explaining his Germanophile links and propensity to support Germany. *"Indeed, my love,"* he answered as one of his sons, George, ran between a servant's legs, also happy to be back at the Tatoi Summer Palace it would seem.

"Your Majesty," said yet another servant, bowing. *"Prime Minister Andropoulos Kostapukis is already waiting for you in the study."* *"Thank you,"* he answered, turning toward his wife. *"Duty calls, my love."* She smiled before turning to the rest of their kids to manage their excitement of being in the new place.

He climbed the winding marble stairway to the second floor and entered his study, where the Prime Minister was indeed waiting for him by the window, looking outside. Kostapukis turned and bowed. *"My King,"* he said. *"Ah, Andropoulos, how are you doing,"* answered Constantine, moving toward his desk. He sat down, running his hand on the polished wood surface. How he liked this place, admiring the large windows, the table in the background with the chandelier. The paintings and the plush green rug were magnificent. He spent most of his working hours in this room when at the Tatoi Palace. He then laid back in the plush chair while Kostapukis patiently waited, sitting in the chair on the other side of the desk. *"What is the news, my dear Prime Minister,"* said the King. They hadn't seen each other in over a week. *"All is well, your Majesty,"* answered the Kostapukis, handing over a folder from his briefcase to his ruler. *"The fleet is slowly getting repaired in Constantinople, the occupation troops in Macedonia and Serbia are doing well against an unruly populace, and the war is going well in general for the Central Powers."* *"That's good news, I like it. No change from last week."* Constantine smiled and then looked outside. The sun was shining, and he was very happy.

Things were indeed going well for Greece since it joined the Central Powers, apart from the loss of a few ships from its precious fleet. It had conquered new territories, and his German Kaiser relative had sent him a few arms and supply shipments (even a new type of artillery howitzer for the troops). *"There is just one thing to discuss, Your Majesty. Berlin continues to ask us to send troops abroad to fight against the Romanians or to help them in the Carpathian frontline."* Constantine made a face. *"Have you conveyed to them that we will not do it? We have joined the Central Powers, but our views are limited to what happens locally. Our army is very small, and we need these troops to defend against a possible Franco-British attack. After all, we do not want what happened to the Italians to happen to us as well."*

"I know and have conveyed our position on this, Your Majesty. Yet, they continue to insist and have mentioned the possibility of stopping the arms and supplies shipments if we don't participate more."

Constantine stood up and walked back and forth in the room, thinking before answering. He came back to the desk and sat back down. *"What exactly is it, and how many troops are they asking for,"* he then said in a defeated tone. *"They would like us to contribute a couple of our best divisions, and have them moved to Transylvania to bolster the southern flank of their Carpathian defense."* The King looked at his Prime Minister with a serious face. *"What do you believe we should do, Kostopoulos? I think, Your Majesty, that we should agree. We are in this for the duration, I am afraid, and not helping the overall Central Powers cause will not help our position if Germany is defeated. Even if he is victorious, the Kaiser will remember we didn't help him, and that won't help us when it comes time to sign treaties and get new territories."*

The tug-of-war between the two men had been an ongoing discussion for a month and a half by the end of April. On one side was the Prime Minister, wanting to agree to German demands, while the King was typically against it. But Kostapukis was insistent, as well, for that matter was Berlin, and the German Ambassador in Athens.

"Very well," finally answered Constantine, who decided that this little bit of discussion wouldn't ruin his good mood, and the happy moment of moving into Tatoi Palace. *"Order the army to send two divisions to wherever the German commands want us to."*

General Brussilov's HQ

Russian-Occupied Austro-Hungarian Galicia, April 30th, 1915

The throng of Russian officers clustered around the Tsar, and the Commander-in-Chief of the Army, Grand Duke Nikolai Nikolaevich, walked in front of the line of 152mm Howitzer field guns, all arrayed and ready to fire. Nicolas II was on a tour of the frontline to bolster morale, as well as to better understand what was happening in the war. He'd taken a train from St-Petersburg, first stopping in Lithuania before the Germans arrived in front of Kaunas. Then, he made his way through Eastern Poland to visit the troops of General Andrey Selivanov. In both instances, he'd been rattled by the apparent lack of supplies, and also because some soldiers didn't even have rifles. Now, at Brussilov's HQ on the eve of the offensive, he was feeling a lot better.

The line stretched as far as the eye could see from north to south. There were two more lines in front and behind, making for an impressive number of guns poised to rain death on the enemy. Behind the guns stood the men, all at attention for their Emperor, giving the military salute as if on parade. Behind the line of men lay the large earthen bunkers built to store the humongous amount of artillery shells assembled for the biggest bombardment the war had seen to date.

The 152mm gun, or, more properly, the *"6 dm polevaja gaubitsa sistemy Schneidera"* as it was called in the Russian Army, was based on a French design, which followed along conventional lines. A gun shield to protect the handlers and a pneumatic recoil system. Along with France, the gun was the most modern in the Entente force arsenals.

"General," said Tsar Nicolas II, the Emperor of Russia. *"This arrayed artillery looks impressive." "Thank you, Your Majesty,"* answered the old imperial officer (Brussilov had been fighting in the Russian Army since the Russo-Turkish War of 1877-1878). *"And you say you have*

enough shells to fire continuously for days?" "Indeed, my Tsar," answered the general as he walked on Nicolas' right side. *"We intend to attack the Austro-Hungarian and German Lines in six different spots with a similar preparation. The idea is as old as warfare. Attack the line, find a weak spot, breakthrough, and exploit the breach. Except that this time, we'll do it with six different armies. We have a great numerical superiority against the Central Powers, and, thanks to the Grand Duke's approval,"* continued Brussilov, nodding to the Tsar's uncle, Nikolai Nikolaevich, *"we will use it simultaneously to overwhelm the enemy. We have enough shells to do a creeping barrage as the troops advance toward the Austro-Hungarian lines and beyond."*

The offensive's architect mentioned the Grand Duke first because the man's ego had to be entertained, but he also referred to a meeting with the Grand Duke and the rest of the generals in January of 1915, where the strategy to follow for the Spring of 1915 had been decided.

Initially, things had looked like the Russian Army would defend against the incoming German offensive in Lithuania and Poland, since it threatened the very core of Russia and the capital, St-Petersburg, and then send some attacks in the Carpathians but nothing truly serious. The country was experiencing, after all, shortages in everything related to war: guns, ammo, shells, food, and even rifles. Regardless of these facts, Brussilov had come to the meeting with a bold proposal. Attack Austria-Hungary with everything the Russians had to knock it out of the war in one fell swoop and sort of accept there would be shortcomings elsewhere.

Most of the assembled generals did not like it. What he'd proposed was a major offensive spanning a front as large as 600 hundred miles. The realities of Russian supplies and logistical capabilities were so terrible that everyone (except Brussilov) doubted the Army could prepare for such an attack. *"Grand Duke,"* he'd appealed to the Commander-in-Chief the following evening (it had been a three-day conference). Brussilov was able to get the man into a one-on-one meeting by inviting him to his tent to have an incredibly rare wine (an

1880 Tzar Alexander III Era Wine), and the Grand Duke, being a wine lover, had accepted the invitation with enthusiasm. With a few drinks in him, the mollified officer listened to what the old general had to say and started to like it. *"With methodical preparation, enough guns and shells, and a different tactical outlook, I am certain we can achieve a breakthrough and possibly knock the Habsburgs out of the war, Sir. Especially if you support the idea. This is the chance you have to look strong in the Tsar's eyes." "Show me how you would do this,"* answered a curious Nikolai Nikolaevich. And the rest was history.

The Russian attack across the line, launched on May 2nd, was the biggest offensive of the war to date in terms of men, with 1,200,000 soldiers sprinkled in six powerful armies. Such an attack would not have been possible in the Fall of 1914, but now that Russian factories were finally starting to make the shells and the guns in reasonable quantities, and thanks to arms sales from the United States, Japan, and Great Britain, it was.

The plan was a mixture of brute force with tactical mobility merged along with the shock and awe of the biggest artillery preparation of the war to date.

Galicia and Prezmysl			
1,200,000 soldiers	Commander	Soldiers	Area of operation
3rd Army	General Nikolai Ruzsky	200,000 soldiers	Carpathians
4th Army	General Alexei Evert	300,000 soldiers	Carpathians
5th Army	General Pavel Plehve	300,000 soldiers	Carpathians
8th Army	General Aleksei Alekseevich Brusilov	250,000 soldiers	Carpathians
9th Army	General Platon Lechitsky	200,000 soldiers	Carpathians
Moscow Front	General Dimitri Doctorov	600,000 soldiers	Carpathians and Bessarabia

And the attack had to work since it *"bankrupted"* the rest of the Russian forces across the Eastern Front. Supply priority was given to Brussilov in all manners of ammunition, shells, machine guns, and rifles. Since the rest of the Imperial forces were to stay on the defensive, it was decided that their lack of supplies would be fine if they did not attack or move out of their positions.

"When is the attack starting, General," asked the Tsar as he walked

up to a gun barrel and ran his hand across it to the stunned (and adoring) face of the sergeant in charge of it. The Tsar was adored by his deeply religious people, and the Army was the embodiment of that adoration.

The Grand Duke, not wanting to be left out of the discussion (he was the Commander-in-Chief, after all), answered. *"The artillery bombardment will start at dusk tomorrow, and the attack is set for the early morning of the 2nd of May, Your Excellency."* Brussilov, walking to face Nicolas on the other side of the gun barrel, also put his hand on it and spoke as well. *"The six armies from Moldova to Northern Galicia will launch an assault that will stun the enemy. We will break through, my Emperor."*

"Very well, this seems like a well-planned operation," countered the Tsar with a smile. *"Now, General Brussilov, didn't you mention a few Vodka bottles in your HQ?"* *"Indeed, Your Majesty,"* answered the General. *"This way, please,"* as he gestured toward a large field tent further out behind the line of guns.

CHAPTER 2
THE EASTERN FRONT

A spray of bullets plastered the ground just before Radno's feet, and Helmut pulled him to his side and behind the cover he was already in. *"Careful, buddy, or else you could die on me,"* he said, to which his Slovene friend smiled as he regained his balance. The Austro-Hungarian soldier had pulled him by his small backpack to move him out of the enemy line of fire he'd just spotted. The Romanian machine gun was well hidden behind a rocky outcrop. *"Thank you, Helmut, that would have been the end of me."* The dust from the rounds that had almost killed his friend slowly billowed in the wind.

Helmut Gottenburg and Radno Karacivs, both private soldiers in the Austro-Hungarian 21st Landwehr Division, were currently fighting in the Oituz Pass, near the city of the same name, deep in the Carpathian Mountains that lay in Eastern Romania.

The Germano-Austrian goal (there were no Bulgarian and Turks in this part of the frontline) was to breakthrough southern Moldova to advance toward the cities of Focsani and Marasesti. The Brussilov offensive had just started up north, and the idea for the southern armies in Romania was to battle and break through to offer a diversion. The general idea remained the survival of Austria-Hungary. If the combined armies of Bulgaria, Turkey, Germany, and Austria could pierce the southern frontline and advance into the Southern Ukraine, the Russians would have no choice but to address it and divert troops from their Galician-Carpathian offensive.

General Przyborski's unit, the 21st Landwer Division, was thus tasked to get across the Oituz Pass and capture the town on the other side to pave the way for more Central Powers troops to move in. As one of its most experienced units, the 8th Austro-Hungarian Regiment was thus at the forefront of the assault. After all, its men (well, those who were still alive anyway) were some of the more battle-hardened in the Empire.

Helmut was from the original stock, while Radno was one of the replacements sent to the unit following its terrible casualties during the first two failed offensives into Serbia by then (now sacked) General Potiorek.

At first, the two men couldn't speak with each other, as Radno didn't know one word of German and Helmut not a peep in Slovene, but they'd eventually learned each other's language, and they were now conversing fluidly in a weird mix of both tongues.

"Do you see where the bastards are," continued Helmut. Several men were huddled beside and behind them as the pass was rocky, and they'd found a big ridge to hide from the fire of the enemy. By the vagaries of war, there were no officers nor NCOs present with them, as the unit was scattered across the ground, and everyone had run for cover when the Romanians started shooting. "No," answered Radno, peering out cautiously. He was rewarded by a flurry of bullets, impacting the rock with a bunch of clicking and ricocheting noises. Smoke and dust billowed all around as the rock splintered into small pieces. *"However,"* continued the Slovene, "I am pretty sure they see us and that we shouldn't move in this direction."

Helmut laughed. *"Rad,"* (that's how he liked to call him now), *"you are very insightful." "Well, thank you, my German friend." "What do we do now,"* yelled one of the men behind the two. *"There is no one to give us orders,"* continued the voice. Helmut spoke up. "Who cares; we know where the enemy is, and that we need to kill him. Let's find a way to do just that."

They spent the next ten minutes strategizing on what angle of approach they should take, and then Radno's idea won out. He proposed to crawl into the small depression in the ground that led to another ridge about fifteen yards away. The whole argument was that, yes, they could see it was a ditch, but a very shallow one. Radno's entire argument was that with the slope's angle, the enemy would not be able to see them if they kept low enough. Helmut wasn't so sure. But the Slovene had won the argument since he'd volunteered to be first.

As he started to crawl ever so slowly (the idea was also to avoid unsettling any dust on the ground), Helmut looked at his friend with nervousness. The man was brave to a fault, but it wouldn't serve the imperial cause to have him killed because of a simple miscalculation. But then, within the first ten seconds, it was obvious he had been right, and that the Romanian machine gunners could not see him. He made it all the way to the other ridge. Helmut thus crawled in the shallow ditch right after him.

Twenty minutes later, the entire group (there were eighteen soldiers) was across. Helmut turned to look back toward the Austro-German lines and saw that most of their comrades were still pinned down by the withering enemy machine gun fire.

In their new position, they had a better view of the Romanian gunners and could see their uniforms. *"We've got a shot, Rad,"* said the Austrian to the other. *"Indeed, we do. But we need to have complete surprise and fire at the same time,"* answered the Slovene, signaling to the rest of the men to prepare to aim and fire. *"Once we send the volley, we sprint towards the machine gun."*

(... Moments later (...)

"Go!!!" yelled Helmut as the smoke from their volley drifted in the air. They stepped over the ridge and into their own smoke to sprint. Both Helmut and Radno could now see the machine gun position. They had actually "appeared" right behind the main Romanian trench, which had ingeniously been built along a ledge partly made of rock and dirt. They were facing maybe three or four companies of startled enemy machine gunners and riflemen. The first few seconds of the fight were one-sided. Explosions (some of the soldiers had Rohr Grenades), bullets, and Austro-Hungarian soldiers with knives did short work of about two-thirds of the enemy before they could sufficiently react to the surprise.

Then, mayhem erupted. Helmut had dropped right on top of a dead enemy that seemed to look at the sky with dull eyes and a gaping mouth full of blood. He rapidly rolled to the side to avoid a Romanian bayonet thrust and certain death, firing his rifle in the man's face. Blood and brain matter washed over him.

While dirt showered onto the assaulting soldiers, with bullets and shells hitting the top of the trench, the sounds of battle were overwhelming. There were whistling sounds of artillery shells, loud thumps, explosions, and the staccato rhythm of machine guns spewing bullets everywhere. He peered a look towards the enemy position, firing on them while the shooting abated somewhat. The machine gun trench was there within another twenty seconds. It was a bloody fight, and the poor Romanian soldiers, as brave as they had been, were no match for the rush of men that swamped them.

Helmut looked down the path leading 100 yards below to the pass the army was trying to force through the mountain. He could see that the troops below had seen their assault and were now advancing steadily. The battle for the Oituz Pass was far from over, but they'd won the first round.

16th Moscow Regiment
The Brussilov Offensive Part 1, May 2nd, 1915

The dust and smoke were barely scattering in the light breeze of the morning when the Russian 16th Moscow Regiment, along with several other units, sprinted out of their defensive positions to charge at the outlying Austro-Hungarian defensive lines.

Within that mass of brown uniformed soldiers lay the 12th company, one of the Regiment's constituent units. That regiment was the home of Private soldier Dimitri Fedorov. Before him towered the daunting sight of the enemy defenses on the rock. A bunch of monolithic rockfaces and hills that still smoked and burned from the recent heavy shelling they had just endured.

They'd been told that the Austrians would be stunned out of their minds by the mass shelling that the very impressive bombardment had inflicted on the fortress since the early hours of the morning. Dimitri had watched in awe while one gigantic explosion after the other rocked the enemy trench line. All during that time, he had felt bad for the poor blokes on the other side. He did not harbor any hate toward his enemies. They were at war, and that was that. Hence why, he felt bad about it, trying to portray the same situation but from his point of view.

When the guns finally fell silent, an eerie calm dropped over the entire battlefield. For a long ten minutes, things stayed still for the Entente and the Central Powers. Nothing moved. There were, of course, no birds or animals. No humans walked the distance between the Austro-Hungarian trenches and the Russian troops. It was a wasteland of mangled earth, small fires, and dark, scattering smoke.

And then it was time. The whistle of Lieutenant Joseph Karatin, one of their officers, blew, giving the signal to advance toward the enemy positions. Every soldier in the 16th Regiment felt confident that they wouldn't be fired at, as they could not imagine anyone surviving the onslaught that the heavy Russian imperial guns had put the defenders through.

They advanced about 100 yards when the first few shots rang out from the opposing side. They had almost reached the mangled line of broken barbed wire when all hell broke loose. At first, Dimitri thought it was just going to be scattered fire as some Austro-Hungarians were bound to have survived the ordeal. But then, as the seconds ticked by, more and more bullets and the noise of rifle fire started to make an appearance. Within a minute, many of his comrades fell on the ground, hit by enemy bullets. Fedorov regretted feeling bad for the bastards trying to kill him and now wished them all dead. Then large blasts started to blossom within the 12th midst, indicating that the enemy still had artillery field guns or their gun emplacement bunkers had survived the heavy shelling of the last few hours.

"Damn, this is a mess," said the soldier as he crouched behind a large boulder. *"Come over here for cover,"* the man yelled, but before Dimitri could answer, a shell landed almost on top of his head, and he was obliterated. The concussion of the blast threw Dimitri to the ground, and he temporarily lost his breath. He lay still on his back for about half a minute, stunned out of his mind and dazed. The enemy fire was heavy. So heavy, in fact, that he could see some of the bullets.

He stood up and sprinted toward a rocky boulder while several rounds whizzed by in his ears. With one last jump to the ground, he made it to the relative safety of the boulder's shadow, where several other soldiers were already sheltering. *"What do you think,"* he heard them say as he found an empty spot on the side of the rock. *"Will they call off the attack? I mean, enemy fire seems pretty heavy, and we already have a lot of casualties. Crossing this open, desolate field is dangerous while the enemy stands guard."* The man facing him made a sour face before answering. *"You know, Pavel, I don't care what's the plan. I am staying here unless an officer comes around and tells me to face this wall of lead over there,"* he pointed toward the enemy trench ridgeline, referring to the murderous enemy fire.

Dimitri had to give it to the first soldier. What he said made a lot of sense, and he'd long learned that being stupidly brave, like some, might give you a medal or two but could also earn you a quick ticket to the afterlife.

The group of leaderless soldiers stayed put while the battle raged, once in a while stepping over the boulder to shoot their rifles, just in case an officer watched, or worse, they were spotted by Sergeant Radetzky, their tough and gritty NCO. They didn't want to get in trouble, but also didn't want to die. This attack was going nowhere, and they knew it, so they decided to be smart about it.

Half an hour later, the attack was indeed called off, and they were ordered back to their trench lines and makeshift bunkers they'd built over the winter months.

A day before, the Brussilov offensive had been launched. The goal of the campaign was no less than knocking Austria-Hungary out of the war. The Dual Monarchy, already shaking on its base because of the defeats of the Fall of 1914 and the Otranto Naval defeat was one big disaster away from suing for peace.

The Russian Army opened the attack with a 24-hour heavy artillery bombardment, thanks to months of accumulating the necessary shells to execute it. As the smoke cleared on the dreary morning of the 2nd of May, 1915, Russian infantry came out of the artificially induced fog, preceded by one hell of a creeping barrage to keep the Austrians pinned down. The Russian 5th Army (General Pavel Plehve) and 9th Army (General Platon Lechitsky) rapidly broke through the first Austro-Hungarian lines of defenses, while other Russian formations were held back (like in Dimitri Fedorov's sector) by more sturdy units (like in the German 11th Army sector, with their commander General Max von Gallwitz).

By the 4th of May, the situation was critical for the Austro-Hungarian

4th Army under the command of General Moritz von Auffenberg, with the losses of a little under 55,000 soldiers, with half of them captured.

By the end of May 6th, the Austro-Hungarian 4th Army's ordeal continued to worsen. It was pushed back twenty-five kilometers, and its trench lines were all conquered, making for an open-field battle like at the beginning of the war. By the end of May 7th, the Austro-Hungarian's 4th Army's retreat was unstoppable, with many elements of the 10th Corps surrendering when caught in the open. 4th Army supplies were abandoned in a major depot (the town of Lutz) and set aflame before the Russians occupied the town.

While the rest of the Central Powers forces struggled mightily to contain the Russian hordes and succeeded with varying degrees of success, the disaster in the 4th Army sector, located in the center of the frontline, created a full panic in Austrian leadership circles.

From one moment to the next, Austria-Hungarians were staring down the ominous barrel of defeat.

The German attack on Kaunas Part 1
Hindenburg Forces launched at Lithuania, May 2nd to May 6th, 1915

The weather was picture-perfect from the Baltic to the Black Sea in the 1st week of May. The sun was shining, and the wind was almost dead, giving the artillerymen perfect conditions to fire and the spotter planes above the perfect view to give them where to fire. Thus, it wasn't surprising to see both the Central Powers and the Entente launching their long-awaited offensives.

In the North, the Russians were in a defensive posture, and thus, the Germans came at them, emboldened by their Konigsberg victory in January. The reasons for the Russians to stay put were multiple, ranging from some supply issues (there was enough ammo and shells but not enough for a large offensive), but the main one was because Brussilov's offensive in the south sucked up all of the Tsar's attention along with all the available supplies.

The German armies, reinforced by several batches of soldiers following the victory in the West (Battle of the Marne), now numbered 550,000 soldiers and were under the direct command of Eric Luddendorf and Paul von Hindenburg, the dynamic duo of generals in charge of the East. The attack into Lithuania was also designed to act as a diversion for the main attack in Poland from General August von Mackensen (the Gorlice-Tarnow Offensive), set to start a week after the attack on Kaunas and the push northward.

Germany– East			
East Prussia			
550,000 soldiers	Commander	Soldiers	Area of operation
8th Army	General von Hindenburg and Luddendorf	300,000 soldiers	East Prussia

To face them, Russian commander General Paul von Rennenkampf possessed a major numerical superiority (albeit badly equipped and supplied), which didn't seem to bother the Germans in the very least.

Northwestern Front (Lithuania and Baltic States)			
1,490,000 soldiers	Commander	Soldiers	Area of operation
1st Army	General Paul von Rennenkampf	350,000 soldiers	Baltic States
10th Army	General Vasily Flug	400,000 soldiers	Baltic States
Northwest Army	General Yakov Zhilinskiy	333,000 soldiers	Baltic States
Southwest Army	General of Infantry Nikolai Ivanov	410,000 soldiers	Baltic States

Rennenkampf's command was spread out, with the Russian 1st Army defending the center in the Kaunas Fortress. The two German generals thus surmised they could take on Russian armies one at a time, and their campaign started right at Kaunas.

The Kaunas Fortress was the largest land defensive complex in the entire Russian Empire and was designed to defend against a major German offensive. Covering a staggering twenty-five square miles, it was built from 1882 to the end of 1914. The setup included no less than nine forts and nine-gun batteries. It was mostly modernized with the latest defensive technologies designed to withstand modern shells, and contained nineteen miles of internal railways, a power plant, a water supply system, a mill, a bakery, a brewery, a food bank, and a telegraph. It was a fully functional, independent fortress. The frontline was about fifty miles away from the fortress by the middle of February 1915.

(...) German 1st Division, 1st Grenadier Regiment, May 5th, 1915, (..)

"Lieutenant Romz, you will go to the right and attack this redoubt, Lieutenant Hamzel; I need you to get your men to this position here," pointed Captain Mikael Lundbeck of the 1st Grenadier Regiment on the map. *"Yes, Sir." "Now,"* continued Lundbeck, *"go to your unit and distribute the orders."* The two men left in the direction of the smoking battlefield that was the German siege trench system in front of Kaunas. The German Army had made good time to the enemy strongpoint since the start of their offensive three days before. Light forces were thus brushed aside as the enemy commander, General Rennenkampf, awaited the Reich in his powerful fortress.

Mikael's war was now finally one of movements, following the long, grueling months of siege warfare in the defense of Konigsberg during the fall of 1914 and early winter of 1915. Relieved by the German counteroffensive under the command of Luddendorf and Hindenburg, the 1st Division he was part of was then requisitioned for the offensive into Russia.

A Captain's job in the German Army (Hauptman) was to lead his men into battle and execute the orders from those higher up. Contrary to most armies of the time, the German Imperial Army gave its officers a great deal of latitude. In short, the man in command on the battlefield had a lot more information to make decisions than the higher-ups. Thus, the higher the orders were, the more general they happened to be. Mickael's orders were to secure his sector, but the details were left to him to execute. He had 240 men under his command (a company) and was tasked with eliminating one of the outlying enemy trenches and a machine gun nest that was detected by a recon plane. He took a deep breath, looking at his watch; his men were now getting in position. He walked out of the small thatched house he'd set his command post in. The place was built into a depression in the ground and thus out of the enemy line of sight. Above him, the loud whistles of passing shells from the German gunners barreled loudly. He also heard the familiar cracks of rifle fire. A large smoke cloud hung over the Russian fortress as it was being shelled around the clock by the Reich's guns. The battle had started, but the real attack was soon. It was 0715 AM, and the attack was set for 0800 AM.

(...) Inside the Kaunas Fortress (...)

"Go, now," said General Paul von Rennenkampf to his assembled officers. Outside, the thunder of the artillery could be heard, like a low and sometimes overwhelming rumble, depending on where the shells would fall. The General HQ was in the relative center of the large fortress complex, inside a large redoubt building fortified against modern artillery bombardment. The Generals and colonels left to go to their units. A shell hit not far from the fortified position exploded, and the ground shook, unsettling dust from the ceiling, which then

billowed lazily around the room.

Rennenkampf walked past the telegraph station, where a soldier was busy sending his orders to units further out since not everyone had been able to come to the meeting. He stopped in front of the small square table, where the map of the Kaunas Fortress was laid down. One of his staff officers had marked the relative position of the enemy units around the area. Putting both hands on the table with his outstretched arms, he hovered above it, looking at the position of the 10th (General Vasily Flug, 400,000 soldiers) and Northwest (General Yakov Zhilinsky, 333,000 soldiers) Armies, north and south of Kaunas, and wondered if it was time to call them to the battle. The full extent of the German offensive wasn't yet known, and he wondered if Hindenburg had any tricks up his sleeve. *"What are you planning, old bastard,"* muttered Rennenkampf. He was already disgruntled at the German general for defeating him at Konigsberg, and the reason he didn't want to move the armies to Kaunas right off the bat was that he didn't want to be outflanked again. He intended to win this time. He lifted his hands, balled them into fists, and landed them hard on the table, startling the telegraph soldier, concentrating on his message. He'd decided. *"Soldier, a message for General Flug and Zhilinsky."*

(...) German field HQ, a few miles behind the frontline (...)

Both generals Luddendorf and Hindenburg were deep in thought, and with their faces creased in worry, as their attack on Kaunas was beginning. The worries had nothing to do with their current situation. Things were doing well in their sector. It had to do with the unfolding disaster in the Carpathians, with the Austro-Hungarian's 4th Army's defeat and apparent rout. The Russians had gotten a jump on them as they launched a powerful offensive from Galicia. While the Central Powers had expected it, they had hoped that the defenses in the Carpathians would hold long enough for the twin German offensives (toward Lithuania and Belorussia) to get into gear and force the Tsar to shift his forces north.

"Damned Austrians haven't even held a week with all the preparations they did," said Luddendorf in a gloomy tone. Hindenburg, more seasoned and experienced, was a little calmer. *"From what I saw in the preliminary reports, the Russians have organized one hell of an attack, and the preparatory bombardment was something to behold. The commanders on the ground say it was the biggest they'd seen since the start of the war."*

The two men were in an austere-looking room with white painted walls and a portrait of the Russian Tsar on the wall. Apparently, this had been the local mayor's residence before the German Army occupied it. The town was nothing special, and its city hall was not much better. It was the only stone building in the entire area, but that was the only thing to make it seem better than the rest.

Luddendorf grunted. *"Nevertheless, Sir, what do we do now? We can hardly let the Russians have their way with the Austro-Hungarians, or else they will crumble. Do you think that this new commander, Boroevic, can salvage the situation?"* Svetozar Boroevic was the new Austrian commander-in-chief, recently named to the position. The man was an expert on defensive warfare and had proved his mettle in the fight for Galicia the year before. *"I Haven't had a chance to meet with him yet, so I don't know, general. But anything is better than that delusional Hotzendorf."* *"Well, sir..."* started to say Eric, before being interrupted by Hindenburg, lifting a finger.

"The real question here is, do we or don't we do something about it right now? The Polish offensive has not started yet; we can divert troops from Mackensen's forces to bolster the front in the Carpathians." Luddendorf, who had been about to go into a rant, was brought back from frustration by Hindenburg's down-to-earth way of seeing things. *"Well, sir, we cannot let Austria-Hungary crumble, and the offensive into Belorussia can be executed at a later time."*

The *old Prussian general laid back in his chair, fingers in his chin, thinking. "What about making the Lithuania offensive the priority? We send Mackensen south to bolster our fledging allies, and we take some reinforcements as well, and push harder than we originally intended, and we forget about the push toward Belorussia."* Ludendorff's eyes lit up at the idea. *"I like it, Sir. It would take some time to organize, but this wouldn't impede us as we are already attacking. From the look of things, that is a very viable option."*

Austro-Hungarian soldier Helmut Gottengurg ducked behind the old Roman-built parapet, holding onto his spiked steel helmet with his hand. Rock splinters fell on it, clanging softly. The Romanians had fired true, and he had almost been killed with that shot. It was weird to be fighting in Roman ruins, but it was what it was. The Romans had conquered Romania eons ago. The territory was called Dacia, and as they did with every other place they included in their empire, they built things like aqueducts, roads, and other wonders of the ancient world. A good part of it was now gone but some of it remained in the remote regions of Romania and Moldavia, just where the 21st Landwehr Division was currently fighting.

Beside him, one of the new arrivals in the division (they'd received replacements after the first two days of fighting in the mountains) smiled hesitantly at him. It was more a nervous gesture than anything else. The guy was just a kid fresh out of the training depots. He was a Slovene, just like Radno, and, of course, his friend had taken it upon himself to help the bewildered young boy. The man didn't speak one word of German. *"Don't worry, Kid, we're good. Just stick with me, and we'll be fine."* The young soldier nodded solemnly. Helmut remembered his first fight in Serbia. It had not been fun, and he was happy to see Rad helping the new guy through it. He spoke up as well, readjusting his helmet as the billowing dust from the bullet hitting the rock dissipated. *"Kid, this is just a minor scrap, and we won't risk our hides for no reason. Just wait, the artillery will smash the bastards."* The regimental spotters had already called for an artillery strike, and the entire squad waited for the shells to start falling before resuming the attack.

The clamor of small arms being fired could be heard everywhere around them. Explosions also rocked the ground. Following their assault on the machine gun nest and the clearing of the first part of the Oituz Pass a few days before, the 8th Infantry Regiment was tasked with crossing the last bit of enemy defenses before the plain and the city of Oituz through a well-known Roman track that crossed the mountain. It was a gently sloped road, solidly built and perfect for soldiers to walk on.

Helmut was the first to hear the low whine of incoming artillery shells. *"Do you hear that?"* he said. The rest of the squad tried to concentrate and then heard it as well. At first, it was just a faraway whistle, like a very distant alarm blaring. But then the sound gradually became more insistent, more ominous.

And then it thundered loudly above the Austro-Hungarians and started crashing in blasts of fire on the Romanian position at the top of the mountain. The entire wooden-rocky area sprouted in fire, and the men spread out in case a stray shell landed too short. No one wanted to get hit by his own side.

The 21st Division had its own supporting gun crews in the form of a battery of Prague-built (near Helmut's home, in fact) Skoda 7.5 cm d/29 Model 1911. Anticipating trouble on the 8th Regiment's ascent, the Divisional commander, General Arthur Przybors, had thus positioned the battery just below the start of the Roman road. These weapons were light and could roll over difficult terrain. With a few sturdy pack horses, they were brought up the pass to help with the last bit of fighting to get across.

After the loud whistling came the uproar of artillery blasts, igniting the entire mountaintop with fire. From a soldier's perspective, it was as if they faced a volcanic eruption. Dirt and fire catapulted in the air, surrounded by dark smoke. Seconds later, debris started falling down the slopes on the Austro-Hungarian soldiers. The 7.5 cm cannons continued to fire in a rolling barrage, meaning they fired a few meters further with every shot, enabling Helmut and his comrades below the top of the beleaguered mountain to advance amidst the pandemonium.

The sergeant and other NCO's whistles started blowing the signal to charge. At that moment, the K.U.K. soldiers started to yell the crazy battle cry of a charge. It was madness, but none of them hesitated. Even the recruits, like that new Slovene kid, lifted themselves up and followed their comrades, all hesitation and fear gone, replaced by the folly of the human charge.

Helmut ran up as fast as he could and quickly outdistanced Radno, who was trying to help the new guy. A few stray bullets zipped down from the rolling mass of fire and smoke, a sure sign that some of the Romanian soldiers kept their wits even amidst the powerful shelling. He stopped for a moment, put his rifle on the shoulder, and fired. He knew he wouldn't hit anything but was doing what he had been taught in training. It was never a bad thing to pin the enemy down while you advanced. When an opposing soldier had his head down, he couldn't fire at you. It was simple logic that he tried to execute every time he had a chance to do so.

As he was getting ready to start running again, he saw the young Slovene sprinting up the cobbled Roman road well ahead of everyone else. The kid was fast, and then he realized that he didn't even know his name. So fast, in fact, that he had reached the point where he was almost on top of the smoking enemy trench. Helmut started running up, wanting to help the brave young soldier. *"Fucking reckless recruit,"* yelled Radno over the tumult of noise permeating the battlefield as he ran past Gottenburg. They both watched, agape, as the young guy disappeared, knife drawn, into the enemy trench up the mountain. His body was swallowed by the billowing smoke.

More and more Austro-Hungarian soldiers trickled into the dark fumes, and soon Helmut was in it, hearing and seeing the struggle of many men in hand-to-hand combat. He had his bayonet fixed to his rifle and plunged it into the back of a Romanian soldier busy hacking away at a fallen comrade on the ground. The enemy yelped as Helmut's blade penetrated deep into his back, spraying blood everywhere.

He could tell that the fight was already further up, and he continued to struggle toward the top of the mountain. More yelling, some bullets visible as they plowed through the hazy dark smoke. Sometimes, he saw them and blinked in momentaneous fear, but he never got hit. *"Forward, forward,"* he heard one of the NCOs yelling some meters beside him. He thought he saw some shapes in the gray dark but wasn't certain.

Then, the artillery bombardment stopped. Its noise had been fading for a while since the artillerymen had fired about fifty yards further with every shot, so it was now landing on the downward slope toward the plain where the town of Oituz was.

He started to hear cheers and shouts of joy in the multitude of languages in the Austro-Hungarian Army. He joined in but didn't understand why his comrades were cheering. Then, he saw why. A powerful gust of wind scattered the smoke enough for him and the men near him to see the shattered battlefield clearly and fully. The entire area was covered with the brown-uniformed bodies of Romanian soldiers while grey-blue-clad Habsburg forces stood triumphant over them. For a moment, he scanned the crowd for his friend and spotted Rad, already busy at work, going through the pockets of a few fallen enemies. He raised his soot-covered face and saw Helmut. He nodded to him with a smile, shrugging his shoulders, and continued on his grim (and profitable) work.

The 8th Regiment had won its battle and was over the last Romanian forces blocking them from going over the mountain and into the Plain. Below them lay Moldavia in all its glory, and they would soon start to go down and conquer it for the Empire. Sometime later, they found the body of that new kid, killed during his mad rush with a sliced throat. Helmut was used to death and to seeing recruits getting killed in their first fight, just shook his head, wondering why the man had sprinted ahead of everyone like that. *"The battle craze got the better of him,"* said Radno as he crouched to check the younger soldier's pockets.

(...) The Battle of Oituz (...)

By the end of the 4th, the Austro-German troops were across the mountain defenses and, the next day at dawn, assaulted the last Romanian troops defending the small border town of Oituz. As the news of the breakthrough spread across the line, more and more Romanian units started to retreat, as they were in danger of being outflanked if they stayed in their fixed defenses in the mountains.

On the 6th of May, the 4th Romanian Army commander, General Constantin Prezan, launched a counterattack in the by-then Central-Powers-controlled town of Oituz, but it was to no avail. His demoralized and badly supplied men floundered on the defenses of the German 49th Division, helped by the 21st Landwehr Division. When Bulgarian General Toshev's Army finally made it across, its troops helped the Austro-Germans to completely overwhelm the Romanian forces. By mid-morning on the 7th, Prezan ordered the entire Romanian line of defense to retreat further East.

The casualties on the Romanian side totaled 26,000 soldiers (dead, wounded, and captured), while on the Central Power's side, the Bulgarians lost 22,000, the Germans 2,500, the Austro-Hungarians 5,500, and the Turks 2,500, for an awful total of 32,500 men.

The outcome of the battle forced the retreat of the entire Entente line further back east toward Iasi and the Dniester River, where a powerful defensive line could be established. It also temporarily checked Brussilov's attack in the sense that the successful Russian forces in the north of the Romanian position were forced to detach troops to send to Moldavia to bolster the fledging forces of Ferdinand I.

(…) 16th Moscow Regiment, near Zborov Castle (…)

The massive Zborov Castle sat on a dominating hilltop over the town of the same name and a large plain in between two sets of mountains in the Carpathians. Throughout its history, the place had been one of the major Carpathian Mountain fortifications, controlling and protecting the routes from and to Hungary-Galicia. Now a relic of the past, it nonetheless represented a powerful defensive fortification that the retreating and beleaguered Austro-Hungarian troops had decided to use to make their stand.

The last week had been pretty eventful for Dimitri Fedorov, a soldier in the 16th Moscow Regiment. After some very stiff initial resistance, the 4th K.U.K. Army crumbled in front of the overwhelming Brussilov offensive. Following several assaults on trenches and fortified mountain positions, and the Russians had finally won the day, pushing the Austro-Hungarians into retreat in several sectors of the front.

Dimitri didn't know because no officers had told anyone in his section, but the Brussilov Offensive was going very well, and had penetrated deeply into the Austrian lines in the center of the front. That much, he could tell because they were advancing. He just didn't know the extent of the success to date, which was incredible. Regardless, he probably wouldn't have cared, for he was a simple man and only cared about surviving the next battle and finding his next meal with some sprinkles of fun and alcohol.

Dimitri and his comrades were now fighting in the Hungarian town of Zborov, as the enemy forces were entrenched in the castle of the same name above the town they now occupied. The ancient fortification, now destroyed, stood watch over the plain. The initial frontline was miles behind them, and they were now in full pursuit of the Austro-Hungarian 4th Army.

The castle itself was a medieval construction and was now a pile of smoking rubble, destroyed by the Russian guns. But that didn't mean the Austro-Hungarian troops were gone from there. Far from it, in fact. Dimitri knew from experience that there were always survivors from an artillery attack, regardless of the number of shells thrown at one given area. The shelling of the Przemysl fortress had destroyed everything standing, and yet, from the destroyed remains, the enemy had fought like demons, and the Russians still had to fight for every inch of the fortress. It could even be argued that destroying a city or fortification and transforming it into a pile of ruins could even help the defenders.

"You be careful, now," said an arrogantly smiling Sergeant Radetzki to Dimitri and the men around him after he ordered them to advance to the pile of rocks above them. *"Sure, Sergeant,"* said one of the men in the group as they stood up from their cover. Dimitri kept silent as he knew that it was no use trying to be a smart ass with the man. Radetzki didn't mean any of what he said, as he believed that they might die assaulting the machine gun nest the Austro-Hungarians had set up in the broken-down tower facing them. The Captain had come moments earlier, giving orders to the Lieutenant that they were to assault the smoking hilltop pile of rubble as part of a general assault from all sides. The Lieutenant had then deferred the choice of who would be in front of the attack to the sergeant, and Radetzky had chosen Dimitri amongst a bunch of twenty soldiers.

The moment they started to make their way across the broken-down pieces of rubble, enemy voices started to be heard, and it didn't take long for rifle fire to swamp the area. Rapidly, several Russian soldiers were hit and fell as Dimitri sprinted for his life in the broken-down building. Soon, the enemy machine gun was brought about and hosed the entire area, and he jumped in between two large pieces of destroyed walls. He and the rest of his comrades had sort of drawn the short stick when Radetzki chose them for the diversionary attack. The idea was to draw the Austro-Hungarian fire in order to have other troops flank them from the other side of the building. Several of his colleagues were now dead or injured, and Dimitri decided that he wouldn't move from where he was until it was over. Anyway, the crusty sergeant could not see him, and thus, he surmised that he would get away with just coming back once the battle was over or else just pretending like he'd fought for the entire time.

The enemy machine gunner continued to fire in his general direction, and he curled into a ball as the ricocheting bullets flew everywhere. Another man near him was hit by a shot that glanced on a rock and right into his left eye. It was pure mayhem. Then, loud whistles barreled above, and the ground shook as the Russian artillery fired a few rounds for good measure. He ventured a look as he was pretty certain the enemy would be busy getting to cover, and he was right; the entire top of the hill blossomed in fireballs and catapulting debris. No more bullets came their way.

"Come on," said one of the soldiers in his group who had been hiding near him. Dimitri stood up, gripping his rifle as hard as he could out of nervousness, and started to make his way upward again. The little group of four soldiers struggled up on the uneven ground and was almost at the ruins when the artillery shelling stopped to avoid killing its own side.

From the haze and smoke of the artillery attack came the usual chattering and clicking noises of the enemy Maxim machine gun that started to fire again. But this time, Dimitri and the others were out of the line of fire since they were just below the Austro-Hungarians, who couldn't see them anymore because of the sloping angle.

The soldier who had urged them on jumped over a large piece of broken wall and fired three rapid shots into the machine gun nest, quickly followed by the rest of the group, including Dimitri. They all yelled out of their lungs and charged once they emptied their ammo clips. What followed was a quick hand-to-hand fight, but most of the enemy soldiers were already either dying or injured, and thus, they made short work of the Austro-Hungarian position.

All across the castle ruins, the same scenario repeated itself as Russian troops overwhelmed the poor defenders, who fought until hope was gone. About half of the soldiers surrendered, and the rest were killed. The battle for Zborov was just an example of the multitude of battles across the broken Austro-Hungarian frontlines as the Russian Army advanced victoriously.

(...) Brussilov offensive success (...)

Before the unstoppable Russian attack commenced, former Commander-in-Chief von Hotzendorf had been satisfied with the K.U.K. forces' preparation in the Carpathians. He had decided that the powerful layered defenses and mountainous terrain would be sufficient to stop any Russian offensives. Across the entire front, the Austrians had thus dug and fortified three trench lines, with good artillery numbers behind for support. They had also installed a thirty-yard belt of barbed wire and positioned the bulk of their infantry in the rear trenches, where they were protected by very large, freshly built concrete dugouts and bunkers. This was done to avoid heavy casualties if the Russians chose to launch an artillery barrage before their attack. The Austrian artillery was placed behind the first trench line, protected by well-built earthworks, sprinkled with concrete bunkers with machine gun nests.

The new commander of the K.U.K. Army, General Svetozar Boroevic, would have disagreed with von Hotzendorf and placed the bulk of the infantry in the 1st trench line to avoid the Russians overwhelming it; however, he did not have time to get to the front and make the necessary modifications, as his nomination was at the end of April.

The Russian attack began with a blazing artillery barrage, with over 1,000 heavy guns and several smaller howitzers pummeling the Austrian trench lines with surprising accuracy. After all, the Tsarist soldiers had had the time to aim properly, the front having been static for months.

The rain of shells obliterated the Central Powers' defensive positions and shredded to pieces any Austro-Hungarian soldier unlucky enough to be in the vicinity, making the area into a new representation of a nightmarish hell. The big shells plowed through the earth and opened up large craters, catapulting rocks, soil, debris, dust, and smoke into the air. Following a full night of shelling, the Russian guns then switched to a creeping barrage as the Russian infantry started charging across the demolished and unrecognizable landscape from the Northern Carpathians to Transylvania.

The Austro-Hungarian troops fought like demons but were overwhelmed by the superior Russian numbers. In most sectors, breakthroughs were made by Brussilov's men, but the situation quickly became critical in the 4th K.U.K. Army sector. By May 8th, the front was distorted, and a large bulge was inflating in the center, threatening the entire Central Powers Frontline. Brussilov's report on the success of the offensive reached Nicolas II and the Grand Duke at the Stavka HQ in Baranovichi, and the Russians started to believe that victory was near.

(…) Dreadnought battleship Setsu, Japanese battle squadron (…)

Japanese Admiral Heihachiro Togo walked the distance from the center of the bridge to the viewport, as he wanted to have his first look at Port Stanley in the Falkland Islands. The islands were a mostly flat affair with mountains in the center, probably of volcanic origins,

The archipelago lay in the South Atlantic, near the tip of South America. It was a British colony, and, as with all far-flung islands, it was also a major Royal Navy base and coaling station. It was from there that the British monitored traffic to and from the Cape Horn sea route. *"Admiral,"* said his chief of staff, Vice-Admiral Jinji Nomura. *"The British have acknowledged our presence and have invited us into the harbor."* The man's words were followed by the blaring horns of the British ships in the harbor, doing this in a gesture of welcome. *"Very well,"* answered Togo, crossing his arms behind his back.

He breathed in deeply as he was finally here and would get another chance at catching that elusive German Admiral Maximilian von Spee and his leftover Pacific Squadron.

JAPAN		
Japanese Imperial Fleet Battle Squadron 1	**Admiral Heihachiro Togo**	
BB Setsu	BC Kongo	2 CA
BB Kawachi		3 DD

After the Battle of Truk and the German Squadron's escape, he had been ordered back to Japan. However, from that moment onward he tried to convince the admiralty and the leaders in Tokyo to let him have one more attempt at sinking the German Fleet. For him, the entire affair had become a matter of pride and a personal duel with his resourceful enemy.

Sailing the large Japanese fleet so far from Japan was problematic, to say the least. Even if one didn't take into consideration the logistical challenge of coaling and distance, the Japanese leadership also wanted its battle fleet in a position to defend the Home Islands. After all, Japan was at war, and while there was no imminent threat as the Central Powers seemed far away, there was always China or else the possibility of a German rabbit-out-of-the-hat trick.

When he arrived in Kure near Tokyo, he lobbied hard to get a few ships to sail once more against the Germans, using his reputation and legendary status (because of his victory at Tsushima in 1905). Von Spee had made a stop in Mexico to repair his damaged boilers following the Battle of Western Samoa with the British, and it thus made it possible for Togo to sail and try to intercept him even if he had to go back to Japan to get his permission.

He finally obtained his go-ahead to sail with the three dreadnoughts Japan had (battleships Setsu and Kawachi, along with battlecruiser Kongo) and followed it up with a visit to the British Embassy in Tokyo, where he learned of Admiral Beatty's plan of waiting for the Germans in the Falklands. Obtaining permission from the British to sail and join their Mediterranean Squadron in Port Stanley, he'd sailed. Following a few stops for coaling across the Pacific expanse, he was finally there, seeing the numerous British battleships in all their glory.

"Sir," said the flag officer walking in from the outside balcony where his signalers were. *"Admiral Beatty is inviting you to diner on battleship Neptune; what shall we answer?"* Togo smiled; he looked forward to meeting with the British admiral. *"Tell him it will be my pleasure. As soon as the ship is at anchor, prepare my motorboat."*

(...) Dreadnought battleship Westfalen (...)

"Plot, what is our position," asked Admiral Maximilian von Spee as he stood on the bridge of dreadnought battleship Westfalen. *"Admiral, we are a hundred and fifty nautical miles from the Island of Recalada,*

near the Pacific entry of the Magellan Strait," answered the sailor, bending over his map as he updated the ship's course and heading constantly.

"Very well, thank you." Von Spee was wondering what was awaiting him in and around the vicinity of the tip of South America. He was pretty certain the British would not let him pass without another battle.

German Pacific Squadron		
Admival von Graf Spee		
BB Westfalen stern and deck damage	CL Emden stern and forecastle damage	Collier ship Oldenwald
BB Kaiserin stern , 1 rear turret destroyed		

He had already elected to avoid the strait as it was too narrow, and if the enemy had ships in it, he would be stuck. It was no place to fight, and thus, he elected to sail around Cape Horn and around Chile.

He looked at his watch after fishing it out of his front pocket and then at the calendar just above the helmsman. He was wondering if Rear-Admiral Felix Funke's 3rd Battle Squadron would make it to the rendezvous point. The last time he was able to communicate with navy command (through wireless telegraph) had been when he was in Manzanillo, and the news had been that the German ships had sailed following a battle between the High Seas Fleet and the Royal Navy's Grand Fleet. Then they'd also agreed on an updated day for a potential meeting in a Fjord on Estados Islands, a small 18 square mile island that belonged to Argentina on the edge of the Atlantic Ocean and near Cape Horn. The place was uninhabited except for a small harbor called Parry Naval Station on the northern side of the island. It was a small fishing area. The meeting of the two German fleets was planned to happen on the southern side in a Fjord called Bahía Capitan Canepa, where a coal collier was already supposed to be waiting for them in order to refill the ships.

Funk's battle squadron was probably already on the way from Swakopmund, the major harbor in the German Southwest African colony.

"How long until we see Cape Horn and we get to Estados Island," he asked once more, looking into the horizon. "Four days, Admiral," answered the plotting station sailor. *"Very well,"* he answered calmly. *"I will be in my cabin; call me if there is anything."*

(…) 3rd German Battle Squadron, Skeleton Coast (…)

The small city and harbor of Swakopmund was located in the northern part of the German Colony of Southwest Africa, in an area called the Skeleton Coast, a place as arid as they got, as it was on the edge of the Namib desert. The small town was founded when the Reich took over that area in the 1890s, and it quickly became the main hub for anything German as it was located at the center of the colony.

3rd Battle Squadron, relief fleet (Rear-Admiral Felix Funke) - Swapkomund		
BB Grosser Kurfürst	BB König	4 CL
BB Markgraf	BB Kronprinz	1 DD

Rear Admiral Felix Funke held his plate and steaming coffee mug as he reviewed the course the fleet would take when it sailed the next day for Estados Island. He was with the plotting officer and his second-in-command, Vice-Admiral Max von Krenk. *"Do you think that von Spee will make it out of the Pacific, Sir,"* said Krenk. *"The last thing we heard about the Pacific Squadron was following the Manzanillo incident. Since then, nothing."* It was normal that no news had been received since the German Pacific ships did not have access to a long-range wireless telegraph station that could only be located on land. Between Mexico and Estados Island only lay neutral countries, and it was thus impossible for von Spee to stop in any harbor on the South American coast unless he wanted to create yet another international incident. The one with the United States had been serious enough, and Funke understood why von Spee didn't want to have any more problems.

"We'll soon find out," added the Admiral. The 3rd Battle Squadron's final mission was to join up with the Pacific Squadron and bring it home. The first part of their orders was completed, as the fleet brought a full battalion of German Marines to help with the colony's defense. The South Africans (part of the British Empire) were pushing hard, and without these reinforcements, the colony would have fallen. Now, with the new troops and the mountain of supplies they brought, German Southwest Africa would continue to resist for a long while. If the British really wanted it, they would now have to invest serious land assets to reduce the 4,000-strong army in the territory.

"Ouch," exclaimed von Spee as he tried to sip his coffee. The liquid was scalding hot. Krenk smiled as if it was a well-known affair; the cook liked to make the coffee super-hot, and the Rear-Admiral never seemed to learn. *"Is everything ready,"* said the Rear-Admiral after putting the cup on the plotting table. *"Sir, the repairs on Markgraf's boiler room number two have been completed, and the rest of the fleet is close to optimal capability. The holds are full of coal, and the men have all been recalled to their ships. By sundown, we'll be ready to go if you wish."* Von Spee thought for a moment and decided that sailing out in the dark of night was not a bad idea since it would give them a few hours' head start from the unavoidable spy reports that would make their way to South Africa the moment they sailed.

(...) British dreadnought battleship Neptune (...)

BRITISH MEDITERRANEAN FLEET (Port Stanley)		
Admiral David Beatty, 1st Earl Beatty	second in command, Rear-Admiral Gordon Moore	
BC Invincible	BC Tiger	9 DD
BB Conqueror	BB Agincourt	4 CA
BB Neptune flagship	Pre-dread BB Russell	
BB Benbow	Pre-dread BB Cornwallis	
	Pre-dread BB Exmouth	

Beatty had to admit he was a little awestruck by his counterpart as they casually enjoyed dinner together, along with their translators and a throng of Japanese and British officers alike. Admiral Heihachiro Togo was a legend in naval history. In front of him was the very man who had commanded the Imperial Japanese Fleet during the Battle of Tsushima in 1905 against the Russian Baltic Fleet.

The man was getting old but seemed to retain all his edge as he entertained conversation with everyone. Beatty also saw the reverence the other Imperial Navy officers gave him. *"Hell,"* he thought to himself, *"if the man's a legend in England, it's hard to imagine he is not a god in Japan."*

The dinner was being held in his admiral of the fleet cabin, which was furnished with a large conference room and table to accommodate fleet meetings and officer events. The Neptune was one of the most modern British dreadnought battleships and, as such, enjoyed the very best in everything. Food, accommodations, facilities, and the like.

Before the meal, he toured the ship with Togo, and the man had seemed impressed, commenting wildly in Japanese, and his translator had relayed very positive comments to Beatty. A visit to the Setsu was planned the next day, and he looked forward to seeing Japanese naval technology, which was said to be quite similar to the British. This was understandable, as most of the Imperial Navy's pre-dreadnoughts were built in English shipyards, and the Japanese employed many British naval engineers and specialists to build their own fleet.

"So, Admiral Togo, can you give me some insights on how this von Spee admiral fights," he said, wanting to move the discussion into more serious territory. The translator took some time to translate the words to his superior, and then Togo answered in a flurry of rapid words. *"Sir, the Admiral says that von Spee fights dirty and that you cannot expect a straight fight from him. He won't just line up for a broadside and hope for the best,"* said the translator, stopping to listen to more words from his commander. *"You can expect something special in the coming fight, and that is if he doesn't succeed in eluding us once more,"* continued the translator. Beatty noticed that Togo's face had noticeably darkened. Togo spoke again, and then the translator did his thing. *"The Admiral apologizes for his rudeness and his apparent*

irritability over the matter. He feels ashamed to have been defeated by von Spee and is very much looking forward to his revenge. It is a matter of honor for us Japanese."

Beatty smiled at Togo and then spoke up. *"Tell the Admiral that I will be honored to share the victory with him and his brave sailors. Also, tell him that British honor has also been tarnished by von Spee following the Battle of Western Samoa. Me and my men are just as eager to finish this."*

The next day, Beatty went to the Setsu and toured the battleship, and the visit was followed by a meeting in Togo's large cabin to discuss the way they were going to find and corner the German fleets. They knew that both the Pacific Squadron and the fleet that had made it to Swakopmund would eventually sail to the area. They just didn't know when and what they would do. The only way to do this was to patrol the area relentlessly and try to root the bastards out. They thus agreed to both sail their fleets and cover a large area, from Estados Island and the Lemaire Strait between Estados and Argentina. The rest of the way to the Antarctic also needed to be patrolled, but it was unlikely the Germans would go this way as it was a dangerous area for icebergs and would consume more coal.

Beatty went back into his motorboat, harboring a smile and in a great mood. They had a plan and knew he had one hell of an ally to defeat the elusive and powerful Germans.

(...) German 9th Army turns south (...)

Germany- East

| German 9th Army | General August von Mackensen | 190,000 soldiers | Northern Carpathians-Hungary-Galicia |

General August von Mackensen, the commander of the German 9th Army, nodded at one of his staff officers, who turned tail and moved out of his field HQ tent to execute his orders.

In the background, soldier chants could be heard, with columns upon columns of grey-uniformed German fighters walking at a brisk pace past the tent on their way southward. Their marching lifted an unimaginably large cloud of dust in the air. Von Mackensen walked out from under the canopy and the moment he appeared in front of them, the soldiers cheered him. The German 9th was in high spirits after comfortably spending a relatively quiet winter in a city. The Imperial Army occupied half of Russian Poland, and the 9th had mostly sat out the cold months in Warsaw itself.

They were now ready for a fight, but the maneuver Mackensen asked of them and his officers was difficult. His entire force had been marching eastward and had already started to skirmish with the lead Russian trenches when he received the order to wheel his troops south and into the flank of the Russian forces in Galicia and the Carpathians.

Even if he didn't like it one bit, he hadn't argued with Hindenburg, his commander-in-chief, because he could read the news, and reports from the Carpathians were speaking of an Autro-Hungarian rout. What that meant in reality was that there was a real chance the so-called *"Brussilov Offensive"* would knock the Habsburgs out of the war altogether.

This would be a disaster for the German Empire and also for the rest of the Central Powers. First and foremost, they would lose over a million and a half soldiers plus the potential for another one to two million new draftees that would join the K.U.K. army in the next months and years. Second, the link between the Reich and the rest of the Central Powers (Italy, Bulgaria, Greece, and the Ottoman Empire) would be severed, creating one hell of a logistical problem for the alliance. Thus, while he would have liked nothing better than to continue onward with the plan to attack Belorussia and destroy the Russian forces in front of him, the survival of Austria-Hungary took precedence in strategic terms.

His orders were to turn his troops south and attack the topmost part of the Russian frontline, which was to the west of his own position. Hence from the looks of it, it was possible he could take the enemy in the rear and even outflank some of its forces. While the overall goal was simply to have Brussilov stop his attack in the center of the Carpathians and redirect troops toward Mackensen to meet the threat, he believed he could be a lot more than a diversion and thus acted accordingly, making sure his officers understood the need for speed and urgency.

(...) Brussilov's reaction to the German attack in the North (...)

Two days later, Russian General Brussilov was faced with a critical decision. The German troops were attacking his northern flank with a lot of vigor. The Army that was already manning the extreme north of the Carpathian Front, the German 11th Army under General Max von Gallwitz, had been reinforced by the German 9th Army under Mackensen, and they were now starting to push his forces back southward.

The Russian commander was in the Lemberg Castle, a city conquered by his troops the preceding fall. The building had been lightly damaged by combat and was thus a fitting place for an army group HQ. After all, he needed a lot of staff, presiding over 1.5 million soldiers stretched over a 600-mile frontline and spread over seven armies.

"What do we do about the enemy attack in the North, sir," said General Aleksander Kratov, his chief of staff. Brussilov remained silent. He could not bring himself to stop his offensive against the Austro-Hungarians. He was so close to success. Some of the lead units pushing back the enemy 4th Army had even reported being in sight of the plains of Hungary. If the Russian forces could spill over into the kingdom, he was certain Hungarians would panic and thus shatter the will of Austria-Hungary to continue the war.

Kratov insisted that it was time to make a decision. The entire discussion had been going in circles for the last twelve hours, as Brussilov was unwilling to release the pressure on the Austro-Hungarians. *"General Brussilov, I must insist,"* the chief of staff continued. *"The enemy has already encircled a division and is moving without much opposition as our forces are heavily engaged at the frontline against the Austrians."* He paused, pointing at a spot on the map they both hovered over. *"We need to engage all of our reserves north of Przemysl to block the enemy attack."*

Russia			
Galicia and Prezmysl			
1,850,000 soldiers	Commander	Soldiers	Area of operation
3rd Army	General Nikolai Ruzsky	200,000 soldiers	Carpathians
4th Army	General Alexei Evert	300,000 soldiers	Carpathians
5th Army	General Pavel Plehve	300,000 soldiers	Carpathians
8th Army	General Aleksei Alekseevich Brusilov	250,000 soldiers	Carpathians
9th Army	General Platon Lechitsky	200,000 soldiers	Carpathians
Moscow Front	General Dimitri Doctorov	600,000 soldiers	Carpathians and Bessarabia

Brussilov made a contorted face. *"I know, General, but I don't like it. If we send Doctorov's Moscow Front north, it means our attack in the Carpathians will lose its steam, as we need his 300,000 soldiers to open the breach and spill into Hungary to finish this war."* The Moscow front Army was 600,000 strong but they had already been forced to engage half of it in Bessarabia and Moldavia to support the fledging Romanians and to protect their southern border from the Central Powers offensive underway.

"Sir, we can break through in Hungary; of that, there is no doubt. However, we will lose Galicia altogether if we don't act now, and if that happens, our troops in Hungary and the Carpathians will be encircled and cut off from any supply." He put both his hands on the map and looked at his commander-in-chief with a piercing glare. "Sir, if we don't move against the Germans, we will be the ones losing this war and knocking out our own country.

Brussilov boiled with rage inside of him but finally relented. *"Bozhe moi,"* he yelled, hitting the table with his fist. *"Send the Moscow Front reserves north, and let's finish this."*

(...) Frontal assault (...)

The fortified position just ahead of the Private soldier exploded in a fury of fire, earth, and smoke. For a moment, it seemed like the hammer of a Norse god had hit the ground. The man was still stunned from the impact but shook himself out of it rapidly as his Captain, Mickael Lundbeck, gave him a hard kick in the ribs. *"Come on, Private. Snap out of it. We are somewhat busy, and I need every able-bodied soldier."* *"Yyyesss, sir,"* the stunned soldier blurted hesitantly. *"What is it, Private,"* answered Mikael. *"Are you hurt, bleeding, something broken?"*

"I... I don't think so, sir. Just a bit stunned, that's all." The Sergeant looked at him for a moment, taking his head into his two hands. *"Listen to me, Private. The fucking Russians are running toward our position as we speak. Can't you hear their damned yelling?"* As Mikael said it, the Russian yell was heard as if to answer or confirm his claim. The characteristic *"oo-oo-RAAAAAAAAAAAAAAAAAAAH"* was something the enemy did when it charged. It was an overbearing sound that even defeated the artillery blasts and the chatter of rifles and machine guns. Thousands of men yelling was something to behold.

Mikael's ears rang like a broken doorbell. He was bleeding from his left shoulder (thanks to a grazing bullet), and he wasn't in a much better condition than the soldier on the ground. However, as a Captain, he was doing his job. He slapped the Private in the face. Then slapped him again. *"Private! I need you with me!!!"* And then the man finally regained his sense. *"Yes, sir,"* he said in a decided tone, picking his rifle up from the ground where he had dropped it after the enemy shell hit. Then, the Private started to hear the enemy coming, and that snapped him out of his funk, as his instinct for survival took over. *"Sir, I can hear the yelling now; I will be okay."* Mikael looked at him for a moment. *"You sure?"* *"Yes, Sir,"* said the man even more confidently as he put his gun on the lip of the trench they'd just taken a moment earlier. *"Is everything all right, Sir,"* said one of his lieutenants, Werner Lotar. *"Yes, all is good, but I need an NCO in this sector."* *"On it, Sir."* A Captain wasn't supposed to play morale booster during a battle, but it was what it was. As commander of his now diminished company (he had 185 men left out of 240), he had decided to participate in the assault on the redoubt the 1st Grenadier Regiment had been ordered to storm.

They were being pounded by a heavy Russian howitzer. Mikael knew it was heavy because of the blast the thing's shells were doing. The assault on the enemy redoubt and fortification had gone well, and they'd stormed it about half a day earlier. But ever since then, the enemy had been trying to reclaim it, attacking them with waves of humans and powerful artillery barrages.

The scene was a barbaric mix of battle, death, explosions, and mayhem. Blasts rocked the area and the by-now very damaged fortress. The Germans had a full battle siege line all along the western ramparts and fortifications, laden with large guns, mortars of all calibers, and thousands of troops. The Russians were firmly entrenched and also possessed a lot of guns, albeit with a slower rate of fire, because they lacked the ammunition to fire in a continuous manner.

If one looked up at the bullet-soaked sky, arcing shells left every other second toward and from the Russian walls and defenses, exploding in cacophonic blasts. The scene that Mikael and his company were going through was repeated hundreds of times across the entire length of the 65 square miles of the Fortress. In short, Kaunas was a cauldron of burning fire and smoke.

Mikael heard the loud humming noise of the "oo-oo-RAAAAAAAAAAAAAAAAAAAAAH" in the field before him as he fired his rifle at the withering mass of men. The Russians charged and moved over to their destroyed redoubt with abandon. He shook his head, again baffled at the immensity of the enemy attack. The Russian Army preferred massed infantry charges because they had the numbers to do so. Mikael wasn't certain it was effective, but then in the end, it worked even if it was costly in men.

He fired his rifle, certain he would hit someone. The writhing and yelling mass of humans filled the view before him. He didn't stay to watch the result, ducking back down because several bullets started to ricochet around him. It was bad; he was certain the enemy would scale the walls this time. *"Lieutenant Lotar,"* he said between two blasts and a shower of dirt on his helmet. *"We are not going to be able to hold this position,"* he said as calmly as he could, putting another clip into his Mauser rifle. It was also called The Gewehr 98 action and had a 5-round stripper clip.

"I agree, Sir," answered the Lieutenant as he emptied his rifle clip with five rapidly fired shots at the enemy charge. *"We've got about a minute before they storm this position,"* continued Mikael as he slammed his rifle on the lip of the half-mangled trench to fire his rounds in rapid succession. *"Get moving and pass the word to the rest of the men this way,"* he pointed right on the fortified ramparts. *"I will go the opposite direction to get the retreat order and get the NCOs and other officers to pass the word as well. We retreat into the tunnels we found earlier today behind us."* *"Yes, sir,"* countered Lotar, understanding why he had to run to talk to the men. The noise was so great that yelling would not do it; he had to move and tell the men to pass the order as quickly as possible. It also had to do with the fact that every able-bodied soldier was busy firing at the incoming charge and had no time to listen or watch for new orders.

Both men ran, slapping the men on the shoulders, stopping when necessary (explosions, blasts, and tracer shells raked the defenses). Mikael tripped on a dead soldier a couple of times, but he eventually made it to the end of the line, just maybe twenty seconds before the first Russians were over the ramparts. He started running down, following the rest of the soldiers, streaming into the large tunnel entrance near their defensive position. The 1.5 kilometers of tunnels had been discovered when they took the redoubt. From the looks of it, all of the Russian fortifications and main bunkers-redoubts were linked from underneath with tunnels. He'd sent men to explore, and they had come back to say that the tunnels split in two directions, one going deeper into the enemy position and the other back toward the exterior defenses of the fortress, now under German control. He had the first tunnel destroyed to avoid having Russians attacking them from below and kept the second direction open just in case they needed to beat a hasty retreat.

Mikael hoped that his unit would be able to retreat as far away from the enemy as possible. The Kaunas Fortress was about to fall, but it didn't look like it in his company's sector, and the local enemy commander still had a lot of men, and was using them as a battering ram.

(...) General Rennenkampf HQ, May 10th (...)

The ceiling shook once more, and dust fell on their head once more, General Paul von Rennenkampf was sweeping his hand across the map he was looking at. He looked up and took a deep breath. "One of these days, Yakovitch, the bastards will land one right on top of us," he said to his Second-in-Command, Colonel Yvan Yakovitch. The room was lit by a dim light bulb, and the ambient air was heavy, with dust hanging in the air. His large and fortified bunker was being pounded by the enemy forces, who weren't far from him. It was May 7th, and the battle for Kaunas was in full swing.

The German forces had penetrated deep into the perimeter, and he'd ordered counterattacks across the entire line for the last three days in order to try and reclaim control of the situation. Furthermore, the 10th Army (General Vasily Flug) and the Northwest Army (General Yakov Zhilinsky) were now finally entering the battle. He'd kept both of them on the flanks as he expected another outflanking move by the

Germans, but the enemy commander had opted for a classic assault across the frontal, southwestern, and northwestern parts of the fortress.

What he had to decide now was either to try and resist in Kaunas, and in this way run the risk of going for broke, or else disengage his forces to try and fight another day.

He was a lot more interested in the 1st option, and was currently implementing a counterattack with his superior numbers. The problem, however, was that the enemy's powerful artillery shattered his forces and didn't seem to be lacking in shell supplies, contrary to his own. Russian ordinance was scarce as priority was given to Brussilov and his offensive. This forced the Russian gunners to hoard their ammo and only fire for about a cumulative total of an hour a day. This was insufficient to break the heavy German forces, especially now that they'd conquered the western fortification; they were using them for protection against the Russian assaults.

His table and the maps laid on them were near the wireless telegraph station, and also where the phone line operators were. The entire Kaunas fortress was crisscrossed with buried telephone lines for battlefield communications. It worked well and enabled Rennenkampf to give orders rapidly to his forces or else be notified of an attack or anything else by the men there. They ran deep in the soil or along concrete tunnels between the main redoubts to avoid them being destroyed or cut by shellfire.

"What are your orders about the enemy breakthrough on the sector of Fort no. 4," asked Yakovitch. *"Shall we launch a counterattack?"* Rennenkampf hesitated. Fort No. 4 was the northern hub of the underground tunnel network. If it was held by the enemy, this would cut the flow of men and the telephone lines underground in the entire northern sector of the fortress. *"What do you think, Colonel,"* asked an uncertain General. *"Well, Sir, I will leave that decision to you; however,"* continued Yakonotivh, pointing to a spot on the map

representing a large redoubt (Fort No.15), "I have ordered the 34th Yaroslavl Regiment to move into No. 15 for the assault you might order."

"Good thinking, Colonel," said Rennenkampf as he smiled at his Second-in-Command. *"Go ahead and launch the counterattack. Let's go for broke."*

(...) German Field HQ, German 8th Army, May 12th, 1915 (...)

"Mackensen's 9th Army has pushed thirty-five kilometers inside the Russian lines in Northern Galicia," said Luddendorf as he read the fresh report they'd just received. Both Eric Luddendorf, and Paul von Hindenburg, were sitting in a room of their commandeered manor near Kaunas. The place was owned by an old, but rich Russian widow who had some German ancestors. Thus, she welcomed the 8th Army's staff into her midst.

The room was a place the widow's late husband had used to receive his guests. It was a large stone-walled construction with a big heart (no fire burned inside it). It had an old but expensive-looking rug covering its floor and a large dining table, where the duo of general's staff had installed all the maps and paperwork they needed. Both men were at the table, while several officers were hurrying about doing their own tasks. The telegraph officer, along with his people, took and sent messages from HQ. Other staff people were busy organizing the flow of information coming in constantly from the outside. The table was large, and a couple of colonels were working on the other end on tactical tasks. The siege of Kaunas was not yet over, and the last few forts had to be assaulted.

Hindenburg grunted in a mix of satisfaction and annoyance. *"Well, this has cost us our grand offensive into Poland and limits what we can do here in the North, but at least it appears to be working. The Russian offensive is petering out and is losing steam in the Carpathians."*

"It seems like it, Sir," answered Luddendorf. *"While the Austrian Army is now almost gone, the Russians are lacking the reinforcements to force the breach open even larger. The attack into the Southern Ukraine and Moldavia has also forced the Stavka to divert men there and to help the failing Romanian forces."*

Hindenburg leaned over the part representing the frontline in the Carpathians. *"Let's not be too hasty in calling victory, shall we,"* he countered. *"The Russians will certainly keep at it; the campaigning season is just starting."* *"Agreed,"* Luddendorf answered with a nod of the head. *"So, now, Sir, the idea is to decide what we do, as it appears we will take Kaunas soon."*

Indeed, the battle for Kaunas was now almost over after a few days when the situation became critical because of von Rennenkampf's powerful counterattacks. But in the end, German artillery (and the feeble Russian guns answer) had shattered the waves upon waves of soldiers who counterattacked as they tried to reclaim the fallen redoubts and bunkers.

Now, the Russians were trying to extricate their forces out of the fortress, and it appeared they might well be able to because of Rennenkampf's positioning of two of his armies on his flanks. While this had given an advantage to the Germans because they launched a frontal assault, it was now saving the Russians from complete defeat as their flanks were still rock solid.

"We need to push the Russians as hard as we can in our sector, in order to force the bastards to send more troops northward and out of the Galicia-Carpathians area," said Hindenburg, *"Eric, have the staff draw plans for the advance toward northern Lithuania. Let's make the Tsar nervous so he recalls his troops."* *"Yes, Sir."*

(...) The Battle for Kaunas and for Western Lithuania (...)

The fight for the fortress ended up lasting a little over ten days, and in the end, the Germans were able to take Kaunas even if the Russians had a large quantitative superiority. This was due to the incredible German superiority in artillery. The things weren't called the gods of war for no reason. They smashed almost every Russian counterattack and also obliterated the fortified walls of the fortress.

Furthermore, it was during this battle that the large difference in industrial capacity between the two empires was made as clear as mountain water. The Germans had the factories to support a modern war, while the Russians had enough to conduct offensive or defensive operations in limited sectors of the front. Stavka's strategic choice of emphasizing in the Carpathians against the Austro-Hungarians did produce results there because every effort was put into sending the supplies to Brussilov. As a result, and to their great dismay, the rest of the Russian forces paid dearly for it.

Svetozar Boroevic, the new Austro-Hungarian Army commander, walked up the narrow path up to the lip of the trench wanting to have a look down at the battlefield. Behind him, as if in a scene from a 17th-century painting, were arrayed the green plains of Hungary. This was how close the Russians had been to breaking through into the rest of the Empire. *"Well, General Westerling, you were right when you said this was the last line of defense,"* he grunted in weird amusement. *"The Imperial troops have been able to stop the Russian attack here and here,"* answered Westerling, always the serious man. He pointed at two areas to the left and to the right of where they were. *"The pass here was defended by the late arrival of the reinforcements you ordered from other sectors of the front and from the new levies, but it was close, Sir."* He also looked back down the slope on the Austrian side. *"The German artillery was also an added bonus and saved the day along with our own."* Boroevic turned to look at the long line of German guns. The duo of Generals Luddendorf and Hindenburg had sent a bunch of heavy howitzer guns, which helped win the day against the Russian offensive.

"These naval guns sure have helped," said Boroevic. The Reich had scrapped the bottom of the barrel and removed several of its coastal defense fortress guns (Konigsberg and several ones along the Baltic Sea) to help the beleaguered Austro-Hungarians weather the Russian attack. The 15 cm Ring Kanone L/30 ended up being the perfect weapon for the intended role.

Before the Great War, most military theorists and planners believed that the fighting would be offensive and that it would move across the land in fast-acting battles. This meant a focus on cavalry and light horse artillery firing shrapnel shells, as it was theorized the artillery would be employed in a supporting role as it moved forward.

Every fighting nation had heavy field artillery prior to the outbreak of the conflict, but none had sufficient numbers of them ready to be deployed, nor was the need for them believed important before the fighting degenerated into trench warfare.

Once the front stagnated and the incredible effectiveness of artillery was realized following the first few months of conflict, the need for high-angle heavy artillery reasserted itself. Naval guns thus fitted the bill perfectly, as they could fire a heavy shell at a high angle and at great distances. Firing high was important as there was nothing to fire at from a direct angle. The trenches were at ground level, and thus, it was incredibly hard to hit them with a line-of-sight gun. Coastal artillery and surplus naval guns thus became incredibly valuable for the fighting nations. Germany had built a sizeable naval defense network across its northern coastline and was thus able to promptly to convert all of them to field uses. The Kaiser's army also captured many more following their occupation of the French Channel and Atlantic harbors. The German generals put them to good use against troops instead of their original intended use. Several were on the frontlines helping German troops, but the urgency of the Austro-Hungarian situation prompted Hindenburg to order a bunch of them south as early as April 1915.

Thus, the hundred or so heavy and powerful 15 cm Ring Kanone L/30 had been one of the deciding factors in the last-ditch Austro-Hungarian resistance in the sector. The other reason the Russians had not broken through was because of General August von Mackensen's German 9th Army's counteroffensive against the Russian northern flank in Polish Galicia. In the end, Brussilov had just lacked reserves to send into the maw of the burning battle.

"The fighting looks to have been quite heavy," continued Boroevic, looking at the number of dead bodies lying by the thousands on the battlefield. Thankfully, a lot more brown uniforms populated the ground than the light blue ones of the K.U.K. Army.

The field of battle was also cratered like the surface of the moon, and it still smoked and burned in several places. The ground itself, well, the part not covered by debris or bodies, was blackened by the incessant explosions and shelling. The foul odor of decaying bodies and of cordite hung heavy, and they mingled together in the weirdest of fragrances.

"Indeed, sir," answered Westerling somberly. The number of dead before them was truly appalling. *"Now, what's next, sir,"* asked the chief of staff. *"For now, we will reinforce our defenses across the area, but in this sector, I would like us to counterattack to give us some breathing space, and in order to organize a defense in depth."* Boroevic paused while he put his fingers on his chin, thinking. *"The trench we are standing on top of was the fourth and last line if I am correct?" "Yes, sir. The Russians hold the three others down that slope,"* answered Westerling, pointing to a line of sandbags and trenches on the other side of the no man's land about two hundred yards away. *"We'll need to reclaim them,"* said the Commander-in-Chief. *"I will get the necessary preparations ready for you tomorrow in the early morning, General."*

(...) How close was it? (...)

The entire ten-day battle was a critical moment in the war. The Brussilov offensive, smashing everything before it, advanced almost through the entire length of the Carpathian Mountains but was stopped at the end of the Hungarian plains. If the Russians had broken through, the war would have been over for the Austrians. But as it was now, they were still in the fight.

The last K.U.K. reserves were also thrown into the battle, as Viktor Dankl von Krasnik's 5th Army, just out of training, had mobilized and moved to the front to bolster the beleaguered 4th Army in the midst of a complete disintegration.

Total losses for the Russian Army were 360,300 soldiers, while the K.U.K. lost 242,000, a number they could ill-afford. Strategically, the battle to mid-May was a strategic win for the Russian Empire, while Austria-Hungary had only won a temporary reprieve that could be shattered the moment Brussilov resumed the offensive.

"We fought over marshland and sand dunes, over bridges and shallow coves. There stood the majestic Fao Fortress, guarding the entrance of the Fao Peninsula. The blood of the Empire was spilled large and wide that day."

Private Soldier's Anthony Edan's private journal, May 1915

The Al-Faw Peninsula was a relatively narrow strip of land guarding the Ottoman's southern coast near Kuwait City and the important town of Basra. The land was accessible from inland by a few large tracks, while to the west, it was bordered by tall, massive cliffs. To the East, lower cliffs could be scaled by troops, the rocky edges giving way to massive sand dunes extending into the land's interior. Close to the coastline, and the water, was a beach, which was large and wide, divided by several small strips of land at low tide that morphed into islands at high tide. At the end of that stretch of beach and those strips of land lay the Fao Fortress, with its many towers and bastions guarding the entrance into the Southern part of the Ottoman Empire.

The entire reason for the operation was that the Viceroy of India, as well as many in London (including, amongst others, Winston Churchill), was to protect the Anglo-Iranian oil company and its refinery in Abadan. Both were becoming critical to the British war effort, as more and more Royal Navy ships used bunker oil as fuel. While the Turks had no such capability and believed the Middle Eastern part of their Empire (apart from the Sinai) was safe from attack, they also didn't see oil as a strategic resource yet, like much of the world. They entertained small garrisons in the Fao Fortress and Basra, but nothing that could be used in any offensive manner. The British, unaware of this lack of strategic vision on the Turkish side of things, therefore took steps to secure Iran.

The plan for the landing was quite simple. Two protected cruisers (HMS Lion and HMS Odin) would approach the fortifications and shell them from afar with their 5-inch guns. A few transports would then move a small contingent (600 soldiers) of the British Royal Marines to storm the fortress. Once secured, a follow-up landing operation was planned with the 15th British Division, composed of Indian soldiers.

(6th Royal Marines Battalion, morning of the 10th of May 1915 (...)

The dim light of the morning outlined the golden sand, and gave the rock on the coastline a bright red color, while the still orange-and-not-yet fully risen sun reflected on the blue ocean. The Fao fortress seemed to shimmer in the foggy, morning haze.

Private James Colborne wondered what he had to look forward to in victory. Everyone in the unit, along with the officer brass and the sailors offshore busily shelling the crumbling walls of the fortress, believed that an easy victory awaited the British Empire on that day.

How wrong they were, as the Turks would prove a lot more resilient than anticipated. For years now, the Ottoman Empire was considered the *"sick man of Europe"* and had not won any land victory in ages. But what the Western World had failed to consider was that it wasn't due to faulty soldiers. Turkish troops had conquered half the known world at one point in the 15th-16th Century, and the terrible results of the last two centuries were mostly due to the incompetence of their leaders, and the technology or training difference with the European armies. The typical Ottoman soldier was as sturdy as any and could fight well under the right conditions, just like at the Fao Fortress.

The British plan was as such: land a first attack of 250 British shock troops and then follow up with the rest of the battalion once a good beachhead was established. Men like Colborne thought that these Ottoman savages would be easy to clear out, but the fight they were about to give them was beyond words.

James came from the London slums, and was an orphan from a very young age. So young, in fact, that he could not remember his mother's face, and he had never met his father, who was never around anyway. Raised by abusive monks, he fled the orphanage by the age of 13 and was taken on a ship as a mate that same year. When he turned 16, he was finally able to enroll in the Royal Marines, and that was where he'd been ever since. James was a veteran of many wars, including the Boxer Rebellion in China and several actions against native rebellions in Africa. He'd also fought in the Boer War. His entire career did not prepare him for what was about to unfold. He and his comrades were not ready for a real fight.

They assaulted the first sector on an island in front of Fao Fortress and under the fire of the old, antiquated Ottoman guns. There were two sections to take in this sector: objective Apples (one of the small islands facing the fortress) and Butter, the beach itself. The Turks had been building their defenses since the outbreak of war in 1914 and had been warned an attack was coming by a deserter a week before. The Royal Marines were thus greeted by a wall of gunfire. James ducked instinctively as the man right in front of him had his head taken off by a Turkish bullet. The fight was on, and they soon got desperate, taking over fifty casualties before they finally took their Apple objective.

An hour later and as the two old British cruisers continued to pound the fortress, the Royal Marines' second attack wave met similar results as they assaulted their second objective, the beach. Many of their assault craft foundered in the water, holed by enemy shells, shrapnel, and bullets. The Ottoman snipers played hell on the Royal Marines as they bravely moved to the beach, soon coloring the golden sand in red. Mortar fire soon joined in and tore into the British ranks, inflicting terrible casualties. It wasn't long before the entirety of the British Marine battalion was pinned down on the beach below the fortress and couldn't move.

General Henry Dobys, the commander of the 15th Division and also of the entire land assault on the Fao Fortress, soon decided to call the entire force out, and the last-ditch assault landing was made. Locked and loaded, the Royal Marine's remnants and the fresh Indian troops charged forth into the slaughter.

Now convinced the Ottomans were devils, James fought as best he could in the maelstrom, and by the end of the day, they were finally firmly installed in their beachhead and ready to make their way into the so-called Sunwada Redoubt, where the Turkish defenders, now much reduced in numbers, awaited them.

The Golden Horn was a horn-shaped fjord on the European side of the Bosphorus Strait. It was a natural harbor where first Byzantine and then Ottoman fleets had anchored, sheltered, and docked over time. This was still the case in 1915. It didn't have the modern shipyards and equipment many of the European nations had, but it had enough to support the Central Powers operating from it.

The three naval commanders were in one of the harbor's many buildings. Behind them were the multitude of ships composing the combined fleet, although some of them had been sunk during the terrible defeat at the Battle of the Dardanelles. The room they were in was high enough to have a great view of the shipyards, the docks, and the warships they commanded. Admiral Wilhelm Souchon, the German officer now commander of the Ottoman Fleet, along with Greek Admiral Pavlos Kountouriotis and the Minister of the Ottoman Navy, Cemal Pasha, were all sitting at the small conference table. They were there on that early morning in May to discuss important matters. The sun shone on the water, with its light reflected brilliantly like a golden hue. Kountouriotis still harbored the burnt scars on his face and neck from the last battle but now seemed fine. All three men had serious faces, because none of them had still quite recuperated from what had happened a couple of months before.

The latest battle in February 1915 was terrible and showed they were not ready nor capable of taking on the British Eastern Mediterranean Squadron, now based in Crete. The defeat also effectively bottled them up into the Bosphorus-Dardanelles and the Black Sea.

The trigger of the battle was when the Germano-Turkish fleet sortied to try and save the Greek fleet being pursued by the Royal Navy. The Central Powers had had the advantage of numbers, minefields and also forts with which to defend and fight against the English. But in the end, it did not go well. Their ships got seriously damaged, with many sailors either dead or gravely wounded. Souchon had not expected such a casualty rate but then he was not necessarily surprised. The Ottoman sailors and ships had performed well against the old Russian ships and shore fortifications in the Black Sea. However, against real opposition and a powerful opponent, it was an entirely different proposition.

The Empire's three dreadnoughts had received extensive damage. First, the Sultan Osman-Evvel had gun and deck damage; then, the Resadiye had heavy waterline damage; the Goeben (Yavuz Sultan) received funnel, stern, and bow damage. And then the real loss, with the pre-dreadnought battleship Turgut Reis still beached on the Asiatic shore of the Dardanelles, with two destroyers sunk.

The Greek fleet made it to the Dardanelles in the end, but not without serious losses. Pre-Dreadnought battleship Kilkis was sunk, along with the modern heavy cruiser Helle and one destroyer. The rest of the fleet was also seriously damaged. The flagship Georgios Averoff had deck and superstructure damage, while the pre-dreadnought battleship Lemnos had one funnel and one engine room destroyed. Admiral Kountouriotis had been evacuated from the ship on a stretcher with serious burns.

The end result was that they were in a quandary. If they sortied into the Aegean, there was a chance they would be completely destroyed and sunk. If they stayed in the safety of the Golden Horn, it was the same result; their fleet was useless. There remained only one option, and it was the Black Sea.

"As I was saying, Gentlemen," said Cemal Pasha, *"the Greek ship's damage has been mostly repaired, thanks to the German naval engineers and repair equipment which arrived last month."* He nodded to the German Admiral as both the translator for Souchon and Kountouriotis gave them the rundown of what the Turkish Navy Minister had said. The Reich was a great supporter, and had excellent naval building techniques, and thus had sent help. The Turks could

man their ships, but they couldn't build them, nor make serious repairs from battle damage. That kind of work required specialized tools, machine shops, and parts that could only be manufactured by a real industrial power, which the Ottoman Empire was not. Germany had thus sent a full battalion of repair and building naval people by rail from Wilhelmshaven. The Austro-Hungarians had also contributed and sent a hundred of their own people from Pola on the Adriatic. The Ottoman government was keen and quick to give them a large building near the Golden Horn docks, and the end result was now a fully functioning machine shop and parts-building setup in Constantinople.

"The Ottoman and German ships are also almost ready to go, and now it appears we have a new enemy in the Black Sea," continued Cemal Pacha. *"Is this confirmed,"* answered Souchon, his face brightening. The Turkish Navy Minister spoke again. *"Indeed, Admiral,"* continued the Minister, handing out folders to the two naval officers. *"Our spies have confirmed that the brand-new dreadnought battleships Imperatritsa Ekaterina Velikaya and Imperatritsa Mariya have been launched from the Nikolaev Shipyards. Along with the pre-dreadnought battleship Evstafi, three armored cruisers, and thirteen destroyers, we now have a powerful enemy to contend with. The Russians will soon come knocking and asking for vengeance after what we did to them since the Battle of Cape Sarych."*

The Russians had indeed (and finally) launched their two brand-new dreadnoughts that had been started in 1912. Their sudden appearance in the Black Sea changed the force ratio dramatically. *"Interesting,"* said Souchon, smiling. *"These ships will require sea trials and some training,"* he continued. *"Do we have any information if they have sailed out of the Nikolayev shipyards?"* The Russian naval base was well protected, as had been confirmed by the raid the Germano-Ottoman fleet had executed in January 1915. The fleet had not been able to penetrate the river leading to Nikolayev. Forts protected it, and a minefield barred its entry, just like the Ottomans were doing to block the British from getting inside the Dardanelles in the strait.

"According to my reports, they have sailed but are staying within the limited confines of Nikolayev Bay, where they can rapidly retreat into the river if we approach."

Any recently launched warship needed to execute sea trials, to first train the crew in live exercises but also to work out the kinks and small things that were overlooked in the design and building phases. They were done following the dock tests to see if the main engines, boilers, and guns worked properly under realistic conditions. The trials were also to see if the ships could reach the given speed in the design specifications and if any adjustments were needed.

"Well, then maybe we should pay them a visit just in case we catch them unaware," said Souchon in a mildly excited tone. The Greek Admiral smiled. He liked the idea but was uncertain if this was in Greece's best interest to attack the Russian fleet. *"Are we certain this is needed, Admiral? I mean, even with these two new builds, we remain stronger in terms of ships and firepower; thus, it is unlikely the Russians will sortie and challenge us, even when their sea trials and training are over." "You may be Right, Admiral Kountouriotis, but at the same time, sinking those ships can boost morale. Also,"* he brought up by lifting his right-hand index, *"the Russians are building more ships, at least a couple more dreadnoughts, and that will put them ahead of us since we aren't making any ships at the moment."*

Kountouriotis grunted reluctantly. *"Very well, Admiral. I will confer with my government on the matter and will get back to you quickly." "Very well,"* countered the German fleet commander. *"Next order of business, Minister?"*

The so-called Sunwada Redoubt was located on the top of the hilly ramparts, overlooking the beach that the men of the 6th Royal Marines had just climbed as they faced a withering all of fire. Its main (antiquated) naval defense guns were destroyed, and the entire place smoked and burned, but that didn't mean it wasn't still dangerous for the British attackers.

Many of the men were either dead or injured, but Private James Colborne was one of the lucky soldiers who got within shooting range of the enemy fortification. The Ottoman position was built on a rocky mound that formed a high ground because of the added walls, giving the enemy directional cover to the northwest and anything coming from the sea and the beach. The entire fortification was pretty beat up as the two old, armored cruisers (Lion and Odin) had smashed everything standing with their 5-inch guns. Regardless, tons of Ottoman sharpshooters and defenders remained in the half-crumbled ruins.

"Watch out," yelled a sergeant; James looked up, seeing the flurry of bullets spitting out of the cleverly positioned and hidden machine gun that had just sprung up out of nowhere. The bullets slammed into several of his comrades while the rest glanced at the rock and debris around them, darting dangerously around, hitting more men. James dropped to the ground, putting his hands reflectively on top of his helmet and closing his eyes. For a moment, he asked God to protect him, and he prayed. *"We gotta move,"* yelled the Sergeant again. *"Anyone who can move needs to get to cover and move forward and leave the injured for now,"* the man repeated.

James stood up as if in a craze, certain to die, and he ran upward, barely keeping his balance on the uneven ground. Bullets zipped by him, and although he didn't feel it yet, one of them grazed his left shoulder. The light injury started to bleed almost instantly.

He finally made it to the part of the Ottoman wall that was still standing, finally safe from the machine gun as the thing was almost right above him, making it impossible for the Turks to fire on him because of the angle of fire. The Sergeant had also made it with a couple of men.

"Okay, guys; my name is Sergeant Kramer. You guys are not from my section, but I am commandeering you. We need to silence these bastards, as they're killing our brothers." After getting all acquainted, Kramer gave his orders. *"You and you, you to go to the left and try to climb this ledge,"* he pointed toward a steep, half-mangled piece of wall. *"That should bring you to the left side of the machine gunners. Pour all the fire you can on them the moment you get in position and see them."* *"Yes, Sergeant,"* they both answered as they turned to execute his instructions.

He then faced James. *"Colborne, you are with me, and we climb here to get on the fucker's right flank."* *"Yes, sir,"* said James as he looked at the treacherous climb the Sergeant proposed them to do. *"Don't think, kid, just follow me."* Kramer had seen the private's hesitation but had chosen to keep him in the action instead of trying to tell him everything would be all right. As he knew it wouldn't necessarily be the case. Ernest Kramer was an old hand of the Marines, having fought around the world, just like James. While he at first thought that this private was a green soldier, he would soon be pleasantly surprised.

Kramer started the climb first, putting his hands on the cracks and pulling himself up. James followed him after having slung his rifle over his shoulder. They moved upward for about ten minutes while the machine gun continued its chatter (James decided it was a German Maxim gun from the characteristic two-men-chainsaw-like sound). As they finally made it to the top part of the ledge and into the broken-down Ottoman redoubt, they both started hearing the sound of rifle fire. *"Good, the other two guys have started firing,"* said Kramer. For a moment, the Turkish machine gunners stopped. They could not yet see the enemy but could see downward in the direction the rest of the battalion was climbing, and when the Maxim started its chatter again, it wasn't in that direction. *"Haha! The fucking bastards have moved their weapons toward the new attackers. We'll see how they like our little outflanking move,"* muttered the Sergeant with a smile.

James heard a voice to their left, opposite the direction they wanted to go to flank the machine gunners, and he tapped the Sergeant's shoulder, pointing left and to his ears. There were definitely voices to that side. Kramer gestured to him they were to go that way, unsheathing a vicious-looking knife. James picked up his bayonet to use as a short sword as he got the NCO's idea. Silencing the Turks on the left with blades in order to avoid alerting the machine gunners on their right.

They moved cautiously between two large and crumpled boulders, hearing the voices more clearly, intersected with rifle fires. The Turks seemed to be in a bunker or something underground, as their voices seemed muffled.

The two British soldiers finally made it to where the Ottomans were hiding, seeing their rifles protrude out of an opening from a brick-walled position that seemed undamaged by the naval bombardment. Kramer put his finger to his mouth to indicate that he didn't want any noise or voices, and then he fished out one of the new Mills Bombs they'd received just before the assault. James had only heard rumors about the things and smiled. Mills Bombs had been recently adopted by the British Army, and were the first hand-grenade in the English armed forces. Designed by a man named William Mills (where they got their name), they were now only starting to get distributed to the troops.

The grenade had a grooved cast shape, looking like a small pineapple with a hand lever to activate it. The casing was easy to grip because of the grooves, James decided, since the Sergeant handed him out one of the Mills as well. Kramer gestured they should walk on top of the small brick-walled fortification and throw the grenades in the hole where the rifles protruded from. James made a sign to let the NCO understand and that he wondered where had gone his idea of being stealthy, and Kramer just gave him a hard stare, meaning, if he could have spoken. *"Are you trying to be a smart ass, son?"* James smiled nervously and nodded that he acknowledged the idea of the Mills bombs.

They moved out of hiding as silently as possible and walked right on top of the small fortification. They could now hear the Turkish voices clearly as the rifle's smoke billowed all around them. All the while, the machine gun chainsaw-like chatter was making itself heard. The two British soldiers lay flat on their bellies and crawled to the edge of the fortification that was built right on the side of the cliff. They both activated their levers and then threw the Mills inside. For a moment, the voices inside stopped speaking, and then pandemonium erupted as they panicked.

Turning quickly on his back, James pointed his rifle toward the fortification's exit, firing a round in the back of the Turkish soldier who tried to run out of the place. The bullet slammed the soldier in the back in a cloud of blood droplets, and he dropped hard to the ground with a loud thud. The next moment, the two Mills Bombs exploded in a fury of fire.

The explosion was so strong (it was in an enclosed space) that it shattered the brick-walled ceiling, and both Kramer and James fell into the exploding debris in a cloud of smoke and dust, landing with a loud thud.

Moments later, James came back to his senses, coughing, trying to see in the billowing dust and smoke all around them. He saw movement to his left and realized the Sergeant had also risen up. *"Quick, Colborne,"* he said as he started stumbling out of the smoking ruins. *"We gotta get to cover!"*

A minute later, they were back to their original climbing spot, coughing loudly and trying to catch their breaths. But something had changed. The machine gun wasn't firing anymore. *"Do you hear that, Sarge,"* said James, pointing toward the Maxim's direction. *"The bastards have either been killed by our guys, or else they retreated inside the fortress."* *"Indeed, Sir. What do we do now?"*

Kramer seemed to think for a moment. *"We move toward the machine gun and see if our guys are still there and alive."* He paused, pointing toward the destroyed fortification. *"But before that, we kill those bastards."* More Turkish soldiers had just arrived at the explosion site and pointed their rifles in every direction, looking for the culprits. One of them, probably the officer or an NCO, barked some orders, and they started to fan out around.

Both Kramer and Colborne thus fired their guns in rapid succession. James had four bullets left while the Sergeant still had the five from his full clip. The rifles barked, and bullets swamped the small group of enemy soldiers who tried to scramble to safety. Then, it was time for both British Marines to reload. Four bodies lay dead or seriously injured on the ground, while two of the Turkish soldiers got to cover and returned fire.

Both Kramer and Colborne dropped to the ground behind the rocks they had fired from for protection. The bullets glanced in bright sparks on the rocks around them, ricocheting everywhere without hitting either of them. The Sergeant fished out yet another Mills Bomb, activated it, and threw the grenade over his shoulder and his hiding place. The muffled explosion shook the ground. It sent rocks and debris flying in every direction, even showering the two British soldiers. James leveled his rifle in case the enemy was still able to fire, but nothing happened. *"They are out, Sarge,"* he claimed. *"Good,"* answered Kramer as he put his hand on his shoulder. *"Nice work, Colborne. Let's go see if our friends survived and what happened to that machine gun."*

CHAPTER 3
THE WAR IN THE WEST

Württemberg Mountain Battalion field hospital
May 9th, 1915

"You are cleared for duty, Captain," said the man after he finished taking Erwin Rommel's pulse. *"Thank you, Captain,"* he answered to the military doctor as he jumped out of bed. Finally, he would soon be back in action!

Rommel had been injured on the side of the head, an injury that sidelined him for a month and a half. It had been in one of the battles following the conquest of Fort Mont Angel. It had been one hell of a tough fight. The next fort for the Germano-Italians to assault on the Séré de Rivières system had been truly high up in the mountains, above a small French town called La Turbie. Compared to the Fort of Bear Mountain (Fort do Mont-Ours) that he'd taken with his men sometime before, it had been the real deal. The very large fort was originally intended to serve as one of the main points of resistance on the border and also as a large artillery support position with a powerful 145 mm gun battery. The thing had been firing every day on the Central Powers' positions, and it was about time that they silenced it.

But after a true feat of heroism and mountain climbing, Rommel and his men had been able to assault the fort's fortified entrance and held it long enough for the main German attack to come from below. The battle had lasted a few days after that, while the French had counterattacked relentlessly.

This was when he was injured, and not even by a bullet. An artillery shell had exploded high above the position he had been defending, and rocks fell down. He was then hit in the head by a sizeable boulder, knocking him unconscious. While this had been quite a bad injury that kept him out cold for several days, he had been one of the lucky ones. Several men in his company were wiped out by the rock avalanche, and many were now dead, or severely incapacitated. Private Stark had survived the ordeal with minor injuries, and he'd been at Rommel's side since then. *"Yes, Sir, about time you get back into the action. The men were starting to think you were relaxing with the good-looking nurses,"* said the man, now Rommel's friend, as they had fought through hell together since their arrival in Italy.

Erwin clapped the soldier on the shoulder and smiled. *"Get me up to speed, Stark."* *"Well, Sir, not much has changed from yesterday. We are still stuck trying to take that damned La Turbie town, but the French are resisting like there's no tomorrow,"* answered the soldier with a sour face. *"We've lost a lot of men,"* he said once more, and Rommel knew what he was talking about. A replacement officer had commanded his unit, and he had been pretty bad at it. Stark had told him all the errors he'd made, and of his arrogance. He was some upstart-well-connected-with royalty types. *"Don't worry, Stark. Go back to the men and tell them I will be back with the unit shortly, and that their time with this idiot will soon be done."*

"Where are you going, Sir," asked the soldier, surprised Rommel wasn't going to his unit right away. *"Gotta report to the Regimental commander."* Rommel was speaking about Colonel Theodor von Dücker, his unit commander, and he didn't expect the discussion to be nice as he had already heard that the replacement captain was to stay with his unit.

More dust fell on the small table, as well as on the playing cards, and Private Soldier Oskar Dantz of the 4th German Division wiped it off in a lazy gesture and then rolled his eyes in annoyance. *"When are those fucking bastards going to stop this relentless pounding,"* said Sergeant Wilhelm, sitting on the other side of the table from Oskar. *"I have no clue, Sergeant,"* said the soldier to his left. *"Your turn to play, Sergeant."* Wilhelm grumbled in frustration as the thundering outside the German dugout kept on going like a bad summer storm. Only it wasn't rain that was falling down on the ground; it was shells. A lot of shells.

Oskar and his section were holed up in one of the first-line trench's dugouts designed to protect the infantry soldiers from enemy artillery attacks. The idea was that while the shelling was in progress, the men needed protection from the incessant shrapnel and explosions raking the trench and defenses.

The place was well-built, as the Reich took the comfort of its soldiers seriously compared to the Entente. The place was extensively dug underground. It sported beds and kitchens and was well-ventilated by three entrances. It also connected the first and second lines of trenches. The ground was also above the dirty water accumulating in every trench of every frontline because the German engineers and builders had put planking above it, like in the trench itself. Compared to their Allied equivalent, the Kaiser's soldiers walked in relative dryness, even when it rained. The only problem was the rats, who also liked the place and thus had infested it.

The small group of men were playing cards because there wasn't much else to do while waiting for the next enemy attack. It would surely come the moment the shelling stopped, but for now, their options were to go outside for guard and sentry duty, sleep, or lounge around like they were doing now. Since no one wanted to go outside unless ordered (the Sergeant sent them one after another through a well-rehearsed rotation system) and couldn't sleep all the time, most of them had *"hobbies"* to pass the time.

They were currently playing poker, and Oskar had a great hand with three kings. Wilhelm also seemed to have a great hand, and soon, everyone had folded except the two of them. The wager was cigarettes, and soon, there was a ton of them on the table. Both men had gone all in, and it was now time to drop the cards.

"You go first, Sarge," said the self-proclaimed leader of the game, the soldier on Wilhelm's left. Wilhelm smiled and dropped his cards. *"Here you go, Dantz. Three queens."* Oskar was about to smile back and drop his own cards when a powerful explosion rocked the dugout, smashing everything in sight. The ceiling dropped on them and soon, it was a scramble to try and get out alive. While dugouts were fine and well to save the soldiers against shrapnel and blasts of fire, they were not designed to withstand a direct hit or two. Since one had already hit the top of the dugout earlier during the French barrage, the second one finished it.

"Out!" yelled Wilhelm, and Oskar jumped to his feet, having the reflexes to grab his rifle. Earth fell on their heads, and dust was everywhere. He coughed hard and ran toward the dim light he could see, which was one of the tunnels giving way to the outside.

He jumped through the haze and exited on the other side, landing hard on the trench planking, soon followed by the Sergeant and a couple of other men. He stood, patted himself out of the dust covering his face and body, and then realized that the artillery barrage was over. The dugouts continued to crumble and soon it was all crumpled on itself in a heavy veil of smoke and dust.

As right as rain, the alarm started to blare out. Several of the officers started to blow their whistles, and more men just yelled *"Alarrmmm!"* out of their lungs. The French were attacking.

The 4th German Division had remained in the Verdun sector following the abating of the enemy offensive, but that did not mean the Franco-British had been done trying to pierce the German lines. They continuously probed the defenses in an attempt to find the weaknesses they believed their enemies had because of all the troops they had to send East to meet the Russian steamroller.

However, the Entente leaders were mistaken if they thought the Germans were weak in France. They had fewer men and thus could not attack, but they had enough to defend and sufficient machine guns with artillery backing them to withstand pretty much anything their enemies wanted to throw at them.

"Dantz," said Wilhelm as he pointed to a spot on the trench facing the enemy. *"Get to the top of the firing parapet and kill the bastards!"* *"Yes, Sir,"* he answered, not wanting to show the crusty Sergeant he was unwilling.

He got to the lip of the trench and dropped his rifle on a sandbag. Bullets snapped the wall of bags he was covering behind, and he winced in sudden fear. The enemy was very close; he could even see the top of their helmets and their bayonet tips through the haze and smoke of the enemy artillery barrage. He emptied his 5-bullet clip into the billowing smoke and reloaded immediately. To his left, a Maxim machine gun nest was hammering away at the half-unseen soldiers, and he saw the bullet slash through the foggy greyness and disappear.

Loud, overbearing whistles started to be heard coming from his back. He smiled as he slammed his third clip into the rifle magazine. The German artillery was joining in. The heavy rounds thundered above and started slamming the no man's land between the two trench lines with explosions. They blossomed in a flurry of fireballs and columns of dirt and smoke. Bullets continuously zipped by him, and he wondered if it was his day to die. Oskar, along with the rest of the German line, cheered in excitement.

"Quick, now, the enemy has crossed our barbed wire line," yelled some Lieutenant behind Oskar. *"I need more clips,"* he yelled, turning back down the trench to some of the runners there, responsible for distributing ammo to the men. *"Here you go, mate,"* said one of the men, handing him five more 5-bullet clips.

He climbed back up to the firing parapet and resumed pouring fire into the incoming enemy. All this time, he hoped that it would not come to a hand-to-hand fight. Those were the worst, as fighting in the haze and smoke was the most difficult.

Minutes later and after having gone down into the trench four more times to get more ammo, the enemy attack abated without anything else happening. *"The enemy's retreating,"* yelled one of the officers.

It was only then that Oskar realized, remembering the card came, that he had been about to win a big pot, and he cursed. He dropped back down into the trench and closed his eyes.

At the onset of hostilities in Europe, Mexico declared itself neutral along with the United States. But many in Mexico City harbored a lot of hostility toward the Yankees because of the recent war in 1846-1848.

The country was also in the middle of a civil war, pitting President Venustiano Carranza against a rebel general named Pancho Villa, who was based in the Northern Mexican states. Villa also constantly raided the United States, especially after the U.S. Army occupation of the Mexican Costal town of Vera Cruz. Most of the fighting was localized in Texas and involved the Texas Ranger Division. It was sort of tolerated to a point by the Americans, but they were getting tired of it and had thus sent troops to occupy the Gulf Costal town of Vera Cruz as a warning to the Mexican President and rebels to get things in order and not involve the United States.

With hostility at its height, the Manzanillo incident happened, and an enterprising Mexican naval battery captain, an admirer of Pancho Villa, opened fire on the American ships blockading the harbor because of the presence of the German Pacific Squadron. What followed was a full-scale battle between the German and U.S. Navy ships along with the forts of Manzanillo Harbor, ending in the sinking of the American ship Galveston.

Thus, Woodrow Wilson and the U.S. Secretary of State drafted a dire warning to President Carranza that no more attacks, raids, or incidents would be tolerated by America and that a full occupation of Mexico would result from any transgression.

Of course, Pancho Vila, being a rebel and a downright bandit, didn't care nor hear about the American warning. He led a powerful raid into Texas on the 14th of April 1915, when a band of approximately 400 mounted rebels crossed the border and raided Los Indios Ranch in

Cameron County, resulting in the killing of several families and twenty Texas Rangers.

What followed the next day was an address by President Woodrow Wilson to Congress, asking the legislative body of the United States of America to declare war on Mexico. With hostility toward their southern neighbor at an all-time high, war was voted unanimously.

Two weeks later, a relatively unknown general was watching his troops as they crossed the border into Mexico. His name was John J. (Black Jack) Pershing. His army was relatively small compared to the ones vying for supremacy in Europe, as the United States of America had not really needed many armed forces until then.

UNITED STATES			
1st Army (General John . Pershing)			
1st Corps	General Hunter Liggett	32,000 soldiers	Texas-Northern Mexico
2nd Corps	General George Windle Read	35,000 soldiers	Texas-Northern Mexico
Texas Rangers Division (Texan volonteers)	Colonel John R. Hughes	4,000 soldierd	Texas-Northern Mexico

With war looming for the country as it looked like the European war could spill over to the New World, there were those who called for an expansion of the U.S. Army, but for now, it was pretty much what Pershing could count on to invade Mexico. A total of 71,000 men, including the 1st and 2nd Corps and a band of Texan volunteers called the Texas Rangers Division. Pershing's troops included cavalry units (11th and 13th Cavalry Regiment) and the 6th Artillery Battalion. While the entire setup along the Mexican-American border was relatively weak compared to their European juggernaut counterparts, it didn't lack motivation in the best spirit of the all-conquering attitude that was taking over the American continent.

"Don't they look magnificent," said Pershing to his young staff officer, a 2nd lieutenant, a fellow by the name of George S. Patton. *"Indeed, Sir,"* answered the young man. Both families were related through marriage, and Patton, who had wanted to be in on the fighting with the Mexicans, appealed to Pershing to participate since his own unit (the 8th Cavalry Regiment) was not going to be in the invasion. *"When*

do we expect our forces to be approaching Monterrey," continued the American General to his aide. *"Sir, we are at least a four to five-day walk to the city, provided we do not fight and that water supply is continuous,"* answered the young lieutenant. *"Very well, Lieutenant Patton."*

Both men were on their horses, as the going on the rugged ground was a lot simpler on horseback. They were flanked by a throng of officers who awaited Pershing's marching order. There was no resistance from the Mexicans at the border, as President Carranza's army was in the south, busy fighting rebel troops. *"Colonel Winn,"* continued the U.S. leader to another officer on horseback. *"Yes, General,"* answered the man as he trotted his horse forward. *"Are the reports still placing Pancho Vila and his men in Monterrey?"* *"At last news, Sir, they were, although we expect the bastard to move out of the way and avoid fighting us when we approach."*

"Very well," grunted Pershing as he turned his horse to go back to his field HQ tent. Lieutenant Patton, as his aide, followed suit.

Capitan Canepa Bay Fjord
The two German fleets join up in enthusiasm and joy, May 2nd, 1915.

(...) Dreadnought battleship Grosser Kurfurst (...)

The Capitan Canepa Bay fjord was located on the southern side of Estados Island. Rugged, snow-capped cliffs guarded its entrance like two stone giants watching for incoming ships. All along the cliffs, Admiral Felix Funke could see the southern swells had dug holes in the rock where small ships could hide.

He saw some of the men on the deck pointing at some spot in the large fjord and saw they were looking at penguins. The beautiful animals plunged into the water as the sight of the big German ships frightened them. On the cliffs above, he saw a herd of goats, probably feral, as there were no reported humans on Estados Island. It was then that columns of smoke were spotted on the high cliffs. *"Rear-Admiral,"* said the lookout officer excitedly as he entered the bridge from the outside balcony, where his men watched for anything out of the ordinary. *"A large fire atop the high cliff over there. The men say a signal team is flagging them a message."* Funke's heart leaped with enthusiasm. Could they have really found the by now famous German Pacific Squadron and its resourceful commander?

The powerful 3rd German Battle Squadron, with its four battleships (Grosser Kurfurst, Markgraf, Konig, and Kronzprinz), four light cruisers, and one destroyer, was about to join up with the remaining ships of the German Pacific Squadron and its two surviving battleships (Westfalen and Kaiserin) and the light cruiser Emden.

3rd Battle Squadron, relief fleet (Rear-Admiral Felix Funke) - To German West Africa		
BB Grosser Kurfürst	BB König	4 CL
BB Markgraf	BB Kronprinz	1 DD

"What does the message say," asked Funke with impatience. *"A minute, Sir,"* said the lookout officer, going back outside on the balcony to get its content. Twenty seconds later, he returned. *"Sir,*

Admiral Maximilian von Spee welcomes you to Estados Island," he said, followed by a thunderous roar of enthusiasm from the men and officers alike on the battleship's bridge.

An hour later, as Grosser Kurfurst's motorboat approaches the Westfalen, Rear Admiral Funke could not help but wonder how the Westfalen had withstood all the damage it sported on its hull. The great ship was scarred and burnt in many places, and it was obvious the ship had not seen a real shipyard since it left Tsingtao in 1914. He'd heard through the scant news he'd received in Swakopmund (the German Southwest African colony had been equipped with a wireless telegraph station) that the two battleships had been forced to stop in Mexico to repair their boilers. But the rest remained damaged. The hull was mangled with holes on the deck and stern. The Kaiserin had its rear turret gutted and had damage on its stern and all across its deck as well. The light cruiser Emden, anchored just to the side, hadn't fared any better, as it seemed it was a floating piece of coal with burnt marks all over. It seemed a miracle the thing was still afloat.

German Pacific Squadron		
Admiral von Graf Spee		
BB Westfalen stern and deck damage	CL Emden stern and forecastle damage	Collier ship Oldenwald
BB Kaiserin stern , 1 rear turret destroyed		

The calm but cold water of the Capitan Canepa Bay fjord made the motorboat ride pleasant. Behind Funke lay the four battleships of his battle squadron, looking pristine and new. He'd given permission to the sailors and officers to assemble on the bridge, and he could hear the roar of enthusiasm coming from both fleets as the joy was overbearing for all. What the Pacific Squadron had achieved to date was something worthy of legends, while the 3rd Battle Squadron, with its dash through the Atlantic, was now also entering the legend that would one day be told in the history books and countless stories about the epic adventure.

Just beside him in the motorboat lay a big pile of large white mailbags. They were the delayed correspondence of the Pacific Squadron's families and friends, and he made sure he brought them over on his first trip. In his pocket, he had the four letters addressed personally to von Spee. Two from his wife, one from Hugo von Pohl, the Commander-in-Chief of the German Fleet, and one from a very admiring Kaiser. Morale was important in war, and for the Pacific Squadron, it was critical. These men had not heard from their families and loved ones in over a year and deserved to have news.

The boat finally docked with the Westfalen's hull, and a large steel ramp was lowered for him and his people to climb on the battleship's deck. He moved in first in line, wearing his best all-white ceremonial uniform like the rest of the men with him on the motorboat. His second-in-command followed suit right behind, and then four sailors with two large mailbags each.

He finally got to the top of the steel ramp and was welcomed by a raucous cheer from the Westfalen's sailors, all assembled on the deck for him. The deck was packed full of men, the bridge, the balconies, and some of the sailors stood on the long protruding gun barrels themselves.

He lost his breath for a moment when he saw the man of the hour in Germany, the legend Admiral Maximilian von Spee. He immediately gave the man, who would soon be his superior, the navy salute. "Welcome to the Westfalen, Rear-Admiral," said von Spee as he returned the salute. To this, every sailor on the deck threw their caps and hats in the air, and they were followed by the men on the other ships looking at the scene.

It was a grand time to be German.

At the same time, on the ships of the combined Anglo-Japanese Fleet

(…) Dreadnought battleships Neptune and Setsu (…)

Discovered in 1616 by explorer Jacob Lemaire, the Strait of the same name was located between Los Estados Island, and the Southern tip of Argentina. The Strait was a shortcut for any ships transiting from the Pacific into the Atlantic and vice versa, saving about twelve hours of sailing time compared to going around Estados Islands. It was thus a logical spot to patrol for the Anglo-Japanese ships of Admirals Beatty and Togo. There was no plan to split the fleet, as the perceived strength of the twin German fleets they thought to be in the area was a staggering six modern dreadnought battleships. It was thus too risky to split the force as each of them would be inferior in strength if they met the two Germans fleets together.

The weather in the Strait was unpredictable, and storms often blew hard, creating treacherous currents with a risk of being blown against the shoreline. A safe naval commander would sail around Estados, but von Spee was not a safe admiral, and thus, both Allied commanders had decided to start with a thorough investigation of the area before sailing to the south side to explore the Fjords. There were a few natural harbors and Fjords on the northern side that needed to be checked as well.

Admiral David Beatty was standing outside on the dreadnought battleship Neptune, hot tea in hand while wearing a warm fur coat and a fur hat. The weather outside was cold. After all, they were close to the South Pole. Hell, they'd even seen penguins, which indicated they were near it, as most of these animals did not live further north.

The Anglo-Japanese fleet was hovering in a large circle as it awaited the result of the investigations they'd ordered into the fjord and natural harbors where the Germans could hide. The teacup was steaming hard in the cold, and he took a sip, feeling the warm liquid going down his throat and into his stomach.

A few miles to the south, Japanese admiral Heihachiro Togo was in his cabin, trying to avoid the cold outside. He didn't like the weather in these southern latitudes. He was also an old man at 66 years old, and the cold was difficult on his bones. The accumulated fatigue was starting to show in his body and mind.

He was sitting alone in his Admiral of the Fleet cabin, lost in his thoughts. How would he have liked to be back at the age he was in 1905 during the battle of Tsushima. That moment had been the prime of his life, and he wished to be back in this type of shape every day since the beginning of this legendary epic chase across the Pacific, and now the Atlantic. He comforted himself in the fact that the gods had seen fit to give him one last shot at glory with this resourceful German Admiral and his elusive fleet.

Togo had also sent patrols into the fjord and potential enemy hiding places, but he'd also sent a few shore parties on the island itself with the mission of crossing it and exploring the southern side. The island was long (about twenty miles), while it was very narrow in length, and it was thus possible for his landing parties to explore several of the fjords on the southern shore while the fleet finished scouring the north. He hoped this would pay dividends.

A young staff lieutenant entered his cabin through the open hatch door and bowed in front of him. *"Admiral,"* he said respectfully, *"the landing parties are reporting seeing some smoke on the southern coast."* The landing parties were equipped with signal flags and were thus in a position to send messages to the motorboats that landed them on the coastline. Those motorboats could then relay the same to the fleet offshore. Togo's interest spiked in an instant. There was nothing like adrenaline to give him his old energy back for a time. *"Do they know what they are?"* *"No, Sir. For all we know, they could just be whale hunters or a few civilian vessels. They are moving further inland to investigate and will report in a few hours."* *"Very well,"* answered the Japanese admiral, hoping this was what they were all hoping for.

Zeppelins, fighters, and a duel
Above Versailles, May 5th, 1915

New fighter pilot Armand Bonnier nodded to his friend and mentor Roland Garros, and then they both began to roll their planes left to plunge down on the large Zeppelin airships below them. The wind slapped at his goggles and scarf-covered face, and he plunged into a thin white cloud. Below, he could already see the enemy machine gunners on top of the big airships firing at him. The plane shook as it was taking in more speed than it was designed for because of the force of gravity.

Armand was nervous as this was going to be his first air action. Both men, along with five others, flew in the Morane-Saulnier L, the first French fighter, as it had been the first Allied aircraft fitted with a machine gun that fired through the propellers. The propellers themselves were protected with heavy metal plates because bullets often hit them as they were not synchronized with the machine gun. It was very dangerous for the pilot, as the bullets could dart in every direction, and even back at him.

Roland Garros, the first French ace (the man already had downed five enemy planes) had been the first to fly the thing in battle. Roland was also the man who had trained Armand for the last two months following his bold move in the Apulia Enclave, where he jumped into a downed plane and took off again. His divisional commander had been so impressed that he'd shipped him back to France to train as a pilot. When he arrived in Vichy, one of the Entente training bases, he was greeted by Garros, a friend since before the war. It was the same man who had shown him the rudiments of flying and the reason he'd been able to take over that fighter in January. Armand was feeling happy and ecstatic as his dream of flying was finally being realized.

Roland was the first air commander in the French Air Force and had been tasked with setting up an air squadron to fight against the growing numbers of German fighters and planes. The enemy also flew

Zeppelins that launched bombs on Allied cities and troops.

Armand tried to concentrate as the looming shapes of the seven Zeppelins grew large below him. He saw Roland was ahead, as he'd picked up even more speed because he had started his dive earlier. He saw his friend's machine gun starting to fire, and the bullets slammed into the Zeppelin's soft skin fuselage. The German machine gunners on the top tried to shoot him down, and Armand decided it was a grand sight. Soon, it was his turn to act, and he chose to attack the same airship as his friend had done. He waited as long as he could (Roland had told him that the typical error was to fire from too far away) and then pulled the machine gun trigger. His bullets streamed between the propellers and on them, sparking in bright flashes as some passed through and some hit them. He felt nervous and hoped he wouldn't die or get injured from a bad ricochet.

His stream of bullets raced down in a curving arc at the German aircraft, and about half of the arc slammed into the fuselage. Two more fighters fired at the same Zeppelin, and then he was past the thing zipping by at great speed. From the corner of his eyes, he then saw a flash, and the next instant, a big explosion rocked the airship as the hydrogen gas inside it ignited in a great fireball. His plane was pushed to the side by the blasts, and for a moment, he struggled to keep control of it. "Damn!" he said to himself.

He pulled on his plane stick, avoiding a couple of bullet streams fired at him by two other Zeppelins hovering near the stricken one. As he did so, he noticed that the Germans were busy dropping bombs on the troops below. The battle was taking place above the Entente frontline near Versailles.

He looked around, trying to find his bearings, as well as where his comrades were. He saw a couple of them busy jockeying with an enemy plane, and he frowned. The German fighter was a triplane, which wasn't rare. But the thing that stood out was that the fighter was painted all in red. He wondered why a pilot would be so stupid as to make sure he would be easily seen and recognized in battle.

And then, one of the French planes was shot down, twirling downward and smoking. He pushed his directional control stick toward the bastard as he decided to join in, leaving the Zeppelins behind. As he made his approach, a second comrade was shot down, and he cursed out loud, hoping it wasn't Roland.

Another minute, and he was almost there, but the mysterious and skillful red plane had already turned away to get back to German lines. He tried to push his engine, but quickly saw the enemy fighter was faster. He decided that Zeppelins would do as targets for today and turned his Morane-Saulnier back toward the big looming airships.

French offensive on the Western Front
May 3rd-May 13th, 1915

(...) Push on Paris (...)

The entire Paris-Nantes frontline lit up in a plethora of fireballs, and a godly artillery hammer descended upon the German defenses as the Anglo-French offensive on Paris opened up in a fury worthy for the ages.

France			
1st Army	General Auguste Dubail	300,000 soldiers	Verdun Area
2nd Army	General de Curières de Castelnau	320,000 soldiers	Verdun Area
3rd Army	General Maurice Sarrail	300,000 soldiers	Verdun Area
4th Army	Fernand de Langle de Cary	315,000 soldiers	Paris-Nante frontline
5th Army: .	General Louis Franchet d'Espèrey	276,000 soldiers	Paris-Nante frontline
9th Army	General Charles Lanzerac	245,000 soldiers	Paris-Nante frontline
6th Army	Général Joseph Maunoury)	300,000 soldiers	Belfort-Swiss Border
8th Army	Newly raised	300,000 soldiers	Vichy area (reserve)

Three French armies attacked first as the British waited to act as an echelon assault a day later. Over 930,000 soldiers attacked across the line once the twelve-hour preparatory artillery bombardment was over. The Entente military leadership would have opted for a few days of barrage, but they just didn't have the shells. The entire operation was thus based on surprise and to quickly overwhelm the German defenses in Paris. The goal of the offensive was no less than the liberation of the French capital. The attack was made on a fifty-mile-wide frontline.

British Empire-West			
1st Army	General John French	112,000 soldiers	Verdun Area
2nd Army	General Douglas Haig (overall comman‹	95,000 soldilers	Paris-Nante frontline
3rd Army	General Smith–Dorrien	95,000 soldiers	Paris Rheims
4th Army	General Henry Rawlinson	350,000 soldiers	Paris-Nante frontline
Reserve Army (England)		300,000 soldiers	Southern England
Imperial forces	Australian, New Zeland, Canadians	100,000 soldiers	Paris-Nante frontline

The next day, following a bogging down of the French attack (as expected by Foch) in the face of withering defensive fire, untouched barbed wire lines, and powerful defensive artillery fire, the British forces launched as well with two armies (the 2nd and the 4th) and 450,000 soldiers.

The effect of the numerous add-ons to the already powerful attack broke the first German lines of defenses, and the Entente forces thus moved twenty miles northward toward Paris, liberating Versailles. Events soon came to a head for the German Army, poised to resist as best they could in their trenches.

Germany– West			
Verdun - Alsace border			
10th Army	General Max von Pritzwitz	200,000 soldiers	Verdun Area
German 9th Arm	General Theodor von Baben	190,000 soldiers	Verdun Area
Paris-Nante frontline			
1st Army	General Alexander von Kluck	300,000 soldiers	Paris-Nante frontline
2nd Army	General Karl von Bülow	220,000 soldiers	Paris-Nante frontline
3rd Army	General Max von Haussen	178,000 soldiers	Paris-Nante frontline
Paris Rheims			
4th Army Gener:	Albrecht Herzog von Württemberg	185,000 soldiers	Paris Rheims

The German Western Commander-in-Chief, General Alexander von Kluck, was quick to recognize the dangers of the overwhelming Allied attack. Lording over 725,000 soldiers in the attacked area, he was outnumbered by a little under 300,000 soldiers and had to adapt to the discrepancy in strength. As the Entente attacked across the entire front line in order to prevent him from moving troops from one side of the front to the other, he soon called the OHL for strong reinforcements. By May 7th, things became quite critical, the Anglo-French forces having advanced another twenty miles and were now within sight of Paris.

North-Channel and Atlantic Ports			
5th Army	Wilhelm Kronprinz von Preußen	92,000 soldiers	North-Channel and Atlantic Ports

Soon, the German 5th Army, commanded by one of the Kaiser's heirs, Wilhelm Kronzprinz von Preussen, which was defending and occupying the French Channel and Atlantic ports before the start of the Anglo-French attack, was called in and put to the line south of Paris, which stabilized the line somewhat.

France			
8th Army	Newly raised	300,000 soldiers	Vichy area (reserve)

By the 13th of May, the Entente forces, now bolstered by more troops from the French 8th Army, which had been held in reserve in the Vichy Area, pushed the German forces even further toward Paris, and by day's end, fighting erupted in the city's southern suburbs, where the Germans had hastily built a new series of trenches and fortified position in the last five days.

The OHL would soon have to take a decision and move more troops to the beleaguered area, or else risk losing Paris to the Entente. Since not many troops were available, the Reich leadership would have to call them from somewhere, and that somewhere was Hindenburg's command. While such a troop transfer would probably solve the French problem, it would put an end to the Luddendorf-Hindenburg offensive that had just stormed Kaunas and was poised to advance deeply into Russia.

Private Soldier Armand Bonnier ducked back down as a flurry of bullets slammed the grass before him. He was lying flat on his belly in a Paris park. The enemy machine gunners were just on the edge of it, about eighty yards north of his position. Left and right, more French soldiers were lying down, some with hands on their helmets, some on their backs.

Philippe was still a member of the 14th Division, but the unit had been moved back to France from the Apulia Enclave in preparation for the push on Paris. The Division was now considered one of the best in the French Army, as it had been fighting since the very beginning, and was composed of many veterans. His friend, Armand Bonnier, had recently transferred to the air service after his stunt in taking the downed fighter in the trench line during a battle. Philippe was also offered a position, but he decided he liked his feet on the ground a lot better after trying his luck with Armand in the sky.

As a member of the 14th, he'd again fought hard as the unit moved northward and fought through trench after trench and artillery barrage after artillery barrage. His section and a few others were now stuck in front of yet another German strongpoint, but this time, it seemed serious, as if the enemy had built another set of trenches and defenses. They'd fought against that in the first five days of the offensive, but following that, it had been easier since they'd kept the Germans on the backfoot.

A runner passed by, crouching low enough to be out of a direct fire line of sight. *"Orders from above,"* said the man to the Corporals and Sergeants near Philippe. *"We launch at three in the afternoon."*

He cursed. Another assault, and in fifteen minutes at that! It was their third one today, and he'd figured they would eventually get a reprieve. However, it appeared the division commander had not received enough casualties yet. *"Merde, saleté de géréraux,"* cursed

Philippe, but loud enough for one of the Sergeants to hear. *"What did you say, Cren?" "Ah, nothing, Sarge, just don't worry about it."* Indeed, Private, that's a lot better," countered the NCO, looking at him with a suspicious glance. A couple of soldiers beside him looked at him almost as if to say, *"damn, Cren, we agree with you,"* and he decided to put his face down on the grass and to try and calm himself down.

(...) 16th Bavarian Infantry Regiment (...)

Private number 148, a member of the 1st company in the 16th Bavarian Infantry Regiment, and also known as Adolf Hitler, ran as fast as he could, clutching the message from Captain Storck to the next officer down the line, in charge of the 5th company. Hitler's role in the army was to be a runner. A runner was the man bringing messages to and from exposed parts of the frontline, and it was a very dangerous job. He'd gotten the coveted posting (it was dangerous but had its perks, as you got to go to the rear often) after he'd won his Iron Cross medal during the Franco-British offensive on Verdun.

Suddenly, he was rocked to the side as a building exploded about twenty yards from where he was. The concussion of the blast rode as a shockwave and slammed him on the wall opposite him. Temporarily stunned, he stood up again, luckily dodging enemy bullets that slammed into the wall, sending rock splinters and dust around him. He was almost in the trench he was trying to reach. The deed was difficult this time, as the communication trench between the main line and the second line had been churned up by a big British mortar shell, and thus, to reach the 5th Company Captain, he had to run in the open.

Private Adolf Hitler joined the German Army in mid-October 1914 and was eventually incorporated into the 16th Bavarian Infantry Regiment. After two and a half months of relentless training and drilling, the Regiment was moved out of Munich right in time to be shipped to Verdun, where the French offensive was in full swing.

The first battle was not easy for the unit, being quickly brought up to the horrors and realities of the Great War. After having endured their first relentless artillery barrage, the men of the 16th were already pretty banged up when a heavy morning fog arose. Through and from it came the Anglo-French horses, firing as they went, and Hitler's baptism of fire was consumed by a terrible hand-to-hand battle involving knives and bayonets.

During the battle, Hitler's platoon leader was shredded to bloody pieces by a giant Frenchmen, as were most of the non-commissioned officers during the fight, except Sergeant Max Amann, who then became their de-facto NCO following the fight. The Bavarian troops had to weather the storm of no less than six assaults to maintain their position.

Months later and with an Iron Cross on his uniform, Hitler was now a runner, having seen enough war to last a lifetime and imprint radical ideas on him for the duration. He was a very lucky man and had already escaped death on multiple occasions. On March 11th, 1915, he was the only survivor of a shell hit, having completely destroyed a dugout and killed nine other soldiers, while he was relatively unscathed with just a minor cut to the back of the head.

His luck again played a role in his survival, as a machine gunner who had taken him into his sight and would have surely sawed him in two was killed by a well-placed German artillery shell. He made it to the first trench line, panting and a little dizzy but unscathed.

After catching his breath, he started to look for the 5th Company Captain. *"A message for the Captain of 5th Company,"* he said as he ran down the trench, where men continuously pointed him south toward the officer.

He eventually made it to the well-built dugout facing a crumbled-down Paris building. The German forces were now fighting in Paris' southern suburbs, and as such, it was their last line of defense before the center of the city. *"Captain,"* said Hitler, handing the man the small steel tube containing the message. *"Thank you, Private,"* answered the officer as he sat on a small wooden chair facing a table. *"Have a seat, Soldier,"* he continued. *"Thank you, Sir,"* countered Adolf. *"Anything else for me?"* *"Yes, Sir. The Regimental commanders want you to know that men from the German 5th Army are arriving to stabilize the line and to bolster our defenses."*

The Captain nodded as he opened the tube, reading its contents. He then signaled for one of his staff lieutenants to bring him a pen and some paper. He wrote an answer to the regimental commander, rolled it, and put the new message in the steel tube. *"Here you go, Private, good luck,"* he started. *"Make sure you get some water and some grub before you make your way back,"* he gestured toward the staff lieutenant. *"Mr. Immelmann here will show you to our magnificent kitchens,"* he finished with an ironic smile. Kitchens were anything but magnificent on the frontline. *"Thank you, Sir. I will get your message safely back."* *"Excellent, private. Now, if you will excuse me, I have other matters to attend to..."*

Clash on Estados Islands
Japanese patrol clash with German soldiers, May 3rd, 1915

The Japanese patrol, composed of ten Marines, made its way to the southern coast through a steep trail of sorts between large cliffs. It wasn't really a trail but rather a goat track for some of the native beasts on the island. It was very slippery and dangerous to negotiate.

The soldiers walked southward in the general direction where smoke had supposedly been spotted (they couldn't see any now) because it meant that there could be the German ships trying to hide in one of the fjords there.

The weather on the island was dismal, with a combo of high-speed winds and icy rain, and none of the soldiers showed any enthusiasm for their mission. Many of them even started to grumble and ask the Lieutenant in charge of the patrol if they should head back as there obviously was no smoke anymore. Whomever or whatever had been there was surely long gone.

But then one of the men in front thought he heard a whiff of a voice in the immensity. The wind was very noisy and loud, but he spoke up and told the Lieutenant that he believed he heard someone speaking nearby.

It didn't take any more for the officer to order his men to fan out in the direction of the perceived voices. The moss-covered rocks gave way to a cliff, and on the side of the cliff, near what seemed to be a natural fissure in the rock, stood a group of men huddled around a cave of some sort.

The Marine officer ordered his men to get in position around the cave and get their guns ready. It was at that moment that one of the men in the cave spotted them as they moved about and prepared for a fight.

Leveling their rifles, they started to fire at the Japanese soldiers, and soon, a full-blown firefight was in progress, heard by other Japanese and German patrols in the vicinity.

The skirmish lasted for about ten minutes as the German troops retreated deeper into the cave, which was a natural rock-carved trail that brought them back down to the rocky beach where the fjord was located.

After the fight with the Germans was over, the Japanese soldiers moved to the edge of the cliff, and they saw the German fleet in all its glory. The Lieutenant quickly ordered a retreat back to the northern coast, his mission accomplished.

The Germans were spotted, and a chase was about to begin.

Fighting in Verdun
4th German Imperial Division, May 13th, 1915

The Franco-British shells were screaming down on them once more; a large cloud of shrapnel burst on top of Private Soldier Oskar Dantz and his comrades. Shouts of pain and calls for help were swamping his ears with unsettling noises. The soldiers around him uttered terrible curses even as they lay, losing blood from horrible injuries. Others, like Oskar, stayed at the bottom of the trench, shaking and shouting. They were not physically hurt but could simply not bear the sight and the horrors around them. To many, it was as if hell had descended upon the land.

Eventually, the Allies ran out of ammo like they always did. Oskar had heard the French were struggling to have enough shells as the German Army occupied the northern parts of the country that were the most industrialized. The Entente didn't lack the resources to make shells and bullets. That, they had in abundance because of their world-spanning empires and colonies. They just didn't have the factories to transform those resources into instruments of war.

Hence, in this lay the main enemy weakness in his opinion. Artillery was a game changer, and he'd seen what it could do when properly applied, and with enough force. In his opinion, what they were going through every time they got shelled was bad, but not as bad as it could have been if the enemy had plentiful ammunition. He'd heard the rumors of what was happening in Paris, where the French apparently had a lot more artillery shells, and he wasn't surprised about the results with the enemy advancing over thirty miles.

Since the enemy was finished firing its guns, the officers called them back outside to the trench in case the French attacked. What greeted them upon their exit from the dugout was a changed landscape. Some of the trench walls were crumbling as they had been blasted out. A smoky haze hung everywhere around the battlefield, with small fires flickering everywhere.

"Alarrmmmm!" yelled one of the sentries on the firing parapet. The enemy was attacking again, but Oskar knew they would fail. The trench had most of its fighters, and the Maxim machine guns had already opened up; the racket of fire rose to its familiar crescendo, and the by-now very experienced soldier (after all, he'd been fighting since the very beginning) knew that the poor French sods walking across the no man's land had no chance.

A few minutes later, the Franco-British troops were charging at their trenches and bunkers as the Germans got busy hosing them down with heavy fire. Entente soldiers fell by the dozens as they tried to reach the main enemy positions. The German Verdun defenses were still fighting off the Allies' onslaught, but things were shaky now following a week of relentless bombing and attacks. The 4th Division was well dug in and had bunkers, dugouts, and tunnels, but human endurance in the face of continuous attacks had its limits. Oskar was no grand strategist, but he knew the enemy would have to run out of men at some point or else irretrievably weaken its own position by expanding too many men in futile offensives.

The Entente might not have enough artillery, but sending enough men at the German trenches made their assault start to have success. Bunkers started to go silent, and Oskar felt things were beginning to get hairy in the sector. He continued to empty his rifle clips as his comrades fought for other positions and tried to do the same. *"The enemy is upon us,"* yelled one of the NCOs. *"Fix bayonets,"* he continued, and his call was repeated many times down the line. Oskar slid his long knife out of its sheath and prepared to receive the first enemy soldier who would be bold enough to jump into the trench near him. And then a wave of blue and brown uniforms jumped, yelling into the trench, and Oskar yelled back in anger and fear.

Quickly, a storm of blades, blood, and death twirled all around him. Within the first minute, he dispatched an ugly-looking Frenchman and a broad-shouldered Englishman. He backed up as he wanted to avoid getting flanked from behind, and he almost fell on two of his comrades who lay dead, blood spreading out into a small pool of water like some bloody halo. One of them looked up at the sky because he lay dead on his back, and he died with his eyes open. The sight checked him for a moment. The man staring upward was one of his buddies from the section he was in. He'd even spoken and shared a cigarette with the guy just the night before.

He was yanked out of his reverie by a couple of enemy bullets that grazed his shoulder and rattled on the wooden plank walls behind him. *"Fight, son, fight!"* yelled a sergeant who was busy sliding his own knife into a bewildered French officer. Moments later, the NCO was dead, taking a British blade to the chest. More yelling Anglo-French soldiers dropped down in the trench, and Oskar struggled to find the bastard with the sword who had killed his sergeant. He looked for him in the melee, but it was hard, as the entire area was crawling with struggling and fighting desperate men.

He eventually spotted the bloody long blade hack up and down over the men and decided that this was his man. He pushed his way toward it. After dodging two other enemy soldiers with their rifles and bayonets, he finally came face to face with the bastard. The man had created a zone littered with bodies around him, and most stayed clear. He wondered why no one had thought of firing on him but decided that it was the same for him; he was in a crazed blood lust, and you didn't think much when that happened, and besides the rifles everyone used were not designed for close in fighting. The Englishmen's attention was to his left, and thus, he lunged with his long knife, surprising him. He planted his blade in the man's side ribs, feeling the blade enter the flesh and grate on the bone. *"Take that, you mongrel,"* he yelled as the man crumbled to the ground in a gust of blood. And then, inexplicably, a shell exploded right on top of the trench. None of the two sides would fire intentionally as their own soldiers were fighting in an area, and thus, it was a stray German shell aimed for the French rear. The entire trench collapsed on itself, burying the fighting soldiers alive.

(...)

Following what seemed to have been an eternity, Oskar was able to extricate himself from the avalanche of earth, swimming and darting through the dirt. Once he emerged from the earth and mix of mangled bodies (the shell had killed a lot of the soldiers when it exploded), he took a deep breath. It had been hard to get out from under, as he hadn't been the only one vying for survival; other people had struggled along with him to get to the surface. The whole affair was a panicked scramble to the top. When he was finally back to his senses and his lungs had oxygen, he looked around and saw that the trench and the surrounding area already looked like a charnel house.

He did a 360 to see what was happening around him and realized the falling dirt had been sort of a godsend because it had stopped the fight, and there seemed to be only German soldiers on top of the dirt.

He peered his head over the mangled trench to look at the overall situation. On his right, there seemed to be a big fight between other troops (they looked like Australian soldiers with their characteristic hats). It was pure mayhem, and he wondered how he could survive this terrible battle if it kept going on.

The ground was still riddled with patches of fire, and smoke columns dominated the landscape. The sound of the artillery shells could be heard even from where he was as the German artillery pounded the enemy rear areas. They were like a loud (but far away) whistle, sometimes flying directly overhead. He could even see the streaking lights of the shells as they arced high and trounced across the ground.

An officer with a fresh batch of troops arrived at the half-buried trench and yelled at them to get back on their feet, and to follow him to get into position for the next enemy wave. The fight was not over.

North of Monterrey, Mexico
Patton pushes on, May 10th, 1915

2nd Lieutenant George S. Patton, reigned his horses as it walked over the desert dune crest where the road took a bend southward. *"Problem, Sir,"* said Arthur Drawbecky, stopping his horse beside his officer. Both men, along with the five others behind them, also stopped.

Patton and his men wore the typical U.S. Army uniform *"olive drab"* with Montana-peaked hats. In addition, the 2nd Lieutenant had holsters on each side of his belt which hung with his favorite weapons, a Model 1873 .45 Long Colt Single Action revolver and a .45 Smith & Wesson M1817, both handguns. His men had regular-issue Army rifles.

Patton wore wool trousers, also in the *"olive drab"* shade. His shoulder belt, which ran across one of his shoulders, across his torso, and on his back, supported a plethora of bullets.

The young and eager American officer was on recon patrol in front of the bulk of the Army. He had heard rumors of Pancho Villa's whereabouts north of Monterrey and had been tasked by General Pershing to investigate.

The young soldiers were a little apprehensive of the man since he had a very strong personality and was one of Pershing's favorites. Some said he was related to the general. And indeed, he almost was, as his sister, Nina, was dating Pershing.

"According to our information, Sir, the Mexican rebels are hiding in this farm over there," said Arthur, pointing to what seemed to be a large cluster of buildings. *"The swine are in there, hey,"* answered Patton, putting his right hand on his pistol.

"Let's approach," he continued. *"Two men to the left, two to the right,*

one in reserve here on the crest to spot if there's anything wrong or trouble coming our way. And you and I, Drawbecky," he said, *"We're going to move in right from the main front entrance."*

Arthur moved back with his horse and gave his instructions to the men, who then proceeded to execute their orders. *"Cover the wall to the south, Patton added to the men moving to the right of the farm buildings."* "Yes, Lieutenant,"* answered the two men before they trotted down the crest and toward their assigned area.

As they moved on their horses like there wasn't a care in the world, they kept a keen eye on the farm, but nothing seemed to move there. *"Sir, the 13th Cavalry Regiment is about twenty minutes away,"* said Drawbecky nervously. *"Shouldn't we wait for them in case the enemy has more men than we have?"*

Patton grunted. *"And let them steal our glory? I am here to find the enemy, Private, and that's exactly what we are going to do!"* Arthur skulked for a moment as he thought it was stupid to approach an unknown group of building with perhaps an unknown number of Mexican rebels in them.

Eventually, they crossed the double gated entrance (the farm buildings were encircled by walls) as it was open. Nothing moved inside the compound apart from a few tumbleweeds rolling by and an eerie wind sound.

Then, a figure exited what seemed to be the largest building. The man wore leather trousers, cowboy boots, a red poncho, and a large Mexican hat. He had two belts crossing his torso in an "X" pattern with bullets in them. By his side, another belt with a handgun.

"What are you doing here, Yankee," said the man in heavily accented English. It was obvious this man was a Mexican. *"My name is 2nd Lieutenant George S. Patton of the 13th Cavalry Regiment. Our forces are moving toward Monterrey, and we are looking for Pancho Villa's*

rebels." He paused to spit on the ground in a desultory fashion. *"I hereby requisition this farm for the U.S. Army."* The Mexican man smiled. *"Are you, now."*

Five more men excited the large building, some with rifles and others with handguns. It was at that moment that Arthur noticed the bleeding bodies on the side alley near them and the other dead people further down on the farm. *"Sir,"* he started, but Patton stopped. *"I have seen them. Get ready."* Arthur saw a weird glint in his young, fiery Lieutenant's eyes.

"Yankee," spoke the Mexican in a firm tone once his men walked to flank him, guns ready to fire. *"I am Pancho Villa in the flesh, and I will give you one chance to leave peacefully; I have an appointment south to prepare to fight your army."*

Patton didn't answer but simply unholstered his handgun and fired, yanking on his horse's reigns to move right to the alley between two of the buildings, while Arthur did the same on the other side. The bullet slammed on the man right next to Pancho Villa, who ducked instinctively. "Kil the bastards," he yelled before running to the side of the main building to get his horse. He was followed by one man while the four others fanned out to find the two impudent Americans.

It didn't take long for two of Pancho's men to find Drawbecky, who had dropped down from his horse for cover. A firefight soon erupted between them, with bullets flying in every direction.

On the other side, Patton had already killed a second man as he fired from behind while he raced through the alley. Pancho Villa and his man just darted for the double-gated exit and made a run for it. Patton saw the Mexican rebel leader zip by, but there wasn't much he could do since the last of the two men was almost upon him, and he needed to face the threat. He cursed as Villa raced below the gate in a cloud of billowing smoke.

The fight between Drawbecky and the two Mexicans was short, as the two soldiers Patton sent to the south walls flanked them. They surrendered without another shot, and George killed the last one.

The entire affair took about ten minutes, by which time Pancho Villa was long gone on his horse. An inspection of the farm building told them what they suspected. Villa and his men had killed everyone, and it appeared the place was plundered of anything and everything of value.

"The bastards are not far," said Patton an hour later, and as the 13th Cavalry entered the farm compound. Pancho Villa's group was near, as there was no way the six men he had seen could have emptied the farm of its food. He decided to reach out to Pershing to give him the news in person and to suggest they thoroughly search the entire area before continuing south.

Estados Island
The German Fleet tries to escape, May 4th, 1915

Following the skirmish between Japanese and German marines, both sides scrambled to action. Both Funke and von Spee quickly decided to sail out of the Capitan Canepa Bay Fjord, raising their steam and creating a very big cloud of smoke visible from the other side of the island. This gave the Anglo-Japanese forces the exact bearing on the German ships, and from there, it was obvious von Spee would work east and north to try and race into the Atlantic.

It took some time for Togo and Beatty to get their ships together, as some patrolled the western coast and others the eastern coast, but within a couple of hours, the combined fleet was underway and was on a north-easternly heading to try and intercept the Germans as they circumvented Estados Island.

The trick for the Germans was to sail before the Allies crossed their path, but from the get-go, both Funke and von Spee saw that they wouldn't be able to avoid a running battle. The only thing they could do, as they saw the long columns of smoke west of their position, was to try and keep the range as long as possible.

BRITISH MEDITERRANEAN FLEET (Port Stanley)		
Admiral David Beatty, 1st Ea	second in command, Rear-Admiral Gordon Moore	
BC Invincible	BC Tiger	9 DD
BB Conqueror	BB Agincourt	4 CA
BB Neptune flagship	Pre-dread BB Russell	
BB Benbow	Pre-dread BB Cornwallis	
	Pre-dread BB Exmouth	
Japanese Imperial Fleet Battle Squadron 1 Admiral Heihachiro Togo		
BB Setsu	BC Kongo	2 CA
BB Kawachi		3 DD

It soon became obvious to Admiral Beatty that his three aging pre-dreadnoughts wouldn't have enough speed to follow the rest of the fleet, and he thus ordered battleships Russel, Cornwallis, and

Exmouth to sail on a northernly heading and to try and cover as much distance as possible, for it was a possibility that the Germans would head for their Southwest Africa colony, in which case the pre-dreadnoughts could rejoin the battle at a later time. Meanwhile, the rest of the fleet, including the Japanese (both Admirals had agreed that Beatty would be in overall command for the duration of the engagement), was ordered to pursue at full speed. When both fleets turned on a full north heading, the range was at 20,000 yards, a very long shot for the gunners. No ship in history had been able to score a hit from this far of a range.

German Pacific Squadron		
Admiral von Graf Spee		
BB Westfalen stern and deck damage	CL Emden stern and forecastle damage	Collier ship Oldenwald
BB Kaiserin stern , 1 rear turret destroyed		
3rd Battle Squadron, relief fleet (Rear-Admiral Felix Funke) -		
BB Grosser Kurfürst	BB König	4 CL
BB Markgraf	BB Kronprinz	1 DD

The German fleet was powerful, but both Funke and von Spee had decided that fighting their way out was only a last-ditch option since the enemy had a significant superiority (9 to 6) in dreadnoughts. Furthermore, the two Pacific Squadron dreadnoughts were damaged and wouldn't stand very well the further damage powerful ships like the Setsu or the Neptune could inflict on them.

The affair now was a matter of will and of machinery. Ships sailing at full battle speed for extended periods tended to break down, and the two damaged-but-repaired-in-Manzanillo boilers were the real question mark for the Germans. Even at optimal performance, the dreadnoughts of all nations weren't designed to run with this kind of speed for more than ten to twenty hours. There were chances of damage, breakdowns and of the coal stoker's fatigue.

(...) Bridge of dreadnought Battleship Neptune (...)

Admiral David Beatty watched in awe as the forward guns on his ships fired with all the power of its four forward 305mm guns. He, like his officers and men, was at his battle station on the bridge near the viewport. The rest of his men were all at their stations and making sure the ship fought and ran at peak efficiency. His view was temporarily clouded by the sudden surge of fire that blossomed out of the gun muzzles, followed by a large, all-encompassing cloud of smoke. The shots were also felt throughout the ship as the structure reverberated.

The maximum firing range of the BL 12-inch Mark XI was 21,500 yards, and thus, the shots could, in theory, reach the enemy ships, hovering at a distant 20,000 yards. But the Admiral didn't hold his breath. Only a truly lucky shot could score a hit. Hell, not even a lucky shot could do it. It would need to be a divine intervention. At below 10,000 yards, naval gunnery accuracy was below 4%, and thus, at 20,000 yards, it was infinitely lower.

(...) Bridge of dreadnought battleship Setsu (...)

"Range to target," asked Admiral Togo to the gunnery officer on the bridge of battleship Setsu. The old commander had his arms crossed behind his back, watching the Neptune, along with the rest of the British dreadnoughts, as they fired in unison toward the Germans. *"A little over 20,000 yards, Sir."*

Togo didn't add anything else, instead waiting to see where the shells would land. Some seconds later, they landed around the Germans without hitting anything but water. Shells fired at a target 1000 yards away had an approximate flight time of just 1.17 seconds. The flight time for the 20,000 yards was thus 23 seconds.

The Japanese ships were about 2800 yards to port relative to the British fleet, but he elected to hold fire, even if he sensed that his men were impatient to do so. He didn't do it to save ammunition because even if he ran out, he knew the British would supply him with more.

His battleships used the same BL 12-inch Mark XI, which was a Royal Navy design. The reason he wasn't firing was that it was useless to do so.

"Helm, keep on it," he said, trying to stay as calm as possible, even if he could see the enemy he had been chasing for months just there in front of him.

(...) Bridge of dreadnought battleship Westfalen (...)

On the other side of the battle, that is, 20,000 yards away, a German commander had a face creased in worry. *"Report,"* he said, as he watched with disinterest the large water geysers rising and falling too far away for that to be the problem that made him afraid.

"Sir, the boiler room says things are holding for now, but the chief engineer says that he won't be able to hold this forever." "What is the problem," answered Maximilian von Spee. *"Sir, according to him, the repairs done in Manzanillo are fine to get back to Germany, but not to be in a running battle for an extended period of time."*

Von Spee walked to the plotting table as if to will a new course that would make his fleet get away from the pursuing Anglo-Japanese. *"Well, that was to be expected, as even brand new, these things aren't designed to run full speed from top to bottom of the Atlantic Ocean."*

He put both his palms on the table with his outstretched arms. *"Anything we could use to get smart,"* he asked to the plotting sailor. By this, he meant: *"Do we have an island or a geographical feature that we could use to try and outsmart the enemy?"*

The man looked at his commander and then spoke. "Well, Admiral, the only spot for hundreds of miles is the Falkland Islands, but that is a British base." "Vice-Admiral Krenk, do we have a better map of the British base?" "Yes, Sir, as per your orders, the men went ashore in

Manzanillo to procure all the maps we could of Argentina, Chile, and the Southern Atlantic. They are in Spanish, but I don't think that is a problem for our current needs." "Agreed," countered von Spee as the map was brought up.

Von Spee put his right-hand fingers on his chin, looking at the shape of the Falklands and seeing the obvious, like Krenk and the plotting sailor. *"Yes, the Falkland Sound..."* he continued, speaking to his own self. The plotting sailor continued along his Admiral's line of thoughts. *"140 miles long from east to west and 12 miles in width and has a typical depth of 22 fathoms (132 feet)."*

(...) Bridge of dreadnought battleships Grosser Kurfurst (...)

"Rear-Admiral Funke, we have sixty-five naval mines spread over our ships," said the signal officer after coming back from outside of the ship to speak to his people. Admiral von Spee had just asked that question to the 3rd Battle Squadron, sort of giving away his idea. His question was followed by a message indicating his intentions to sail to the Falkland Sound and get the Anglo-Japanese to pursue and then drop mines to block their way.

As his flag officer relayed the questions to the other ships in the squadron, he looked over the Falklands map with his people and decided that the Admiral's plan was not a bad idea.

"Excellent, signal the Admiral the quantity and that we are awaiting further orders."

Submarine Warfare
The Sinking of the Lusitania, May 11th, 1915

"Clear bow shot at 700 [meters] . . . Shot struck starboard side close behind the bridge. An extraordinarily heavy detonation followed, with a very large cloud of smoke (far above the front funnel). A second explosion must have followed that of the torpedo (boiler or coal or powder?) . . . . The ship stopped immediately and quickly listed sharply to starboard, sinking deeper by the head at the same time. It appeared as if it would capsize in a short time. Great confusion arose on the ship; some of the boats were swung clear and lowered into the water."
—*Extract from official Kapitänleutnant Walter Schwieger's diary*

From the start of the Grear War, the Reich and its Kaiserliche Marine enacted a powerful and destructive U-boat campaign against Franco-British merchant vessels. The idea was to choke the Entente of its lifeline. The breakout of the High Seas Fleet into the Atlantic further intensified the German pressure on the waves. When that happened, Admiral Hugo von Pohl started to send his armored cruisers and light cruisers on raiding missions. Added to the U-boat depredations, things were starting to get pretty tough for the British and the resource-starved French.

When the war started, and things still remained sort of clean, U-boats obeyed *"prize rules."* In essence, it obligated the submarine captains to surface prior to attacking and give the opportunity to crew and passengers to get away on lifeboats

While this was honorable, the German ships (subs and surface raiders alike) were open to being attacked, especially after the British introduced merchant ships with hidden guns. These ships waited for German ships to approach and then attacked by surprise, often sinking them or inflicting enough damage that they had to get back to port.

Following their defeat at the Naval Battle of Brest in the middle of March 1915, the German leadership at the OHL saw the writing on the wall. As long as the Reich played nice, the Franco-British wouldn't be choked into submission.

The logic was that as Paris and northern France were already in

German hands, the Reich only needed a great victory in the East to bring everything back to bear in the West and show the Entente that continuing to fight was futile. For the time in between, the war could be brought to a successful conclusion against the Franco-British if Germany could isolate Britain, the real industrial driver in the Entente. English industry relied mostly on exterior trade with the imperial colonies, as there were not enough resources in the Home Islands to feed the many war factories needed to prosecute the war.

On March 19th, 1915, Berlin declared the British Home Islands a no-go zone (in essence, that it was a war zone). Any merchant ship seen in this area would thus be sunk without warning.

This unrestricted submarine warfare didn't go very well with neutral nations like the United States, who had a lot of business going on with the Entente. The arms dealers, in particular, were making a fortune off the never-ending needs the French and British had in terms of ammo, military supplies, artillery guns, and rifles. U.S. factories on the East Coast were booming with new business, and it was not like America to stop making a profit when it could.

With tensions already running at an all-time high with Germany because of the sinking of the USS Galveston in Manzanillo at the beginning of the year, the announcement was not well received in Washington D.C.

U.S. President Woodrow Wilson called for a meeting with the German Ambassador, during which he outlined America's opinion on the Kaiser's decision. And it was not an acknowledgment of the U.S. willingness to comply and stop sailing into British waters.

Wilson and Lansing told the German ambassador, in no uncertain terms, that the Kaiser's decision was unacceptable, and that America would start the very next day to escort its merchant ships. As per the President's own words, sort of prophetic in a sense, war was already in motion. *"Don't get me wrong here, Ambassador von Bernstorff. If*

Germany sinks one American ship, or costs the lives of American citizens as you attack a ship sailing under a neutral flag, we will respond with all the might of the United States of America and smash Germany to oblivion." Wilson's very direct way of handling diplomatic affairs was not something the old European monarch liked, but at the very least, the President's words had the merit of being in the clear, without any flowery diplomatic niceties.

Things would come to a head, and Wilson's words would soon engulf America in the Great War.

(...) May 11th, 1915 (...)

Being a British passenger liner, the HMS Lusitania was not sailing under an American flag. Hence, to Kapitänleutnant Walter Schwieger, the commander of the German U-boat U-20, it was fair game. The man couldn't have known the ship had 128 American citizens on board.

To the Reich's credit, President Wilson's harsh words had the OHL, and then the Kaiserliche Marine Command soften their unrestricted policy to exclude any ships sailing under an American flag. This state of affairs held for almost two months before disaster struck. In all fairness, the German leadership knew it was bound to happen, but had decided that war with the USA needed to be risked. There were many in Berlin, including the Kaiser, who did not believe America was capable of having a major impact on the conflict. First, the Yankees were an ocean away, and they didn't even have a 100,00 man standing army. Second, they just didn't believe they had the stomach to fight as hard as what was currently happening in Europe. But they should have paid attention to a conflict not so far removed in the past when America had fought against itself and seen that these so-called Yankees were capable of fighting, and fighting really hard.

Be that as it may, the match that would ignite the already pretty full powder keg between the two powers sailed right in front of

Kapitänleutnant Walter Schwieger's periscope that day. "British ship in view. It appears to be one hell of a fat cruise liner," said the U-boat commander as he turned to signal the weapon officer to get the torpedoes ready.

U-20 had caught sight of the British ship in the distance as he lay in wait on the surface near the sea lanes. The ship was quickly ordered below the waves, moved to a firing position, and within another few minutes, everything was ready to go. The distance was 765 yards, an easy shot against such a slow ship. "Fire," said Schwieger.

The weapon traveled the distance in no time, and then a resounding explosion rocked the ship (the hit was squarely in the center). The U-boat captain watched as a second, even larger explosion rippled across the ship and the surface of the water, catapulting debris, fire, and smoke into the air. The ship's main boiler room had just exploded.

Within a few minutes, the ship listed heavily and was sinking rapidly, covered in fires everywhere. Several lifeboats, already loaded with people, slammed into the water as the ship suddenly lifted in the air. He could then clearly see the name of the vessel on the bow, noting that it was the Lusitania. Then, the ship slid down into the water, followed by bubbling, foaming water and surrounded by swimming and desperate people trying to save themselves.

Schwieger lifted the periscope apparatus and took a deep breath. The Sight of all those people dying and despairing was terrible, and he decided it would be hard to sleep that night. Unbeknownst to him at the time, the ship he had just sank, and the chain of events the attack would trigger, was even worse than he'd thought.

Wurttemberg Mountain Battalion
Monaco, below the Dog's head and La Turbie, May 10th, 1915

"It's good to have your back, Sir," said Private Theo Stark as Captain Erwin Rommel exited the staff car that brought him from the field hospital ward to the recently occupied French town of Monaco.

The Wurttemberg Mountain Battalion was below one more fortified mountaintop in the Séré de Rivières defensive system. The Germano-Italian forces were making good progress toward the pivotal French town of La Turbie, having taken Fort Mont-Angel above. It was now time to assault the fort defending the small city, Fort Massena.

"Captain," said a couple of men, obviously happy as they smiled broadly at Rommel's sight. *"It's good to see you, Sir." "Likewise, Private Stumran,"* answered the young officer. Both Rommel and Stark were walking into the trench, a full-on wooden and sandbagged position built for the duration. It was as if the high command expected an attack.

The unit, along with several Italian mountain and infantry regiments, were entrenched all across Monaco and below the tete de Chien, a steep mountainside where an old Roman paved road snaked its way to the looming silhouette of Fort Massena. No attack had been launched as of yet since Monaco had just been secured the week before. However, regimental Commander Theodor von Ducker had told Rommel that an assault was going to be ordered within the week. He was thus intent on getting the men ready, but before that, he had an important call to make on the officer who was his replacement while he had been gone. Stark had told Erwin that the man had been an incompetent disaster, and that many of the company's men were killed because of his incompetence and arrogance. *"Where is the new captain's command post,"* he asked to his maverick sidekick. *"Sir, don't you want to go see the men first? They are all waiting to see you?" "No, let's start with the most obvious problem to solve." "Right this way, Sir,"* answered Stark, gesturing toward a large redoubt in the trench.

Two tough-looking men Rommel didn't recognize blocked the redoubt entrance and stopped him. *"Sorry, Sir, you can't enter,"* said the first of them, lifting his hand in a stopping gesture.

Checked because of the man's sheer boldness in the face of a captain instead of his obvious hostility, he stopped for a moment. He quickly got back on his game. *"It's just as I told you, Sir,"* said Stark in a low voice. *"The new captain has his own people."* *"Well, Private, that can be easily fixed."*

Meanwhile, many soldiers of the battalion recognized Rommel but kept their distance and watched the scene in eager anticipation. They knew their old commander would not let the matter stand. Several of them sent for the others, and soon, a bunch of them were by the redoubt entrance or close by, waiting for what would happen.

"Private, I order you to stand aside," finally said Rommel in a firm tone. *"Captain, I am under orders to let no one pass while Captain von Broberg sleeps."* Again, Erwin was temporarily checked by the sheer audacity of this private, and of the fact that this stupid captain was sleeping during the day. Manfred von Broberg came from a prominent noble family related to the Kaiser, and had the attitude that went with it. Arrogance, incompetence, and an air of impunity about him that only rich noblemen could have.

Out of nowhere, Rommel slammed a punch in the first private's face, knocking him unconscious. The man dropped to the ground like a heavy sack of potatoes amidst a cloud of billowing dust. He turned to the other guard, who was about to raise his rifle, but he was stopped midway by Stark, who gestured to him that it was a bad idea with his own handgun right to his face. *"Now, Private, will you let me pass, or will I also first knock you out, and second put you under arrest?"* The man made a sour face but stepped aside, raising both his arms in a sign of acquiescence.

Rommel stepped inside the darkened redoubt and heard a grumbling voice. *"Private Kramer, who dares to disturb my sleep?"* *"I do,"* said the young captain as he moved right up to von Broberg, who was sitting on the bed. The entire place (ten beds) was empty, and that itself was a problem because it wasn't just a resting spot for one person.

"Who the hell are you," asked the still sleepy captain, now starting to wake up pretty fast. He then stood up. Rommel smiled, gently pushing the other man on the chest, unbalancing him, and sitting him down once more. *"My name, Captain, is Captain Erwin Rommel, the very commander you have replaced and who is now back to take command of his unit."*

Initially surprised, von Broberg quickly regained his composure and tried to stand up again. Rommel pushed him once more, this time more firmly. *"Stay down, you bastard. Now, I understand from von Ducker that I am to be nice to you and take you under my wing to show you the ropes of command. I am senior to you, and you will now be under my orders."*

Broberg didn't like that one bit. *"I am a noble and related to the Kaiser; I am the senior one here,"* he answered firmly. *"Well, you can verify that with the Colonel, then, as he'd just told me I was back in command."* Rommel continued as if the other wasn't entitled to speak. *"We'll start by making sure insubordination is not tolerated anymore, and place the unconscious soldier outside under arrest. Then, you will go to this table,"* he pointed toward the small wooden stool and a half-crumbled chair, *"and write up a report on what has transpired during my absence. I want a full rundown of the unit, the casualties, and its readiness."*

CHAPTER 4
Politics, Strategy, East-West

WASHINGTON HERALD
LUSITANIA SUNK BY GERMAN SUB!
Over 1,400 passengers dead, including 100+ Americans
President to make statement this morning

"Well, that does it, Robert," said American President Woodrow Wilson to his Secretary of State. *"I agree, Mr. President,"* answered Lansing. *"Should I call upon the German Ambassador?"*

"The time for diplomacy is over," grumbled Wilson. *"How dare they defy us? First Galveston and Mexico, then this,"* continued the American leader, pointing to the headline news in that morning's newspaper before them on the Resolute Desk in the Oval Office.

Both men were having their morning coffees, and Wilson had his staff people cancel all of his day's schedule. Instead, he'd called upon Congress to meet in the late afternoon to ask for a formal declaration of war on Germany and the Central Powers.

"No, Robert, we are done speaking with the Germans. Get me the British and French Ambassadors to setup for a meet later today when my speech to Congress is over." *"Yes, Mr. President."*

(...) A few hours later, United State Congress building (...)

(...) I have called you all here today to ask you for something momentous. Something that our nation tried to avoid as the flames of war engulfed the European continent. I cannot do this myself, and I need you, the Congress, to make the decision.

Imperial Germany and its allies have been conducting a war of aggression in Europe, and now in the waves. Furthermore, they have befriended our enemy to the South, Mexico. Then, they killed over five hundred sailors in the sinking of the USS Galveston off Manzanillo last February. And now this unspeakable act of horror and cowardice from a German U-boat, sinking a passenger liner that included over 120 American citizens.

The entire Congressional room broke into raucous boos and yells. Not one of the Congressmen was happy about what had transpired in the last two months, and now the situation had reached a crescendo.

This war below the waves by these dastardly submarines is an attack on all nations of the world, as clearly shown by the sinking of the Lusitania yesterday. American blood has been shed; our ships have been sunk, and the rest are under threat every time they sail out in the Atlantic. Must I also add that the Pacific is not safe from German attacks, as the sinking of the Galveston has clearly shown us?

We will not be looking for revenge or else the good old European ways of "might make Right," but only the just return to peace and human rights.

It is thus with a profound sense of the solemn and even tragical character of the step I am taking... I advise that the United States formally accept the status of a belligerent that has thus been thrust upon it by Germany's action, and the need for the country of liberty to rise to the challenge and return peace to the World.

We will fight for the liberation of Europe, the people under the Kaiser's yoke included. The world must be made safe for democracy....

In the Senate, the resolution passed 84–5 (with 7 absentees) following a record-short debate. In the House of Representatives, the resolution passed late at night by a vote of 383–40 (8 absentees).

America was going to war.

Black Sea
Near Imperial Russian Coast, May 12th, 1915

(…) Bridge balcony of dreadnought battlecruiser Sultan Yavuz (…)

Ottoman Navy- Admiral Souchon	
BB Sultân Osmân- Evvel	CA Hamidiye
BB Re;adiye	CA Mecidiye
BC Yavuz Sultan -Goeben (Flagship)	6 DD
Pre Dreadnought BB Barbaros Hayreddin	

Admiral Pavlos Kountouriotis	
CA Giorgios Averof (flagship)	6 old DD
Pre-Dreadnought BB Lemnos	

German Admiral, now commander of the Greco-Ottoman Navy, watched toward the Russian coastline in the distance with his binoculars. He was standing on the steel balcony surrounding the battlecruiser's Goeben's bridge, the Yavuz Sultan, formerly called the Goeben that is. Vice-admiral Hubert von Rebeur-Paschwitz, his chief of staff and second in command, was beside him, also with binoculars in hand. They were in the vicinity of Nikolayev but far enough not to be fired at by the defensive forts they had fought with a few months prior.

The Central Powers fleet was on the hunt for the new Russian ships, said to be busy with sea trials and training in the area. There was also news of the leftovers of the former Black Sea Fleet from Sebastopol, having joined the newly-built dreadnought battleships Imperatritsa Mariya and Ekaterina Veliyaka.

Under the command of former Vice-Admiral Alexander Kolchak, now named to top command in the theater, it was now a serious challenger to Ottoman dominance in the Black Sea. The presence of this new and powerful fleet was a threat to the Turks and the Central Powers because Constantinople was very vulnerable to an attack from the sea.

The Russians, with such a fleet, could also contemplate the possibility of landing troops near the capital along the Bosphorus Straits to try and force the naval lanes to the Aegean Sea. Combined with the presence of the powerful British Eastern Mediterranean Squadron in Crete, it was a threat that could simply not be ignored.

While Souchon had discarded the idea of again challenging the Royal Navy's supremacy in the Aegean Sea (the Brits were too powerful), but that was not the case with the Russian's, as they were composed of the former outdated ship's he had defeated at the Battle of Cape Sarych back in 1914, along with two newly-trained crews of still-to-be-fully operational dreadnought battleships. His idea was to catch the enemy as they were bringing these ships up to full fighting shape.

It was why he'd sailed the combined fleet to Nikolayev, in the hopes of catching the Russians unaware, or else tempting the new enemy admiral into battle. After all, the blotch on Russian honor that was Cape Sarych (Souchon had sunk four pre-dreadnought battleships there and effectively eliminated Russian naval power for the time being) would need to be avenged one day. What Souchon was thus trying to do on that clear day of May 1915 was to tell Kolchak, *"Hey, you, I am here; why don't you come out for a fight."*

"Do you think those smokestacks are from the Russian warships, Vice Admiral," said Souchon as he lowered the binoculars to see if the lookout sailor on the mast would signal anything more interesting than what he could see from his vantage point. But the man in the sky was just busy looking through his optical equipment into the distance. *"Well, Sir, I don't see what else they could be. It's a pretty heavy concentration of smoke, and the lookouts have reported high masts consistent with battleships,"* answered von Rebeur-Paschwitz. *"What do you want us to do, Admiral? Should I order the ships toward Nikolayev, and those smokestacks?"*

"Mmmm, said Souchon," hesitating for a moment. It wasn't that he was afraid of fighting the Russians; it was more because of their proximity to the coast. This meant that if he moved in to fight them,

he would also have to contend with the fort's defensive guns as well. There was also the possibility that the Russians had laid mines to the approaches of the harbor following the Ottoman raid in January. There was also the not-so-simple matter of getting the Greeks to collaborate with the fleet.

The secular hostility between Turks and Greeks was not making collaboration very easy for the combined fleet. Yes, Greek King Constantine and his new Prime Minister, Androlos Kostapukis, had agreed to sail their powerful fleet into the Dardanelles and to join up with the Ottoman-German fleet, but first and foremost this was to protect itself from Royal Navy depredations, and defend or eventually engage the British Eastern Mediterranean Squadron. Fighting the Russians in the Black Sea was not exactly in any set of Greek national interests, or objectives. In the end, he'd gotten the go-ahead to have the ships, but he didn't think that damage on the precious Lemnos or Georgios Averoff would help his cause, and certainly not make it any easier to continue to get the Greeks to further collaborate with him.

"Let's move in, Vice-Admiral," he began. *"Order Admiral Kountouriotis to keep his ships behind our three dreadnoughts. We know that is what he is going to do anyway, so let's give orders he will follow to keep the appearance that we are in full command."* Von Rebeur-Paschwitz smiled. *"Very well, Admiral."*

(…)Bridge of dreadnought battleship Imperatritsa Mariya (…)

Russian Black Sea Fleet	
Admiral Alexander Vasilyevich Kolchak	
BB Imperatritsa Mariya	3 CA
BB Imperatritsa Ekaterina Velikaya	13 DD
Pre-Dreadnought BB Evstafi	

Newly minted Admiral Alexander Kolchak was sipping his hot tea on the bridge of his new and pristine warship when the news came of the appearance of smokestacks on the horizon. *"Any expected convoys or ship arrivals for today, or this week?"* "Sir," answered the captain of the battleship (also doubling as his second-in-command), Captain Vladimir Trubetskoy. *"Not that we know of. These most certainly belong to the enemy."*

Kolchak put his teacup on the small armrest of his admiral of the fleet's chair and stood up. He walked slowly to the viewport and looked to the horizon, where the smoke was in plain view. *"Yes, this much smoke can only be coming from the enemy fleet."* *"Orders, Admiral,"* countered a nervous Trubetskoy. "Yes. Let's implement our plan."

Kolchak was of a very different breed than the former, and defeated Commander-in-Chief of the Black Sea Fleet, Admiral Andrei Eberhardt. Kolchak had been there during the battle of Cape Sarych and had commanded the only surviving battleship that day, the pre-dreadnought Evstafi. Eberhardt had paid for his incompetence with his life and, unfortunately, the lives of thousands of his sailors. Only his maneuvering and quick-thinking had saved his ship from destruction that day.

Thus, he had not simply sailed his ships out of Nikolayev to wait for Souchon to attack him. He'd taken steps to make certain he would first be able to move back to the safety of the shipyard in the river and the defensive forts, and second, he wanted to show Souchon that he wasn't the only big bully in the Black Sea. His plan had been simple. While continuing the maneuvers and the sea trials, his smaller ships, destroyers, and cruisers screened the area around to watch for enemies. Furthermore, he'd laid a pretty dense minefield in the likely route the enemy ships would take.

The plan was thus simple. Fire a few shots from afar and pretend to scramble for safety. Hopefully, the aggressive Germano-Ottoman commander would try and pursue.

"Ship's raising steam as we speak, Sir," said Captain Trubetskoy. *"Our*

turn will be completed in minutes. The enemy ships are still well over 30,000 yards and thus no danger to us." "Very well, Captain. " countered Kolchak with a smile, hoping Souchon would take the bait.

A new ally
Entente reactions to the U.S. entry into the war, May 13th, 1915

The news took European capitals by storm. The United States of America had just declared war on the Central Powers following the sinking of the Lusitania and the mounting tensions between Berlin and Washington. The Americans were already involved in a war against Mexico, triggered by the major international incident in Manzanillo, where the German Pacific Squadron had sunk the U.S. Navy cruiser Galveston.

Anti-German sentiment had been bubbling to the surface following the start of the conflict in 1914, with news of atrocities in Belgium and Northern France, but most especially with the German unrestricted submarine warfare strategy. As much as it had tried to avoid sinking American ships or avoid hindering their interest, the Kaiserliche Marine was bound to smash something it wasn't supposed to. After all, the United States' trade with Britain was humongous and with the war, had increased to a crescendo. British factories and armies were buying all the resources and weapons they could. It was the same situation with the French, who were lacking in everything because the industrialized part of the country (the North) was under German occupation.

French leadership was ecstatic at the appearance of such a new and powerful ally. Just a few hours after Wilson's address to Congress, the American Ambassador met with President Pointcarré and Prime Minister Viviani to discuss an immediate increase in American arms shipments and the possibility of having U.S. Army troops on French soil.

While America was in no position to send troops to Europe in May 1915 (it was busy fighting Mexico and didn't have a large army anyway), arms manufacturers could increase their production to sell even more weapons and ammunition to the very needy French forces. Hence, American entrepreneurship started to gear up for a major uptick in industrial production. Companies like the Winchester

Repeating Arms Company, Remington Arms Company, Lefever Arms Company, and Merwin, Hulbert, and Co. all soon and enthusiastically increased their collaboration with the French government. Most had already opened offices in Bordeaux, and the American declaration of war would only increase their efforts in Europe.

The U.S. Navy was also going to be greatly expanded. Shipyards on the East Coast went mad with Government orders and demands. Some even came from France, as most of the "hexagon" shipyards were occupied. They included the Boston Navy Yard, the Philadelphia Navy Yard, the Hunters Point Naval Shipyard (which had the largest drydocks in the world), and the Washington Navy Yard (the very one that had built the giant Panama Canal locks).

In Britain, the reaction was also very positive. While the English didn't need the American factories as much as the French did because the British Home Islands were free of any German occupation, they were very happy to see the powerful U.S. Navy joining the fight.

The American fleet had climbed from the 10th largest Navy (in 1898) in the world (in size) to third behind the Kaiserliche Marine and the Royal Navy and the very close Russian and French navies (4th and 5th in tonnage). This was done under the guise and leadership of President Wilson and his top naval adviser, the great strategist and naval theoretician Alfred Thayer Mahan.

In the Spring of 1915, the U.S. Navy sported a total of 32 battleships (a mix of dreadnoughts and pre-dreadnoughts), 37 cruisers, 45 destroyers, and a bunch of smaller escort vessels and submarines.

In fact, it was powerful enough to face the by-now diminished German High Seas Fleet in the Atlantic, and U.S. President Woodrow Wilson gave orders to the Navy to sail into the Atlantic as soon as it was ready, with the mission of first escorting its merchant shipping to Europe, and second to sink any German ships.

ATLANTIC FLEET

BB Michigan	Pre-dread BB Maine	Pre-dread BB Lousiana	CA Milwaukee
BB South Carolina	Pre-dread BB Missouri	Pre-dread BB Kansas	Ca Charleston
BB Delaware	Pre-dread BB Ohio	Pre-dread BB Minnesota	5 CL
BB North Dakota	Pre-dread BB Illinois	Pre-dread BB New Hampsh	30 Destroyers
BB Utah	Pre-dread BB Alabama	CA Seattle	
BB Wyoming	Pre-dread BB Wisconsin	CA Charlotte	
BB Arkansas	Pre-dread BB Kearsarge	CA Missoula	
BB New York	Pre-dread BB Kentucky	CA Pittsburg	
BB Texas	Pre-dread BB Indiana	CA Huntington	

PACIFIC FLEET

Pre-dread BB Virginia	Pre-dread BB Massachussets	CA San Diego	15 Destroyers
Pre-dread BB Nebraska	Pre-dread BB Oregon	CA Pueblo	5 CL
Pre-dread BB Georgia	Pre-dread BB Iowa	CA Frederick	
Pre-dread BB New Jersey	Pre-dread BB Connecticut	CA St-Louis	
Pre-dread BB Rhode Islands	Pre-dread BB Vermont	CA Huron	

The reaction in Britain was thus one of relief and certainty that the Entente would be the master of the waves. Along with the eventually-arriving American soldiers, it meant that the Allies had gained several points in the grand strategy analysis of who would win the war in the end.

The Second Battle of Nikolayev
Souchon attacks again, May 12th, 1915

Souchon was almost startled by the opening salvo of Goeben's main guns. The shots shook the ship, and a fire mushroom blossomed from its forward guns. Within moments, the first salvoes from Sultan Osman-Evvel, Resadiye, Barbaros Hayreddin, and Lemnos soon followed.

The shots slammed into the water, not anywhere near the enemy ships, as they made for the safety of Nikolayev. This was totally normal, as the distance between the two fleets was still 17,000 yards, an almost impossible shot. The three Russian battleships guns soon responded, as it was obvious from the flashes of their own guns (the rear-facing ones). Souchon didn't even blink as he knew the enemy would also miss unless they were blessed with a miracle. The shots whistled loudly above the Turko-Greek fleet and exploded harmlessly over a thousand yards further back.

There were two forts protecting the entrance of the Nikolayev Channel. Both were relatively modern since they were built following the Russo-Japanese War in 1907. Fort Ekaterina, the first of them, was bristling with coastal defense guns ranging from the modern 203 mm 50 caliber Pattern 1905 to the ancient smoothbore cannon. Fort Nicolas, on the other side, also had 203 mm 50 caliber Pattern 1905 and 203 mm 45 caliber Pattern 1892. The bigger guns also opened up and fired their salvoes. Both forts had been badly damaged during the January raid but had now been repaired somewhat, and most of their destroyed guns had been replaced.

"The enemy fleet is making for the safety of the river, Sir," said Vice-Admiral Hubert von Rebeur-Paschwitz. Nikolayev Shipyard was located twenty miles inland and thus was the perfect place for the enemy admiral to hide. Souchon could smell the kill and got excited by the fleeing enemy, just like a wolf running after a terrified prey. Perhaps too much, in fact.

Then, the second salvo blossomed from the Ottoman-Greek-German ships. More geysers of water, this time closer to the Russian battleships, sprouted high in the air. Some of the shells (pre-dreadnoughts Barbaros Hayreddin and Lemnos had been ordered to concentrate on the forts) slammed onto the two forts, as an unmoving object with known coordinates was a lot easier to know with exactitude.

The third salvo was fired after the Russians retaliated, and again missed. Souchon's ships again blasted out fireballs of fury and might, slamming into the fortress and also missing the enemy ships. With every shot fired from the powerful dreadnoughts, the water in front of them rippled because of their blasts. The fortified buildings at the river's entrance were alight with fiery burning infernos.

"Range 12,000 yards, Sir." For a moment, Souchon wondered how his ships had closed the distance so fast. There was only one reason this was possible, and it was if the enemy ships had slowed down. His mind computed for a few seconds, and the reasons for such a slowdown were obvious. It could be an enemy maneuver or a problem with the engines. But that seemed unlikely as none of his ships had hit any of the enemy's. And then, he understood. *"Order all ships to stop and turn,"* he yelled. *"Sir?"* countered von Rebeur-Paschwitz. *"Just do it,"* started Souchon before a resounding explosion slammed the dreadnought battleship Sultan Osman-ı Evvel.

"Sir," said the lookout officer about the obvious that everyone could see. *"The Sultan Osman-ı Evvel has been hit by enemy gunfire!"* Souchon's face darkened. *"It's not enemy gunfire. Signal every ship in the fleet to stop moving in on the mouth of the river and to turn around as tightly as they can. The Russians have laid a minefield since our last visit!"* No one else countered anything after that and just went about their business of trying to survive.

On the other side of the battle, Admira Kolchak smiled. *"Take that, you bastard,"* he said out loud, watching the large explosion on one of the enemy dreadnoughts. Then, the two rear-facing guns of his own ship fired, blossoming into a red fireball. For a moment, he wished his gunner would hit something, but the range was still too great, and the enemy was maneuvering wildly in a tight turn to avoid the minefield. There was almost no chance to score. But the mines did what they were supposed to do, and a large explosion followed by many secondary ones slammed a Turkish protected cruiser, almost stopping him dead in the water. The immobilized ship was slammed a minute later by a shell from his own battleship as well as from the forts, worsening the size of the fire, smoke, and secondary explosions. *"Admiral, we're entering into the river,"* said the Battleship Captain.

And that was that, said Kolchak to himself. His first action as commander-in-chief was a victory. While not a major one, it did show the Turks that he was no pushover, and that they had no business gallivanting near Nikolayev. He hoped he'd spooked them enough since it was soon to sail his fleet to the main naval base in Sevastopol. After all, another dreadnought was in construction in the shipyards, and he very much hoped to have it added to his fleet when it was completed in 1917.

(...) A couple of hours later, battlecruiser Goeben (...)

Vice-Admiral Hubert von Rebeur-Paschwitz dropped the folder containing the preliminary after-action report and the fleet's damage. *"Sir, the final tally is that the Sultan Osman-ı Evvel has heavy damage to its waterline and can only do twelve knots for now. It will need to be towed back into the Golden Horn for major repairs. It's taking in water, and if it goes faster, it will sink."* The man paused, putting a darker shade on his face.

"The protected cruiser Mecidiye is gone, Sir. As you know, it was seriously damaged by a mine that killed its speed. The forts and the enemy battleships soon afterwards slammed it with hits. It sunk a few minutes later, according to the lookouts on the masts."

Souchon opened the folder to start reading it, not really wanting to know how many of his sailors had died. They might be Turks, but he'd come to respect and love them as much as his own men. *"Thank you, Vice-Admiral, that will be all." "Thank you, Sir. The fleet is about ten hours from Constantinople."* Souchon didn't answer, instead skulking into his frustration.

A new enemy
Meeting of the OHL, Konigsberg, May 13th, 1915

"You worry too much, Minister," said the Kaiser to von Falkenhayn, the Minister of War, waving his arms in a desultory manner. *"The Americans are a paper tiger. They just don't have the troops." "Well,"* countered General Paul von Hindenburg in a hard tone. *"Your majesty should take note of the U.S. Navy's 30-plus battleship fleet. It could, after all, sink your precious High Seas Fleet."*

Everyone around the table held his breath, as this was not the way you spoke to the German Emperor. But it seemed Hindenburg's influence (and thus his arrogant attitude) was growing equally. The victorious general was becoming very influential. Surprisingly, Wilhelm II didn't seem fazed by his favorite military commander.

"Admiral," said a now uncertain Kaiser to Alfred von Tirpitz, the State Secretary of the German Imperial Naval Office. The man was the architect of the German fleet resurgence, and the man behind the naval buildup. He was not involved in military matters anymore, leaving this to younger men like Hugo von Pohl. Rumors were speaking of his soon-to-be retirement. *"Is this true?"*

Tirpitz, trying to manage his ruler's susceptibilities by not wanting to confirm Hindenburg's words, would have stayed silent but now had no choice but to speak. "Indeed, your Majesty. The United States Navy has 32 battleships, including ten dreadnought battleships. Our information network in Washington speaks of a large building program that will soon be voted on that will exponentially increase the size of the fleet."

"Well," countered the Kaiser, *"they don't matter; we still have more dreadnoughts than they have."* Wilhelm slapped his open palm on the table of the conference room they were in (the meeting was being held in Fort no.7 near where had been the frontlines against the Russian forces). Everyone else around the table stayed silent, seeing

the petty answer for what it was.

The discussion had been moved to Konigsberg to enable Hindenburg to be close to the action. The meeting was more or less one about the Eastern Front, and thus, no Western generals were present because they were quite busy fighting the French offensive in Paris.

The men present were Helmut von Moltke, the Chief of the General Staff (and thus head of OHL), the Minister of War, Erich von Falkenhayn, and the Chief of the Information Division (intelligence), Lieutenant Colonel Richard Hentch. The Chief of the Operations Division, Colonel Gerhard von Tappen, was also absent as he was busy in Northern France getting things organized.

At the head of the table and facing them all was the Kaiser, Wilhelm II, flanked by Hindenburg to one side and Eric Luddendorf on the other. To the right was Rear Admiral Roman Berger, the Chief of the Admiral Staff's deputy for this meeting, as Admiral Hugo von Pohl was still in Brest, France. And, of course, the German Foreign Affairs Minister (and Imperial Chancellor), Theobald von Bethmann Hollweg, along with Tirpitz, who had just spoken.

The discussions were supposed to be about the victory in Kaunas and the successful attack by General von Mackensen on the Russian right flank in Galicia, saving Austro-Hungary from total collapse. Instead, one enterprising U-boat captain's actions had changed the subject, along with the strategic aspect of the entire war.

"Lieutenant Colonel Richard Hentch," interjected von Moltke, the Chief of the General Staff. *"We know the American fleet is powerful, but what about their army? We know it is very small, but the real question is, how big can it get?"*

Hentch cleared his throat since he knew none of the assembled men around the table would like what he had to say. *"Considering the fact that the United States official census puts their population numbers at*

101 million citizens versus our own German numbers at 64 million, I believe it can indeed get pretty big." Everyone gasped, some audibly, some silently, but the general consensus was that they were stunned.

"And they seem to have the fleet to transport them to Europe," countered Hindenburg with a cocky face. *"How long do we have before they raise the millions of soldiers that they can certainly train and equip,"* said von Falkenhayn. *"It's hard to say, Sir,"* continued the Lieutenant Colonel. "They are currently involved in a land war against Mexico that involves most of their standing army. Thus, those are not going to be available."

The Kaiser had finally regained his composure and spoke up. *"Your best estimate, Lieutenant Colonel?" "Ten months to a year, Your Majesty. After that, the Yankees will be in France by the millions."*

From there, everyone around the table knew what that meant. If they could beat the French by then, they would remain in a good position as the Allies would be stuck with only being in the British Islands and would have to try and find a way to land back on the continent. If not, well, the war might be as good as lost.

"Then, we'd better get to it, gentlemen," said Hindenburg, slowly regaining his composure. *"Let's beat the damned Russians, and then, we can move the might of the German Army back to the west and smash the French."*

The British conquest of Basra
Kut-az-Zain mud fort and Basra, May 14th 1915

"Here's the fort," said Sergeant Kramer to Private James Colborne. Both men had fast become friends following the difficult assault on the Fao Fortress. *"It looks pretty bland,"* continued the NCO. *"Sure does, Sarge. Do you think the Turks have a lot of troops inside the city?" "That, Private, I do not know."*

From a bird's eye view, the entire British procession was one hell of a long brown and light brown snaking line, spreading for kilometers. Following the successful landings in the Fao Peninsula (the fortress was declared secure on the 13th), the 14th British Division (Indian) and the 6th Royal Marines started to advance toward their next objective, the Ottoman city of Basra.

The troops were arrayed on the barren dune sprinkled with shrubby vegetation, while the artillery in the rear got organized to pound the fort into oblivion. The high-command's idea was that this type of fortification could not hold against modern artillery, and by smashing it from a distance, it would save men.

"Here it goes," continued Kramer with glee, hearing the reverberating whistle (sounding more like a giant Hornblower) of the first shells thundering above them. Moments later, a plethora of explosions started to pepper the ground around the fort and slam upon its fragile walls. Rock, clay, and mud exploded in every direction as the British Royal Artillery did its demolition work.

"Do you think it will be enough, Sergeant," said Colborne. *"It will, James, it will. Thus, this type of forts cannot withstand modern guns. We should be on our way within the hour."*

As sure as night follows day, within sixty-five minutes, the fort was leveled to the ground and pounded to dust while the Ottoman troops defending it retreated northward and toward Basra.

"Forward," said one of the Captains, the order quickly relayed by the lieutenant and, most especially, by the NCO surrounding James and his comrades. *"Come on, you maggots,"* yelled Kramer. *"Basra isn't going to fall while you lounge and twiddle your thumbs in the Turkish desert."*

(...)

The 6th Royal Marines arrived within sight of the Ottoman city of Basra on the 18th of May, and they entered it without a fight, because the scant Turkish troops supposed to defend it had fled the day before.

Beside the road lay the Shatt Al-Arab River and the protected cruiser Odin, which had been able to sail up from the Persian Gulf. The river was formed by the confluence of the Tigris and Euphrates, flowed down for 120 miles, and passed through Basra. It then went to the Persian port of Abadan, where the all important Abadan oil refinery was located. That strategic asset was the entire reason why the British had decided to invade Iraq.

"I didn't know ships could sail up the river all the way to Basra, why didn't they just keep us on the boat? We could have sailed right through," asked Colborne to Kramer. *"Well, son, that isn't the case. They like it when us ground-pounders walk, and besides, the Fao Fortress was guarding the entrance to the river. There was thus no other option but to send us, the great and terrible Royal Marines, to take care of the guns there."* A few soldiers beside the pair laughed at the Sergeant's ironic words.

"And now what, Sage," said one of the laughing men. The section was walking on a sandy road. There was so much dust in the air from the thousands of men walking and disturbing it that a large and thick cloud of yellow dust hung over everything. Their faces were dirty with soot and sand, and several of them had pretty bad sunburns, even if

they wore hats or strips of clothing on their heads like the Arabs. *"Now we walk in, boys, and we have a bit of a break,"* answered the NCO.

James decided that he liked the concept of a break after the difficult last week. The fighting for the Fao Fortress had been rough, and the walking from there to Basra was almost as bad because of the sun, the heat, and the lack of water.

Basra was now in British hands.

Battle of the Falklands Part 1
May 7th, 1915, approaching the Falkland Sound

(...) Bridge of dreadnought battleship Westfalen (...)

Admiral Maximilian von Spee moved to the bridge's viewport, watching the outline of land on the horizon. And here it was; he now had a full battle fleet, was in the Atlantic, and steamed northeast toward the Falkland Islands. His idea was to repeat the maneuver that enabled him to escape the Japanese fleet in Truk some months before.

The trick had been to steam hard for one of the three lagoon's exits and drop mines so Togo couldn't follow or else risk sinking his ships. With the situation regarding the boilers on both his damaged battleships, he didn't have a choice but to attempt a repeat, as he needed to distance himself from the enemy to slow down the pace. The boilers had been repaired (summarily) in Manzanillo, but the Mexicans weren't exactly a naval power and didn't have the parts they needed to make them work like new. They were working but could not be pushed to their limit for a prolonged period of time.

The idea he'd had was thus to steam for the Falkland Sound in between the East and West Falklands. It could be mined as he sailed by, and if the enemy followed him, then it would be forced to stop because of the minefield he would lay down. At 140 miles long from east to west and 12 miles in width, if the enemy commander took the bait, It would be von Spee's fleet's salvation. By the time the Anglo-Japanese fleet either cleared the mines or turned back to go around the western part of the Falklands, von Spee and his ships would be long gone. The number of mines they had was limited, and thus, it would be in no way a heavy minefield. But he hoped it would be enough to make the enemy commander hesitate.

He wasn't certain it would work since he didn't know what the British had in store for him in the Falklands and didn't even know if there were naval defenses in the Sound. It was a desperate and too-quickly conceived plan like at Truk. But he didn't have a choice. It was either that gamble or turn around and fight the superior numbers of the enemy.

"Any change in orders, Sir," said his Chief of staff, Vice-Admiral Max von Krenk. The standing orders from von Spee were to sail right into the Sound and steam right past it while the rear ships spewed their mines. *"Order two of the light cruisers and the destroyer from the 3rd Battle Squadron to sail ahead of the main body of the fleet." "Yes, Sir."* Von Spee wanted to make sure there weren't any unpleasant surprises for him waiting there, although he suspected he would still try to force the waterway to try and outpace the enemy ships. *"Lookouts,"* he said matter-of-factly. *"What is the pursuing enemy ship's distance?" "Still about 18,000 yards, Admiral,"* answered the Lieutenant near the plotting table. "Yes, that seems about right," he answered, looking at the geysers of water behind his fleet as the British continued to fire at them.

(...) Falkland Islands (...)

While von Spee's idea was not a bad maneuver and could have been a good idea, Beatty had anticipated his move. The German admiral wasn't aware that Japanese Admiral Togo had been in the Falklands and had met with Beatty before they sailed to Los Estados Island. During their discussions and as they planned how they would trap their enemy. Togo unavoidably explained to the British commander how von Spee had escaped his clutches in Truk.

The two admirals had thus planned accordingly, and they found their German counterpart's idea of mining the Sound excellent. Beatty and Togo had a total of 123 mines in between all their ships and dutifully mined the center part of it to trap the German admiral if he dared to enter. It was a bit of a long shot, but it was what it was. They also laid some mines on the approaches to Port Stanley, just in case the German admiral decided to fork east.

The idea was that once he was in, he would never get back out, as the Anglo-Japanese Fleet was right behind. Furthermore, the Sound was protected by two aging but still operational BL 6-inch Mark VI guns. These guns would have been more useful against ships from the 1880s but could still pack a decent punch. They were protected by a 7-inch gun mantle and were built into concrete casemate. There was one at the western end (and it was about to fire on the approaching German fleet) and another one on the other end.

As Beatty sailed away to try and catch von Spee on the open sea, he had not left the defenses of the islands to these two guns and a minefield. Two pre-dreadnoughts had been left in Falklands, under the command of Captain Heathcoat Grant, also the commander of the battleship Canopus. The decision to station them there had as much to do with the defense as the fact that they didn't have the speed for a chase against the modern enemy battleships anyway.

Falkland Islands

Captain Heathcoat Grant.
Pre-dread BB Canopus   Pre-dread BB Vengeance

The two ships (battleships Canopus and Vengeance) were powerful enough to face the Germans or, at the very least, give them pause. Since they wouldn't need to maneuver a lot in the coming battle, they would end up doing pretty well. The Canopus-Class of pre-dreadnought battleships were 14,000-ton warships armed with 305mm guns. They didn't have the speed to match the approaching German ships, but the British plan didn't rely on speed.

The plan was hopefully to have the Germans enter the Falkland Sound and trap them in it, while both the coastal defense guns and the Canopus, anchored in Goose Green near the center of the Sound and where the minefield was located, would fire from a distance.

Goose Green was a small village in East Falkland. It lay on Choiseul Sound, on the east side of the island's central isthmus. The reason pre-dreadnought battleship Canopus was anchored there was because of its proximity to the Falkland Sound. The ship's 305mm BL 12-inch Mark VIII naval gun could cover the sound since Goose Green was eight miles from it. With land in between and some distance, the battleship gunnery system and spotters couldn't see any passing ships through the sound. But Beatty had installed a network of lookouts and flag signalers to give firing solutions to the ship if the Germans came through the Sound. The idea was thus to have Canopus firing on the passing Germans without them realizing where the shells came from and without the capability to fire back.

The Vengeance's part in the plan was to stay in Port Stanley, the Islands' capital and main harbor, first to protect it, but mostly to move in and react to any of the enemy's moves. If von Spee did engage in the Sound, the Vengeance's mission was to sail through the eastern entrance and block the way for the Germans, as they would undoubtedly try to force the minefield and sail away.

(...) Bridge of battleship Neptune (...)

"Admiral," said one of his bridge officers. *"The lookouts report that the enemy fleet is about to enter into the Falkland Sound as you predicted."* *"Perfect,"* answered Beatty with a predatory smile. *"Helm, keep it steady. Flag, signal all ships to prepare for battle."* Togo had been right, and it was now time to kill the Germans.

(...) Bridge of battleship Setsu (...)

Togo smiled and thanked the gods in a silent prayer as he watched the enemy fleet's dark plumes head for the center of the Falklands, right where they wanted it. His people were speaking and going about their business, but he'd given his orders and was now waiting for the start of the battle. There wasn't much more to say. They had the bastards trapped.

He was sitting in his Admiral of the Fleet's chair and had his elbow on the armrest, with his fingers on his chin. He'd adorned his best and cleanest uniform for the battle and looked resplendent. All white, with his cap and even his Tsushima medals. He knew, deep down, that the coming battle would be the last in his long and illustrious career, and he intended to make certain it would end with a resounding victory.

Poison Gas, Infanterie-Regiment Graf Schwerin
The Horrors of War and Chlorine, May 17th, 1915

(...)The next thing we heard was this sizzling—you know, I mean, you could hear this damn stuff coming on—and then saw this awful cloud coming over. A great yellow, greenish-yellow cloud. It wasn't very high; I would say it wasn't more than 20 feet up. Nobody knew what to think. But immediately it got there, we knew what to think, I mean we knew what it was. Well, then, of course, you immediately began to choke, and then word came: whatever you do, don't go down. You see, if you got to the bottom of the trench, you got the full blast of it because it was heavy stuff, it went down (...)
British officer Martin Greener, as witness to the first gas attack in Verdun, May 1915

(...) German lines (...)

The orderlies and runners were going around the unit, giving out gas masks to everyone. The things looked eerie, and Oskar wasn't certain he would like to fight with these things on his head. Called the *"Lederschutzmaske"* (mask with leather protection), it was made from tanned sheepskin, dipped in an oil sealant solution. He put it on to see what kind of vision he would have through the two goggle-looking eyepieces and cursed. *"Damn, Sergeant,"* he said to Wilhelm. *"We will only be able to see forward with these ugly things."* Several of the men beside him in the deep part of the trench they were in grumbled in acknowledgment. Not one of them liked the masks, or looked forward to fighting with them on their heads. *"Are we supposed to put our helmets on top of that,"* he added. Wilhelm turned to face him. *"Dantz, just do what you are told and shut up. These things are designed to keep you alive, and believe me, once you see what it does to the enemy, you will be happy you have it on."*

Oskar shut up, not wanting to attract more of the NCO's ire, but continued to grumble to himself. *"Damn mask, damn war, damn trench, damn everything."*

Above them whistled the loud, horn-like sounds of the German artillery, unusually heavy as it was preparing the enemy trenches for the planned German attack. The battlefield's no-man's-land was a pandemonium of exploding ammunition, catapulting earth and debris, and bullet streams being fired on both sides. In the sky, planes were fighting with each other in a grand ballet of death, while the entire area was covered in a cordite-smoke fog permeating everything in a hellish landscape.

As it all unfolded, German engineers and special troops toiled about (to Oskar, they didn't look like soldiers, but more like civilians or scientists) to install steel cylinders embedded in the ground and linked to large tanks in the redoubts.

The idea, as Oskar had been told, was to release a toxic gas toward the enemy lines when the wind permitted it, like today, where a pretty steady breeze blew from the East toward the West. The cylinders protruded about a meter from the ground to ensure maximum dispersion into the wind and were placed about five meters ahead of the trench. Some of them were installed during the night to make sure the enemy didn't spot them.

The French Verdun offensives looked like they were over, as the enemy forces were now concentrating on the Paris offensive. Oskar had heard that the German forces there were not holding the line and that something had to be done elsewhere to release the pressure while more troops were moved into the French capital.

The Infanterie-Regiment Graf Schwerin, like all other units in the sector, was exhausted from the non-stop fighting of the last few months and because of the difficult conditions they lived in. But that didn't seem to compute with the generals at the top, as they were sending them into yet one more attack.

"This time, it will be different, men," said one passing-by captain, tasked with explaining to them how to use gas masks and also what the gas would do to the enemy. *"You will be able to walk in the enemy trenches without fighting, and the gas will sow confusion into the enemy ranks. With its help, you can break through the enemy line and storm Verdun for the Empire, just like your grandfathers!"* Germany had indeed won a victory here during the 1870-1871 war, but Oskar wasn't certain they could do it again. War had changed a lot from that

time.

Poison gas was *"not permitted"* by the Hague Convention of 1899. Europe's competing military powers had met and decided to sign a pact to ban its use in war. But this was not to hold as a stalemate, and the warring powers wanted to win. The first to move were the Germans.

Headed by a brilliant scientist named Fritz Haber, who believed he could change the course of the war with his inventions, the German gas warfare program was ready to go on that fateful day of May 17th, 1915. The first weapon that was ready to deploy was Chlorine gas. The stuff was pale green in color and was reminiscent of a mix of pineapple and pepper. It reacted with water in the lungs and basically filled them with water. Thus, the idea was to *"drown"* the enemy soldiers.

With a sizzling noise, the gas started to go through the piping laid about in the trench and outside in no man's land when the order to put their mask on was given.

(...) Entente Lines (...)

> (...)A panic-stricken rabble of Turcos and Zouaves with gray faces and protruding eyeballs, clutching their throats and choking as they ran, many of them dropping in their tracks and lying on the sodden earth with limbs convulsed and features distorted in death (...)
>
> Officer Fred Chappy, 5th Royal Rifles.

The German fire was heavy, as rifles and machine guns saturated the space above the trench. The damned Krauts had been hammering them for the last two days, and everyone in the units around Verdun expected an enemy attack. After all, they were done with theirs, and the normal course of events was that the generals on the other side called a counterattack to see if they could break through. But on that day, instead of raising the alarm because enemy soldiers were starting to make their way on the no man's land toward their trenches, the hunkering-down soldiers started to hear a sizzling sound like a gas stove of some kind. Some of the more enterprising ones lifted their heads only to see an ominous (and approaching) yellow-greenish cloud coming toward them.

The cloud seemed to have a life of its own and was about twenty-five feet high. Then, a weird smell of fruit and pepper started to appear, and it was at that moment that the choking and the yells of horror began. Men started clutching at their throats with bulging eyes and a panic-stricken face. None of the Franco-British soldiers that day had gas masks. Why would they, as a gas attack was not expected.

Then, men started to die as they choked to death in a horrifying moment of death and suffering. None of the men in the affected trenches knew what to do or what to think, and thus, they did the only sensible thing: run, run away as far as possible from the terrible cloud of death.

(...) German lines (...)

The whistles blew hard across the entire German force, and the order to advance was given. Oskar felt the usual dread of the moment as he climbed to the top of the trench and then over the sandbagged walls. This was the moment the enemy bullets and, often, the artillery shells started to explode or whizz by him.

But he was only met with an eerie, gas-riddled, and foggy silence. The yellow-greenish substance billowed everywhere, and it was difficult to walk with his limited vision. But at no time was he tempted to remove the mask.

Through his heavy breath, he could hear through the mask breathing apparatus; he also heard the yells of pain and desperation coming from the Franco-British side. Damn, he couldn't see a thing in this muck. He was worried he would walk right into barbed wire or fall into a deep shell crater as he walked to the enemy line. Once in a while, a loud horn-like noise blazed above, a sign that the German artillery was still at work. The blasts of explosions could then be heard far into the enemy's rear.

The gas billowed around him and his comrades as they slashed through it. It was as if he was walking through a thick morning fog that wouldn't go away.

And then he was at the enemy trench, looking down, without being fired at. Some of the bravest amongst the German troops jumped into the trench, only finding corpses lying about everywhere. Confusion in the ranks was at an all-time high. They didn't know where they were, and no orders came to continue to advance or assemble.

Eventually, the sizzling sound stopped, and the heavy, greenish-yellow muck lifted, drifting west into the wind. Oskar finally started to see normally again, and what he saw horrified him. Hundreds upon hundreds of enemy soldiers lay dead on the ground. And what killed them wasn't bullets. It was the damn chlorine gas.

He started to hear cheers through the ranks coming from far away as the German troops started to register the immensity of what had been done there. The first and second lines of enemy trenches had been taken, and this without one casualty. The enemy was either dead or had fled away. The cheer came and went over Oskar and his nearby comrade, and he followed suit, uncertain of what they had achieved.

For he might have been one lowly, relatively uneducated private, but he knew that this new horror wouldn't go unanswered forever. The Entente would also deploy gas and kill them by the thousands. He shivered at the thought.

(...) The outcome (...)

As it happened, the Franco-British troops completely emptied the defenses for five miles in and around Verdun, and a five-mile by a four-mile deep gap opened in the Allied lines. However, the German generals, stunned by their resounding success, failed to exploit the moment and, by the end of the day, contented themselves with the first two lines of trenches. The German troops advanced to the base of Verdun's biggest forts (Fort Douaumont), as its occupants were protected by the walls of the building from the gas cloud. This was enough for the German leaders to call a stop to the attack.

(...) 16th Moscow Regiment May 14th, 1915 (...)

Private Soldier Dimitri Fedorov grabbed his rifle from the ground, put a knee down, and slammed the bayonet in its socket. A blast of an artillery shell rocked him, and he fell to the ground as he was hit by the concussion wave. Dirt half-buried him, and when he rose, he fought through a thick cloud of cordite-smelling dust lifted by the explosion.

As weird as it may sound, he was now fighting northward and against a powerful German counteroffensive into the Russian right flank. "Get readyyyy," yelled Sergeant Radetzki. And then a flow of grey uniforms flooded their trench.

All across the field, German troops charged the Russian lines and yelled out at the top of their lungs while artillery shells from their guns flew above them, smashing into the Russian ranks. Bullets blazed about everywhere, and Dimitri sort of tried to make a void in his mind about it all. He'd found that it was the best way to stay concentrated during an assault. In the air, German planes flew, and he also saw a couple of the big Zeppelin airships dropping bombs from above.

A big brute of an enemy soldier dropped from the top of the trench right in front of him, and he dispatched the man with a shot from his rifle to the belly. For a fleeting moment, he looked right back at Dimitri with empty eyes and then fell backward. A thumping sound behind him alerted his senses that another German had landed near him, and he turned in a slashing motion with his bayonet blade, catching the poor bastard in the back. The blade slammed on his side and penetrated between two ribs. He yelped in pain and then crumbled in place.

Dimitri heard yelling above at the top of the trench and leveled his rifle, seeing another enemy, this time a saber-wielding officer about to jump in while urging the rest of his men on. His weapon banged hard and recoiled on his shoulder, the zipping bullet slamming home into the man's chest. The now limp body twirled in place and fell in a bloody cloud of blood right beside Dimitri.

The moment was desperate, and brown uniforms mingled in a deadly dance with grey uniforms, both sides intent on killing each other. The place they were fighting in was called Radom, a Polish city on the edge of Austrian Galicia.

(...) Big picture (...)

Germany- East			
Poland			
German 9th Army	General August von Mackensen	190,000 soldiers	Northern Carpathians-Hungary-Galicia

The German 9th Army, under the command of General August von Mackensen, was in the middle of a powerful counteroffensive aimed at unhinging General Brussilov's attack on the Austro-Hungarian Carpathian front defenses. The Russian offensive had started from the moment the weather cleared and the snow melted sufficiently in the mountain passes to enable proper troop movement. The attack had been so powerful and well-prepared with artillery and numerous troops that it smashed the Habsburg defenses and even pushed Max von Gallwitz's 11th Army backward in confusion.

Germany- East			
Galicia-Carpathians			
	Commander	Soldiers	Area of operation
German 11th Army	General Max von Gallwitz	160,000 soldiers	Galicia-Carpathians

The first phase of the Brussilov offensive only stalled when it was almost through the mountains and in view of the Hungarian plain. The Austro-Hungarian forces of the new K.U.K. commander, General Svetozar Boroevic, had their backs to Hungary, and a few meager lines of trenches but had held the line.

By all intents and purposes, they should have been destroyed, but were saved by the timely German counterattack decided on by Eric Luddendorf and Paul von Hindenburg, the Eastern German commanders. General August von Mackensen was thus ordered to cancel his planned attack East of Warsaw and move his army southward to create a large and impossible-to-ignore flanking diversion.

The trick had worked, and the victorious Brussilov was forced to relinquish his pressure on the Carpathians just as he was about to break the Austro-Hungarians. It was either face the German outflanking attack or else risk all his armies being encircled and rendered out of supply.

By May 14th, well over five Russian corps had been removed from the Carpathians frontline to face the attack from the north, and while it looked like the German offensive was losing steam as more and more Russian troops entered the fray, it was nonetheless sufficient to continue to stall Brussilov in his attempt to finish off the Austro-Hungarians.

General Svetozar Boroevic also scrambled everything the Empire had in these critical days and railed them toward the frontline. Thus, the last K.U.K. reserves were also thrown into the battle with Viktor Dankl von Krasnik's 5th Army, just out of training. Things looked like they were going to be stabilizing for now in the Carpathians because of the new reinforcement's arrival combined with Mackensen's attack.

But it was unlike Brussilov to just let go. During the initial phases of the German counterattack, he was able to convince Grand Duke Nicolas to send him more reserves. Well, not reserves, but troops from one of the quieter fronts. From the very start of the Mackensen attack south toward Radom and the other northern Galician towns, the Russian general had thus understood that the German forces, formerly poised to advance into Belarus, were now going south. In a meeting at The Stavka headquarters in Baranovichi (in western Belarus, he'd correctly surmised to commander-in-chief Grand Duke

Nikolai Nikolaevich and his staff that the troops would be more useful in supporting his offensive.

Russia			
Galicia and Przemysl			
2,100,000 soldiers	Commander	Soldiers	Area of operation
3rd Army	General Nikolai Ruzsky	165,000,000 soldiers (-35,000)	Carpathians
4th Army	General Alexei Evert	175,000,000 soldiers (-25,000)	Carpathians
5th Army	General Pavel Plehve	282,000,000 soldiers (-18,000)	Carpathians
8th Army	General Aleksei Alekseevich Brusilov	208,000 soldiers (-42,000)	Carpathians
9th Army	General Platon Lechitsky	182,000 soldiers (-18,000)	Carpathians
Moscow Front	General Dimitri Doctorov	600,000 soldiers	Carpathians and Bessarabia
12th Army	General Aleksev Churin	200,000 soldiers	East of Warsaw and Belarus

Thus, when the man got back to the frontline, it was with a promise that General Aleksev Churin's 12th Russian Army would move to his area as soon as possible. The Russian rail and logistical system being what it was, the troops only started to arrive on the 16th, and Brussilov sent them immediately toward the Austro-Hungarian lines, seeing that his moves northward had stalled Mackensen and that he was hitting a wall of trenches along with having logistical problems, being far from his starting point.

The Russian attacks on General Svetozar Boroevic's beleaguered defenses started to hit their stride on the 18th of May. Thus would begin the biggest crisis in Austria-Hungary since the Hungarian revolt of 1848.

The French offensive on Paris stalls
German eastern reinforcements arrive, May 14th-20th, 1915

Faced with a major crisis, and lacking the troops where it mattered the most, the German OHL leaders were forced to put an end to all offensive movements for the time being and reinforce the threatened and critical areas under attack. The Entente forces were attacking in a coordinated fashion and from both sides of Europe, and it was not an easy feat for the Germans to stay afloat.

Germany- West			
Verdun - Alsace border			
10th Army	General Max von Pritzwitz	200,000 soldiers	Verdun Area
German 9th Army	General Theodor von Baben	190,000 soldiers	Verdun Area
Paris-Nante frontline			
1st Army	General Alexander von Kluck	300,000 soldiers	Paris-Nante frontline
2nd Army	General Karl von Bülow	220,000 soldiers	Paris-Nante frontline
3rd Army	General Max von Haussen	178,000 soldiers	Paris-Nante frontline
5th Army	Wilhelm Kronprinz von Preußen	92,000 soldiers	North-Channel and Atlantic Ports
German 12th Army	General Max von Fabeck	220,000 soldiers	East of Warsaw
7th Army	General Josias von Heeringen	125,000 soldiers	
Paris Rheims			
4th Army General	Albrecht Herzog von Württemberg	185,000 soldiers	Paris Rheims
North-Channel and Atlantic Ports			
Minimal garrisons			
Belfort-Swiss Border			
6th Army	General Konrad Krafft von Dellmensingen	110,000 soldiers	Belfort-Swiss Border
Reserve, Western Germany			
New levies- training, Germany			

The Entente offensive on Paris pushed the Central Powers defenses to their limit, and major reinforcements were poured in from May 13th to May 20th. First of all, the abandonment of the Offensive in Poland made it so that the Eastern command could do without General Max von Fabeck's 12th Army, and it was quickly railed to northern France. The reserve army under General Josias von Herrigen was moved from Central Germany, where it was training, and sent right into the hungry maw that was the battle for the French capital.

Already weakened by the moving south of pretty much all his forces except his original 8th Army of 550,000 men, the 525,000 new levies training and getting equipped in Germany were rushed to Eastern Prussia. The moment was critical, and it was thus decided these young men would just have to train on the job.

Germany- East			
East Prussia			
550,000 soldiers	Commander	Soldiers	Area of operation
8th Army	General von Hindenburg and Luddendorf	550,000 soldiers	East Prussia
German 14th Army	(Reserve) – new levies	525,000 soldiers	

The arrival of the fresh troops stabilized the frontline and also helped the German forces regain some of their lost territory. The battle moved from the center of the capital into the southern suburbs, and by the 20th, things were finally stabilizing for the Reich, with the Franco-British losing steam as they ran out of reinforcements, shells, and ammo to keep pushing northward.

(...) 16th Bavarian Regiment, May 19th, 1915 (...)

Private soldier, and message runner Adolf Hitler felt elated as his feet felt light. The German Army was winning once more. After being pushed to their limit (he'd even seen the Eifel Tower at one point) to the center of Paris, a large number of reinforcements arrived for a week and bolstered the Reich's position. During this time, he had been quite busy running around getting messages to units, but this time, they were orders to advance.

The ground rocked as the enemy artillery blasted all around him, but he didn't care and kept running. He was trying to reach the 14th Wurttemberg Regiment's colonel to give him an important message. The Unit had advanced far and wide and was the forward-most German unit on the front.

Well, too far-in-front, in fact. The aircraft spotter above had seen that the enemy was moving troops for a large counterattack in their sector, and they needed to retreat immediately. There were no telephone lines laid down as they had just taken the forward-most enemy trench, thus no way of reaching the unit commander, who probably thought he had other units on his flanks to keep them secure. But that wasn't the case. The 14th was 500 yards ahead of everyone else and in grave danger of being encircled and then overwhelmed.

Hitler took his role very seriously and felt invested in his mission. He was solely focused on running and avoiding the enemy shells and bullets. In front of him was just a jumble of destroyed buildings and broken-down areas. He negotiated the entire length of the 500 yards within thirty minutes, taking insane chances. During his trip to the front, he also saw that the enemy forces had already started to flank the 14th Wurttemberg. That motivated him to run even faster toward his goal.

(...) 14th French Division (...)

Private Soldier Philippe Cren walked in the billowing smoke, and on the broken ground of the no man's land in the rear of the enemy unit, they were trying to flank. The going had started to get difficult about six days ago as more and more enemy reinforcements arrived, and then a couple days before, it got really hard. They'd fallen back a few miles. They had been so close. He'd even seen the Eifel Tower and the damaged dome of the Pantheon. Damn Germans and their luck, he thought sourly.

Ahead of them, a rolling barrage thundered and blasted its way forward, clearing the way for them. The blossoming fireballs and catapulting geysers of dirt looked eerie in the drifting smoke of the battle. They walked without being attacked, and for once, the air boys like Bonnier had been right. A German unit had indeed advanced too far in front, and it was now vulnerable.

A movement caught his attention from the corner of his eye, and he leveled his rifle. *"Look, Cren, a fucking Kraut runner,"* yelled his friend and comrade Max Killerman, a man in his section. "Let's kill the bastard," he answered. Both men put both of their rifles on their shoulders and aimed. Bang! Bang! Both shots rang into the air, barely audible because of the ambient ruckus. *"Did we get him,"* said Max inquisitively. Philippe tried to spot the German runner in the smoke, thinking that, yes, they had killed him. But then he saw whiffs of smoke billowing in twirling circles further down toward the German unit's forward positions. *"Look, the fucking bastard is still alive and kicking,"* he said, putting his rifle back to his shoulder and firing once more. Max did the same. Bang! Bang! Again, both bullets whizzed into the swirling smoke. More trying-to-see-if-he-was-dead, and then, nothing. They looked at each other, smiling.

(...) The runner (...)

Adolf panted hard as he was completely winded from his running and now recently sprinting to avoid the enemy soldiers who had tried to kill him. He cursed at them silently with his fist and then slammed his back on a half-broken wall to catch his breath. He then slid down to the ground, sitting there for another half minute. Then, he got up and ran like the devil toward his objective, this time unseen by the two French soldiers, thinking him dead.

A new frontline on the Dniester
Central Powers troops reach Iasi, May 19th, 1915

Private Helmut Gottenburg, a soldier in the 8th Austro-Hungarian Regiment of the 21st Landwehr Division, walked past the throng of men looking out in the distance.

The last two men moved to the side, and he finally made it past the group of soldiers. In the distance was a long and snaking river. He could see far away because the ground was sloping downward. The Central Powers forces had finally broken through the last Russo-Romanian defenses in the Carpathians and were now invading Moldavia proper. Beyond Moldavia was Podolia and then the Ukraine.

Things were going well for Helmut and his unit, but the same could not be said of the Empire as a whole, and the frontline in the Carpathians. The offensive movement in the south had even slowed down because of the lack of supplies and several troops' transfers to Hungary. Helmut had heard the enemy forces were about to break out into the plains and smash the last defenses in the mountains. If that happened, Austria-Hungary would be in real trouble.

There were already rumors going through the troops about desertions and whole units disintegrating in the face of the Russian unrelenting attacks and advances.

Following the victory at Oituz, the 21st Landwehr Division and the rest of the Turco-Bulgarian-German forces pursued retreating Romanian General Constantin Prezan and his men. In order to avoid the front collapsing completely, the Russian Commander-in-Chief, Grand Duke Nikolai Nikolaevich, transferred General Andrey Selivanov's Russian 11th Army from Poland, as he could tell the Germans were also thinning out their forces there. The Russian troops arrived well before the retreating Romanians and dug an extensive network of trenches along the Dniester River.

The river was ranging from 100 to 250 yards wide, making for a formidable defensive barrier. A few rearguard actions were fought by Prezan's forces in which Helmut was involved, but all in all, most of the demoralized and demolished Romanian troops (they had lost close to 40,000 since the beginning of the Spring) were able to move across the river and then all the bridges were blown up to block the Central Powers from moving over as easily.

MOLDAVIA: ROMANIA and RUSSIA			
405,000 soldiers	Commander	Soldiers	Area of operation
1st Army	General Ioan Culcer	268,000 soldiers (-12000)	Moldavia
2nd Army	General Alexandru Averescu	48,000 soldiers (-7000)	Moldavia
4th Army	General Constantin Prezan	65,000 soldiers (-9000)	Moldavia
11th Army (Russian)	General of Infantry Andrey Selivanov	250,000 soldiers	East of Warsaw and Belarus

"Well, Helmut, that's some obstacle," said his Slovene friend Radno Karacivs. Several of the men around them grunted. The scene was sort of quiet compared to the battles they had been unlucky to participate in so far. The Austro-Hungarian and German artillery wasn't yet setup and thus not firing on the enemy defenses, and the Russians, for one reason or another, weren't firing. Helmut didn't know why, but the reason was simple; they just didn't have enough ammo to use. Everything was being funneled toward Galicia and the Carpathians.

"Come on, you maggots," said one of the Sergeants near them. *"Move forward, we've got trenches to dig."*

Atack on the Dogs Head
Württemberg Mountain Battalion, May 19th, 1915

Monaco was a very small principality on the coast of the Mediterranean, bordering France. In fact, it was sort of part of France but also a sovereign state. The Prince thus declared its neutrality at the start of the conflict. But the Germano-Italians quickly moved in once they broke through the first French fortified defenses across the Alps.

The country's only armed forces were a little over 80 palace guards, who had been mobilized into the Anamakaze forces. The Central Powers thus took the city easily. It wasn't a large area, but it enabled the Germano-Italians to be in a good position to assault the next fort in the serré de Rivières defensive system, Fort Masséna.

Fort Masséna was built at the end of the 19th Century to guard the important mountain city of La Turbie from Italian attack. It was also below Fort Mont Angel, now occupied by the Central Powers.

It was built atop a towering peak over Monaco and could see the Mediterranean Sea approaches from both sides. Its approaches were very steep and rose 1800 feet above sea level. On all sides except one, rock walls protected it from attack, and the only road up was through La Turbie, a small town that the French also occupied and had fortified.

There was another path up, and it was through the old Roman road. During Antiquity, the Roman Empire built a large monument near Fort Masséna called the *"Trophy of the Alps"* in order to commemorate the conquest of Gaul. Exceptionally, this path wasn't paved like most Roman roads of the time, as it was mostly used to get to the monument and wasn't part of the imperial road system. But no Romans lived up there apart from the priests and a few soldiers protecting the trophy itself.

The small path, which snaked upward for over 1,500 feet, was, of course, protected by the French, who had built trenches and redoubts to repulse any enemy assaults toward Fort Massena.

"Captain," said Private Stark as he put his hand on his helmet to protect himself from the falling rocks after a burst of machine gun was fired toward him and the small rock he was sheltering behind. "Yes, Private," answered Erwin Rommel as he also ducked to avoid the spray of bullets trying to hit him. For his part, he was hiding in the confines of some old, broken-down Roman shrine. "The bastards sure have some guns up there," continued Stark. "You have any Stielhandgranates, I'm out?" Stielhandgranate was a hand grenade or more like the German version of it. The things were small round cylinders at the end of a half-foot-long wooden stick and could be thrown over enemy strong points to destroy them.

"I do," answered the Captain, picking up his side satchel and throwing it in a large arc toward Stark's hiding place. Both men were about ten feet apart, and it wasn't an easy throw, but Rommel was pretty good at it, and thus, the small bag landed almost on Stark's lap. Rommel smiled when the Private gave him the thumbs up.

"This is no place for an officer of our rank, Captain," said his new colleague, Captain Manfred von Broberg, the man who had replaced him while he was injured. Erwin didn't answer right away, as he was busy looking at what Stark would do with the grenade. "Did you hear me, Captain Rommel?" "I did, Captain. But I am a little busy at the moment." "We should go back down and direct the men from the field down there," continued von Broberg as he pointed down the path in a worried voice.

Erwin took a deep breath. "I have told you that my leadership style is to be in the field, not in a tent, asking men to die for me." Von Broberg made a sour face. "But that is what they are teaching us in officer school, Captain." Erwin ignored him, instead concentrating on the flying Stielhandgranate. Stark lobbed one right over his hiding place, and it arced high and then fell right into the machine gun nest. A few yells were heard, and then a loud thumping explosion, with French soldiers flying out of the hole in bloody, gory body parts.

"Forward!" yelled Rommel to the rest of the assembled men. *"This is crazy,"* said von Broberg. But Rommel wasn't listening to the coward, as he was busy sprinting toward the next part of the path up to the Dog's head.

Brawl in the Falklands Sound
(Battle of the Falklands Part 2, May 7th, 1915)

3rd Battle Squadron, relief fleet (Rear-Admiral Felix Funke) - To German West Africa		
BB Grosser Kurfürst	BB König	4 CL
BB Markgraf	BB Kronprinz	1 DD

German Pacific Squadron		
Admiral von Graf Spee		
BB Westfalen stern and deck damage	CL Emden stern and forecastle damage	Collier ship Oldenwald
BB Kaiserin stern, 1 rear turret destroyed		

(...) Dreadnought battleship Westfalen (...)

Admiral Maximilian von Spee stood resolute on his battleship bridge as he watched the two light cruisers and the destroyer from the 3rd Battle Squadron enter the Sound. *"Sir,"* suddenly said the lookout officer, walking from the bridge balcony to inside where he was. *"The cruiser Koln reports that he is being fired on." "Yes, I can see that,"* answered the famous naval commander, seeing the flash of a big gun at the mouth of the Sound.

"Gunnery, what's the range on that coastal battery," he continued, watching the three German ships returning fire, and the rock promontory on which the gun was built started to light with flashes, smoke, and explosions. *"We are about 8,000 yards from the entrance and the supposed position of that gun, Sir."* Von Spee smiled. *"Order all ships to return fire immediately."*

Another minute elapsed while the Koln got hit by one of the British BL 6-inch Mark VI gun shells. A large fireball sprouted on the small cruiser. Then, finally, the German battleships answered in kind, firing a coordinated volley with their forward guns. In total, the salvo included 24 guns (each of the German battleships had two twin turrets able to fire forward.

The shells traveled to the British coastal battery in no time, and from one moment to the next, pandemonium erupted on the rock promontory. A flurry of explosions raked the area, some landing near the guns but most firing wild. From a distance, the sight was impressive. Bubbles of fire erupted in succession, followed by smoke, dust, and scattering debris everywhere. A bunch of them fell toward the Sound, followed by dust and smoke, making for what looked like a giant landslide. The debris slammed into the water, producing a large wave that hit the three small German ships making their way inside the sound.

The wind, always prevalent on the islands, soon scattered the large dust and smoke and pushed it away northward. *"Sir, the lookouts report that the gun is destroyed." "Very well. Signal all ships to continue with the plan. Range to enemy fleet behind us?" "17,000 yards, Sir. We're fighting strong head currents, and the Kaiserin has lost a little bit of power from its boiler,"* answered his Chief of Staff, Vice-Admiral Krenk. Von Spee crossed his arms behind his back, looking at the still smoldering ruins of the British gun battery on the destroyed rock promontory, and took a deep breath. This was going to be tight.

(...) British pre-dreadnought battleship Canopus (...)

Falkland Islands	
Captain Heathcoat Grant.	
Pre-dread BB Canopus	Pre-dread BB Vengeance

"Ready to fire, Sir," said both the gunnery and flag officers at the same time to the Captain of the battleship Canopus, Heathcoat Grant. *"Very well. Where is the enemy fleet reported?" "Last flag signal puts them past the now-destroyed gun battery, Sir." "Very well, this is one of our firing markers,"* answered Grant. *"By all means, mister Luddock, fire when ready."*

The Canopus was in Goose Green, a small town not 8,000 yards from the Falkland Sound, and lying in ambush for the passing German ships. It could not be seen by them, nor could he see them, as there was no direct line of sight from Goose Green to the Sound, but the British had set up a lengthy network of spotters on the rock promontory dominating the Sound. They could see the ship and signal the enemy's coordinates for the Canopus. In a sense, the old British battleship was firing blind, but it wasn't. Before the battle, Canopus' gunners had also calculated several firing markers, a set of pre-determined coordinates that the flag signalers could give to them for quick firing. The moment the Germans approached one of them, then they would fire at it without having to give a complex set of instructions and coordinates. *"All guns firing on marker one,"* answered the gunnery officer.

Canopus was armed with four BL 12-inch Mark VIII naval guns and twelve QF 6-inch 40 caliber naval guns (of which six could fire as there were half of them on each side of the vessel). The 10 naval rifles fired all together, making for one hell of a broadside.

The British shells traveled to the German fleet in no time (the range was 7450 yards), and they started to land all across von Spee and Funke's ships, straddling them. None hit, but many of them exploded very near the hull, causing secondary damage and killing sailors with their expanding shrapnel pieces.

(...) Bridge of dreadnought battleship Westfalen (...)

"What the..." exclaimed von Spee in surprise. From one moment to the next, loud, whistling, and horn-sounding shell noises thundered above and beyond them in a powerful echo. The shells started to land everywhere around his ships, lifting great geysers of water and blasting out the hulls of his ships.

The surprise was complete, and for a few fleeting seconds, the staff on the bridge, including von Spee, were startled and stunned into inaction. *"The enemy fleet has found the range,"* yelled one of the men on the bridge. *"Unlikely,"* said the gunnery officer. *"The enemy is still 15,000 yards away. It's either a very lucky shot, or we're getting fired at from somewhere else."* *"Lookout,"* started von Spee, now back from his stunned silence. *"Instruct your men to check for anything firing at us."* The Lieutenant went outside to give his instructions and then came back. *"Sir, one of the men from Kaiserin says he saw the arcing shells coming from the eastern part of the island."* As if on cue, the next shell salvo announced its arrival with loud horn-like sounds.

This time, two of the six-inch shells connected with a ship, the Grosser Kurfurst, Funke's own flagship. Bright explosion blossomed on the dreadnought, which was sailing right beside Westfalen. *"It's confirmed, Admiral. The ships guns firing at us are doing so from the other side of the island."* Von Spee opened his mouth, then closed it without a sound. He knew this spelled trouble. Some of the shells calibers falling around his ships were big, and that could only mean a very large gun battery or a battleship.

He shook his head, as there was no point in worrying about it as his fleet was committed inside the Sound, and there was no turning back now. If he ordered that maneuver, then the enemy fleet would be on him in no time. *"Flag. Instruct Vice-Admiral Funke to start laying down the mines,"* he finally blurted out. *"Yes Ad..."* A resounding boom was heard coming from the Westfalen's starboard side(and interrupting the flag officer), the sure sign of a very large explosion. Then, a second one rocked the Emden, just ahead of the Westfalen. The blast could be seen clearly, as it originated from below the waterline.

A shiver of pure ice ran down von Spee's spine as he understood the implications of those two explosions. *"Admiral! Battleship Markgraf to our starboard side has run into a mine!"* Running to that side of the bridge and exiting on the balcony, the Admiral put both his hands on the steel rail and watched the horror unfold. A very large explosion was still expanding across the ship's waterline, also engulfing its central funnel. A large gust of smoke shot up in the air, followed by debris. *"Admiral,"* said one of the signal flag sailors on the balcony. *"You need to get inside; it's not sa..."* The man's words were cut in mid-sentence as a large shrapnel piece slammed into his back. Blood oozed from his mouth, and he fell to the ground. More metal pieces hit the hull and the balcony. *"Admiral, get inside,"* said another sailor (it was one of the German Marines on the security detail), manhandling him inside the bridge and closing the steel hatch.

Another explosion rocked yet one more battleship, the Konig, also hit below the waterline near the bow, mangling it and giving way to rushing water. The explosion slammed it backward a bit, but then it rapidly started to plunge forward as seawater penetrated its insides.

"Helm, move away from the Emden," yelled Vice-Admiral Krenk, as the hit on the light cruiser had completely killed its speed, and it was sinking rapidly, engulfed in a large and twirling vortex of fire and smoke. The ship responded by moving to port in a sharp maneuver, unbalancing everyone by the suddenness of the course change.

Without any intention to give the Germans any respite, Canopus' next salvo arrived right after. One of its 305mm shells slammed on the already sinking Emden, obliterating it in a spray of fire and dark debris, splintering everywhere around and on the ships of the fleet in a starlike fashion. Two more of the 6-inch shells landed on yet another battleship, the Kaiserin, and the men on the Westfalen bridge could see it clearly as the smaller caliber slammed on the central control tower in a resounding and noisy blast.

As pandemonium erupted all around him, Admiral von Spee tried to make sense of what was happening, and to decide what to do next. His options were limited. He could stop to avoid hitting more mines. That would, however, be problematic because he would have to face the rapidly approaching Anglo-Japanese battleships. Or, he could continue onward and lose more ships. Anyway, and as much as he computed it, there were no good options. But the only one giving a chance for some of his ships to get away was to rush through the Falkland Sound and hope that the enemy minefield wasn't heavy enough to kill them all. With Funke's dropping of his own mines, he thus hoped that if some of his warships made it across, they would be saved.

"Vice Admiral Krenk," he said with a resolute voice. *"Order all ships to keep plowing forward at full speed regardless of the danger from the mines."*

(...) Dreadnought battleship Setsu (...)

Admiral Heihachiro Togo grunted in frustration. *"Just as I expected,"* he said out loud to no one in particular. *"Sir,"* answered his chief of staff, Vice-Admiral Jinji Nomura.

The Imperial Navy commander took a deep breath. *"A Japanese admiral would have turned around and faced death with bravery. Instead, our foe will try to elude us yet again."* Togo tightened his hands into fists as he felt a growing frustration. The minefield across the Sound wasn't heavy enough, and if the German admiral continued to sail ahead, he would call their bluff. He hoped the enemy fleet would be slowed down enough for his own vessels to be able to fire.

(...) Dreadnought battleship Neptune (...)

"Range to enemy ships," asked Admiral David Beatty. *11,000 yards, sir. Well,"* paused the gunnery officer as he smiled, *"that is the range to the ships still moving, Sir. The three immobilized ships are at 8,000 yard range."* *"Good,"* answered the Royal Navy commander, watching the Japanese battleship Setsu, Kongo, and Kawachi fire their first volley at the unmoving German battleships Markgraf and Konig. Their guns blossomed in bright trails of fire, the water before them rippling in small waves from the force of the coordinated concussion. In the distance, he could see the Kaiserliche marine behemoths were not about to give up without a fight. Flashes from their guns could be seen. *"Fire at the immobilized ships just like the Japanese are doing."* *"Yes, Admiral."*

(...) Duel (...)

The first Japanese salvo landed in the area where the two stranded ships were adrift, slamming into the water in a straddling shot. One of the shells ignited one of the British mines, creating yet another gigantic explosion from the sea. Water sprouted and rained down on the two German dreadnoughts as they retaliated with their own guns.

The mine had damaged their hulls, not their weapons. The two Kaiserliche Marine battleships might have been stranded, but they still packed a punch and weren't going to give up without a fight. In the background, the rest of von Spee's fleet plowed on, triggering more mine explosions, while still being shot at by the unseen Canopus.

Both ships still remained somewhat maneuverable, and their captains moved them to present their full broadside to the approaching Anglo-Japanese ships. Both Markgraf and Konig thus thundered back in anger with five twin 12-inch gun turrets. For a moment, their large silhouettes were shrouded in expanding clouds of red fire and smoke. The British salvo, fired from Beatty's six dreadnoughts, crossed the sky above at the same time as the German ones, and both landed at about the same moment.

Again, both fleets only scored straddling hits, peppering the area around their enemies with large geysers of water and shrapnel clouds. The first ship to score a hit was the Japanese battleship Kawachi (12-inch guns) on the Markgraf. One of the shells slammed hard on the forward part of the deck, creating a huge detonation that lifted the frontal part of the ship upward, destroying the forward-most turret in a furious blast.

Konig was one of Germany's most modern dreadnoughts, had a top-of-the-line gunnery system, and was the next to hit. Four of its shells plowed deep into Imperial Navy battlecruiser Kongo, who, unfortunately, was the least armored of the Imperial Navy ships that day. It was faster but less resistant than Setsu and Kawachi. The rounds penetrated right into the shell magazine, and the next moment, a world-ending clapping sound snapped. The ship exploded in a catastrophic display straight from hell.

Konig's sailors didn't get the chance to rejoice for long; a minute after they congratulated themselves in cheers, it was the turn of the British to slam home some shells. Battlecruiser Agincourt, Tiger, and battleship Conqueror all scored twin hits on the German vessel, raking it with explosions. The modern warship withstood the hits like the big boy it was, but over 500 sailors were killed on impact, a funnel was destroyed, and two main gun batteries were put out of action. A large wall of fire rolled across the length of the ship burning everything it touched to a crisp in mere seconds. It was at that moment that one of the British mines touched the stricken ship's hull, drifting right on it. The following discharge of fire and power opened the ship's hull like a cracked egg, igniting no less than four secondary explosions in the process. It was at that moment that all power went out on the ship leaving the gunners to their own devices in their turrets to fire away blind.

(...) Meanwhile (...)

"Damn!" yelled von Spee as the Koln also slammed into a naval mine. The poor ship was rocked to the side and received a giant hole with an accompanying fireball for its troubles. It was soon also engulfed in another straddling shot from the unseen guns of the enemy battleship or artillery battery firing at them from the East. The destroyers and the other light cruisers were already gone.

"Status," he said out loud for Krenk to give him news of what was happening behind them to Markgraf and Konig. *"Sir, Markgraf and Konig are dead in the water but fighting back..."* the lookout officer said, and then he paused. *"Sir, the Konig had been hit by a flurry of enemy shells and has exploded."* *"Is the ship still there,"* countered Krenk with an anxious voice. *"Yes, Sir, the lookout report it is, but it's crippled,"* answered the officer after getting the signal from his men on the masts. *"Markgraf,"* added von Spee. *"Markgraf has also been*

hit but appears to be in better shape."

Another large blast rocked the ship as the Collier Oldenwald slammed into an enemy mine. The ship disappeared in the vortex of a raging inferno. *"I thought we were done with mines,"* said Krenk in exasperation.

"This is a disaster," said von Spee as he knew his decision to sail for the Falklands had sealed the fate of many of its sailors. After this moment of discouragement, his revolved steeled itself once again. There were still many sailors left to save.

(...) The duel continues (...)

"Admiral," said one of the Japanese officers, looking in the Kongo's direction. The ship was gone. *"Don't worry about the dead, Lieutenant. Worry about the enemy that can still kill you,"* yelled Togo in rage. His feeling came both from the younger officer's panic and from the loss of the magnificent Kongo, the most modern ship of the Imperial Navy.

As if on cue, another salvo from both Kawachi and Setsu thundered away, shaking the ship to its core. The two Japanese battleship's gunners didn't have time to ponder on the fate of the Kongo, and just kept on with their training and the duel they were engaged in. Just as the shells started to fly toward the two German battleships, the Konig exploded in godlike fury from the British salvo.

Then, the Japanese shells landed amidst both dreadnoughts, peppering the area – and Markgraf - with their shells. Two of them plowed through the central funnel and the forecastle, igniting more mayhem on the ship. Another large plume of dark debris and smoke rose in the air. Markgraf rocked hard, and two lances of flames shot horizontally from its starboard and port sides. All power died on that ship as well, with the raging fires taking over.

(...) Battleship Neptune (...)

"Sir, we're entering into the sound, and the two enemy battleships are dead and sinking," said the helm officer, yelling over the noise of battle. *"So far, so good,"* said Admiral David Beaty, watching as the burning hulks of the German behemoths filled his view. What about the other... A resounding explosion rocked the Neptune as if a giant hand had taken it and pushed it roughly to the side. The next moment, a clout of smoke slammed on the bridge, exploding all the windows. And knocking everyone but Beatty and a few others unconscious as they hit the steel deck.

The Anglo-Japanese fleet had reached the edge of the freshly laid German minefield. "Mines," yelled Beatty, who then knew his chase was over. Anyway, the incredible amount of smoke produced by the dying pair of enemy battleships obscured the view of his gunners, and thus ended the duel.

(...) One last obstacle (...)

"Report," said a passably disgruntled and worried von Spee to the lookout officer. *"Sir, we can't see anything behind us. There is too much smoke and fire. The good thing is that our enemy can't see us either." "Well, that's something."*

For a fleeting, very short moment, the German commander thought the ordeal was over and that his ships would exit on the other side of the Sound without more fighting. But he was to be disappointed. *"Sir!"* yelled one of the sailors on the bridge. All the attention had been focused behind them, but a ship was rounding the edge of the northern Sound's entry point. *"Another battleship sighted!"*

And as right as rain, that is what it was. The pre-dreadnought Vengeance, stationed in Port Stanley and under orders to join the fight in the sound but from the northern entry point, was sailing right into the teeth of a very powerful German fleet. Von Spee and his ships were bloodied and damaged, but they still had a lot of firepower. *"And Admiral, there also appears to be yet another gun battery on the rock promontory on top of the Eastern Falkland Island."*

"All ships: engage at will," ordered Vice-Admiral Krenk.

(...) The Final Brawl (...)

As it happened, Vengeance did not stand a chance. It was a well-armored ship and had 12-inch guns, but it was no match for the array of dreadnoughts barreling down toward it. The Germans, already enraged by the day's outcome, fired at it with a vengeance. Kronzprinz, Grosser Kurfurst, Kaiserin, and Westfalen all unleashed their 12-inch guns at the Royal Navy ship. The duel was as intense as it was short. Since the fight happened at 3,200 yards (very short range), both sides scored hits almost immediately. Vengeance slammed Kaiserin with four shells, destroying its two main forward turrets and killing 250 sailors, blasting out the bridge windows, and injuring its captain.

The German ships outdid the brave vessel, scoring no less than ten 12-inch hits in under a minute, rapidly transforming Vengeance from a proud and powerful-looking ship into a burning hulk. Not one part of the battleship was left intact. To its credit and to the one of its designers, it didn't explode or sink. It just took the hits like a big boy. The German ships thus sailed right beside it to port and starboard as it burned fiercely.

"Finish it," said a very angry von Spee. A minute later, both Kaiserin, Westfalen, and Grosser Kurfurst slammed another series of shells on the poor vessel, and then it met its end, exploding in a spectacular fashion. Meanwhile, Kronzprinz finished the lone gun battery at the top of the rock in yet another display of firepower and death.

(...) Aftermath (...)

Admiral Maximilian von Spee's battered ships eventually rounded the exit of the Falkland Sound and made toward the northeast, toward German Southwest Africa and the harbor of Swakopmund.

Not one German ship was unscathed and undamaged, ranging from light (Kronzprinz and Westfalen) to heavy (the rest that was afloat). The losses were simply terrible, with the sinking of two dreadnought battleships (Markgraf and Konig), four light cruisers, including one of the three last remaining original ships from the Pacific Squadron, which sailed out of Tsingtao in 1914, collier ship Oldenwald and the lone destroyer. Thousands of sailors were dead, and German morale had reached an abysmal low of lows.

However, the epic adventure of Admiral von Spee and his brave sailors continued, and as long as they were alive and afloat they would try and reach the Reich to be welcomed as heroes and see their loved ones again.

The British side only lost an aging battleship, while the Japanese mourned the loss of their newest dreadnought, the battlecruiser Kongo. The battle could be called an Entente victory, but a bittersweet one. The damned and epic tale of the German Pacific Squadron wasn't over yet, and as long as it was afloat, German hope in naval glory would remain.

EPILOGUE

As fate hangs in the balance...
Mighty nations clash in a maelstrom of fighting and death.

If something was certain, it was that one side or the other would break at some point in 1915. Not that the war would end. But some nations were about to be broken to such an extent that, like the Romanians, they would be beaten down to a pulp and no longer be a major factor in the war.

The new age of conflict brought upon by the eruption of the Great War across the entire globe involved completely new concepts of fighting and industrialization. No longer was it possible to win with courage and good generalship. Now, armies needed artillery, bullets, and good supplies to have a chance to win it all.

Those who were not ready to face the music were about to feel the pain of their unpreparedness. The old world was clashing with the new, and from there nations would fall.

The situation was critical for the French and the Austro-Hungarians, while new, powerful nations like the United States were only beginning to gear up for battle.

Lots of tears, fighting, and death remained before a victor emerged. This is the story of the First World War, as it might have been. The clash of nations was about to explode in full fury.

THE STORY WILL CONTINUE IN BOOK 5 OF THE WW1 ALTERNATE SERIES:

CLASH OF EMPIRES

Thank you very much for reading my work.

I HAVE A NEW FACEBOOK PAGE! PLEASE GO AND VISIT:
https://www.facebook.com/profile.php?id=61558770082344

*** Please review my book(s) on Amazon and Goodreads.com and try not to be a troll.

.

*** Send me an email at **souvorov@hotmail.com** if you feel like chatting with me. **I respond to every email.**

Some of the books that I have published will soon be for sale on:

www.maxlamirande.com

THE BLITZKRIEG ALTERNATE SERIES

BY MAX LAMIRANDE

Book 1: Blitzkrieg Europa – 2nd Edition – 20 December 2024
Book 2: Battle Europa 2nd Edition – January 17th, 2025
Book 3: Battle Russia – January 24th, 2025
Book 4: Struggle Europa 2nd Edition – winter 2025
Book 5: Fortress Europa 2nd Edition – winter 2025
Book 5: Stalemate Europa 2nd Edition – TBD
Book 6: Staggering Europa 2nd Edition – TBD
Book 7: Faltering Europa 2nd Edition – TBD
Book 8: Crumbling Europa 2nd Edition – TBD
Book 9: Falling Europa 2nd Edition – TBD
Book 10: Soviet Europa 2nd Edition – TBD
Book 11: Red Europa 2nd Edition – TBD
Book 12: Climax Europa 2nd Edition – TBD
Book 13: The Walder Chronicles Part 1
Book 14: The Walder Chronicles Part 2
Book 15: The Walder Chronicles Part 3

THE PACIFIC ALTERNATE SERIES

BY MAX LAMIRANDE

Book 1: Blitzkrieg Pacific
Book 2: Battle Pacific
Book 3: Struggle Pacific
Book 4: Staggering Pacific
Book 5: Burning Pacific
Book 6: Sallying Pacific
Book 7: Siege Pacific
Book 8: Faltering Pacific
Book 9: Crumbling Pacific
Book 10: Collapsing Pacific
Book 11: Shattering Pacific
Book 12: Overwhelmed Pacific: March 2025

THE NAPOLEONIC ALTERNATE SERIES
BY MAX LAMIRANDE

Book 1: *Austerlitz Alternate*
Book 2: *Friedland Alternate*
Book 3: *1809 Alternate – Winter 2025*

THE AXIS ALTERNATE SERIES
BY MAX LAMIRANDE

Book 1: *The Bear and the Swastika*
Book 2: *World War*
Book 3: *Axis Triumphant*
Book 4: *Axis Victorious*
Book 5: *Axis Overwhelming*
Book 6: *Stalemate*
Book 7: *Axis Resurging*
Book 8: *Axis Siege: February-March 2025*

THE GREAT WAR ALTERNATE SERIES
BY MAX LAMIRANDE

Book 1: *Schlieffen Alternate*
Book 2: *Great War Alternate (Summer-Fall 2024)*
Book 3: *1915 Alternate*
Book 4: *Weltkrieg 1915*
Book 5: *
Book 6: *

Also, from the same author:

BLITZKRIEG PACIFIC

The year is 1942.

The world is at war. Almost every major nation has declared for the Allies or the Axis. Europe is occupied by the Third Reich, and the British Islands have been invaded and conquered by the Germans. Metropolitan France has fallen, along with its North African colonies. Spain and Turkey have joined the Axis. The Middle East is Axis. The USA and Soviet Russia are also at war with the Third Reich.

Only one major power is still on the sidelines. Imperial Japan, already busy in its war of conquest in China, dawns on the idea of conquering the Pacific and Southeast Asia following German successes in Europe and the subsequent weakening of the resource-rich Franco-British and Dutch colonies.

The United States, following Japan's occupation of the French colony of French Indochina in 1940, froze all of Tokyo's assets, stopped scrap metal deliveries, and is just about to stop delivering oil to the hungry Japanese military machine, a move certain to trigger a reaction from the warmongers in Tokyo.

President Roosevelt's decision to do so is about to have dire consequences for America. The Imperial Navy has set its sights on the main US base in the Pacific, Pearl Harbor. And all across the Japanese-held islands of the Pacific, the forces of the Rising Sun prepare for a full-scale invasion that they hope will give them control over the resources the country needs to continue on its expansion.

This is the story of the War in the Pacific.

Also, from the same author:

AUSTERLITZ ALTERNATE

DECEMBER 2ND, 1805

The War of the Third Coalition rages in Europe. Battles have been fought, and Napoleon Bonaparte's Grande Armée sweeps everything before it. After a big victory over an Austrian Army in Ulm, the French occupied Vienna, the capital of the Austrian Empire.

The Russians entered Austria to come to the help of their Allies and under pressure from the British. The Austro-Russians and the French are about to clash in a small, unknown town called Austerlitz.

And then everything changes. The French stop trying to retake the Pratzen Heights, and the day's battle ends in a stalemate for both armies. Kutusov, the allied army's leader in the absence of young Tsar Alexander (who fell ill and is still somewhere in Galicia), decides to retire the army northward with the Austrian Emperor's approval. The news galvanizes the Revolution's enemies and the Empire, jealous of Napoleon's success and wanting him gone. The Prussians decide to join the war and move their troops into Austria to link their forces with the two other powers. The German states and other countries like Naples rethink their stances in the conflict. And the French Emperor's internal enemies, ever wishing the old regime's return, start plotting to overthrow the government in Paris.

All the while, the Ottoman Empire, convinced by the French several months earlier to enter the war, has decided to intervene in favor of Bonaparte and invade southern Hungary with an Army. Austria is on the brink of annihilation, but Napoleon's Grande Armée also has a big challenge ahead since it now needs to defeat three major powers simultaneously.

Everything will come down to either Napoleon's genius to overcome the odds and win regardless of the troops arrayed against him or his defeat and the end of the French Empire.

This is the story of the Napoleonic Wars.

Also, from the same author:

SCHLIEFFEN ALTERNATE

Europe, August 1914.

The world explodes into war as Austro-Hungary declares war on Serbia following the assassination of the heir to the throne, Archduke Franz Ferdinand. Russia follows suit and mobilizes, while Germany supports its ally and declares war on Russia. France then joins the conflict, as it is Russia's ally.

The British intervene when the Germans execute their Schlieffen Plan and attack through Belgium to outflank the French defenses. And then pandemonium explodes everywhere. The Austro-Hungarians attack in Serbia and Galicia, the Russians invade Prussia, and the Germans smash into France. In the Middle East, the Ottoman Empire declares for the Central Powers, while Italy stays neutral.

The German Army is unstoppable and closes in on Paris as the Allies retreat in disarray all along the front. The fate of the world hangs in the balance as a big battle looms for Paris. However, no gains come without giving something away. While the German Army is busy conquering the French and beating the British Expeditionary Force around, the Russians storm Prussia and roll over the German 8th Army. The Reich has all of its remaining troops fighting in the West and nothing fresh to put in front of the Russian steamroller. Koenigsberg falls and the Austro-Hungarians fail before Belgrade and in Galicia. Something will have to be done, or else Berlin will fall to the Russian Imperial forces.

This is the story of a war that might have been.

Also, from the same author:

THE BEAR AND THE SWASTIKA

The year is 1939.

The World rocks with the news of the signing of the Germano-Soviet pact. A dark veil soon falls on Europe as Poland is invaded and destroyed by the overwhelming forces of the Wehrmacht and the Red Army.

France and the United Kingdom can only sit by and watch the two military juggernauts obliterate the Polish state. No one believes the two totalitarian regimes can agree in the long term as their ideologies completely contradict each other.

Russia wants influence in the Balkans, has eyes on Finland, and wants an opening to the Mediterranean. Germany needs Romanian oil to keep its war machine operational, and Hitler is adamant about not letting the Bolsheviks gain another inch of ground in Europe. At least not more than he has already given out in the treaty of non-aggression signed before the Polish campaign.

The year is 1940.

The French campaign then unfolds with a disaster for the Allies, and the Germans win an incredible victory over the combined forces of the United Kingdom and France. British forces narrowly escape to their island with the remnants of their armies, and France surrenders. Half of the country is occupied by the Germans. It seems that the swastika will conquer the world, especially with the Russian bear watching its back.

Germano-Soviet Axis talks were organized in October 1940 concerning the Soviet Union's potential entry as a fourth Axis Power during World War II. The negotiations include a two-day conference in Berlin between Soviet Foreign Minister Vyacheslav Molotov, Adolf

Hitler, and German Foreign Minister Joachim von Ribbentrop. The two powers will try to agree on a formal alliance to divide the world.

The fate of liberty hangs in the balance.

Also, from the same Author:

BLITZKRIEG EUROPA – 2nd EDITION

September 1st, 1939.

Germany invades Poland, igniting a major European war. A few months later, the French are also invaded, and the Allied armies are utterly defeated. Then the Dunkirk disaster happens, and the United Kingdom loses most of its land army. Soon, the British Isles are also attacked, and the British are hard-pressed with a serious German invasion. The French struggle to resist the Axis forces bent on conquering all of their mainland home country and West African colonies. Watching from its safe shores, America cannot stay still while Western Europe and all of the Mediterranean fall to the forces of the Axis. And when the Afrika Korps plunges over the Suez and invades the Middle East, the Soviet Union finally decides to join.

And through it all, a hero emerges. Erich Walder, tank commander, will have to fight on all fronts and attempt to survive what the enemy will throw at him.

This is the story of the Second World War.

Also, from the same author:

SPACE WAR, An Empire Divided

The Empire built by Haakon the Great is no more. It's 4124, and the Human race has spread to the stars in four different star clusters by discovering light speed and wormholes. A civil war has broken out between the different human enclaves to see who the next Emperor of humanity will be.

The Ptolemy and Hadesian Star Nations are invading Elysium, allied with New America from the Alpha Perseis Cluster. Large battles are being fought in star systems between former comrades of the Imperial Fleet. In space, battleships unload their powerful weapons at each other while giant battle mechas fight for control of the ground.

The opportunity is too great for the evil Cybernetic forces in the Caldwell 14 Star Cluster. Having fought – and lost – a terrible war against the Empire two hundred years ago, they are gathering for a return engagement against humanity.

A thousand years before, Haakon had dreamed and foreseen a terrible time for humanity. The Black Death is coming to consume all, and his Empire will not be there to fight it.